MATRIX

An Underground Vengeance MC
Romance, Montana Chapter

Liv Brywood

Copyright © 2023 Liv Brywood

No part of this book may be reproduced in any form or by any electronic or mechanical means including information storage and retrieval systems, without permission in writing from the author. The only exception is by a reviewer, who may quote short excerpts in a review.

This book is a work of fiction. Names, characters, places, and incidents either are products of the author's imagination or are used fictitiously. Any resemblance to actual persons, living or dead, events, or locales is entirely coincidental.

Cover design by Jacqueline Sweet

Cover photograph © Wander Aguiar Photography

www.livbrywood.com

"Being deeply loved by someone gives you strength, while loving someone deeply gives you courage."

- LAO TZU

CHAPTER 1: MATRIX

For some people, sleep is a luxury. For me, it's filled with nightmares. I haven't slept through an entire night since Blackstone became the governor of Montana. Cutting myself isn't an option anymore. The last time I tried it, I fucked up and ended up in the hospital for a few days. I sliced a little too deep and hit an artery in my arm. Blood shot all over my office at the clubhouse. The guys had to rip out the carpet to remove the stains. What a fucking mess.

The guys in the MC have treated me like a child ever since. They're constantly checking on me, not trusting me enough to leave me the hell alone. All I wanted was to get out of my body for a while—to free myself from the prison of my mind and get to that floaty place where nothing could hurt me. The others will never understand. We all spent years trapped in Blackstone's dungeon, but we deal with it in different ways. Some of them fight. Some of them fuck. Some of them kill. But none of them cut themselves. They never learned to harness the pain and float away as I did. That's my fucking superpower. I can escape my body whenever I want. All it takes is pain.

Since I can't sleep and I can't cut myself anymore, I've only got one option. Instead of lying in bed suffering through flashbacks of those hellish years spent in Blackstone's dungeon, I'm going for a run. Scar, the MC's president, can't stop me from running. He put an end to the cutting by threatening to kick me out of the club. I believe him. He'll toss me out on my ass if I ever do it again. Scar doesn't put up with any bullshit from anyone, not even his club brothers. Out of respect for him, I stored my knife downstairs in the basement. It's on a shelf next to Reaper's *special* tools, the ones he uses to interrogate our enemies. I miss the sharp sting of the blade slicing through my skin, but Scar's right. I could have died. Now, all I can do is run. Run to escape the past. Run to escape the pain. Run until I get to that floaty place where nothing and no one can touch me.

I throw on a pair of gray sweatpants and a black hoodie, then grab a platinum gray knitted winter hat and pull it over my shaggy blond hair. The hat was a Christmas gift from Nina, the woman who took us in after we escaped the dungeon. When she found out about the cutting from Scar, I thought she would whoop my ass. Fortunately, I'm a full foot taller than her five foot two, so my long legs made it easy to outrun her. I feel like I've been running ever since, but no matter how many miles I put between my demons and me, it's never enough.

I check the weather app on my phone. It's January in Montana. It's also four in the morning, so it's well below freezing. This run will suck, which is exactly what I need right now. A blizzard would be helpful, too. The more suffering the better. I can't get to the floaty place as fast as when I'm cutting, but I can still get there on my runs. It just takes longer.

When I open my bedroom door, silence greets me. No one else is awake in the clubhouse. Now that Scar and Nitro have moved into their own homes with their wives, the only other people living here are Talon and Reaper, my club brothers, Tucker, the prospect, and Daisy, the club girl. Her bedroom's down the hall from mine, closer to the kitchen, and her door's closed. She's probably sleeping. Not that I care. Not that it matters.

My footsteps slow as I pass her room, but I force myself to keep walking. She's been a pain in my ass since Scar invited her into the clubhouse last year. She's a prissy, country-bumpkin of a girl who's always flitting around in the same damn outfit: jeans or cut-off shorts and a t-shirt. She looks like a farmer's daughter with her long, brown hair tied up on each side with matching ribbons. She's gorgeous in that girl-next-door kind of way, but she annoys the fuck out of me. I don't know what the hell Scar saw in her that made him bring her into the fold, but I wish she'd leave. She's too sweet and innocent for club life.

As I stroll into the kitchen, I don't bother turning on any lights. This isn't the first time I've stumbled out in the middle of the night looking for something to take the edge off my nightmares. I shouldn't drink and run, but there's no one around to stop me.

I open the refrigerator door and pull a beer off the top shelf. After closing the door with my foot, I grab the magnetic bottle opener off the fridge. I'm about to pop the top when a sound breaks the silence.

I freeze. The softest creak echoes from somewhere down the hall. The first footfall has me on full alert. I reach for my gun but realize I left it in my cut, which is in my room. Fuck!

Sliding back into the shadows of the kitchen, I reach behind me for the knives in the butcher block and grab the seven-inch hollow-ground santoku knife. This will cut through anything, including an intruder. I don't know how the fuck they got past my perimeter security, but I'm about to find out.

A petite shadow glides out of the hall, past the kitchen, and into the living room. I follow silently, using all the stealth of a predator. As the figure passes through a shaft of moonlight, I relax my grip on the knife. It's fucking Daisy.

What the hell? I'm about to make my presence known when she stops at the front door. She punches the security code into the box, disarming the perimeter alarm. What's she up to?

She glances back toward the hall but doesn't see me hiding in the darkness. Satisfied that she's alone, she carefully twists the doorknob before slowly opening it. I wait until she slides out into the night before following.

After her footsteps hit the ground outside, I pull the door open wide enough to slip out. She's trudging through a foot of snow but she's moving fast. She's getting away. Fuck, I need my boots. I jog back inside, grab my boots from the mudroom, and quickly lace them up before taking off after her.

As soon as I'm outside, I pull my phone out of my pocket and type in the security code to rearm the clubhouse. I don't know what the hell she's up to, but I'm not leaving the others unprotected. Satisfied that the house is secure, I follow her trail. It disappears into the woods, but it's easy to track. Last week, a massive storm dropped several feet of snow. Her boot prints are clearly visible.

Trudging into deeper snow, I curse my sweatpants. I enjoy tough runs, but I hate being wet. Cotton is the worst fabric to wear in these conditions since it gets bogged down with moisture. If I'd known I'd be up to my knees in snow, I would have worn something else. But I didn't think I'd be doing this shit. I was supposed to be running on the plowed trail alongside the highway, not chasing our crazy club girl through rough terrain. Where the hell is she going?

When I finally spot her, I get a better look at what she's wearing. She's dressed in all-white snow gear, including waterproof pants and a thick jacket. She's also carrying a white backpack. A bulge on one side of her jacket makes me think she might be carrying a gun. But she doesn't have a gun—at least not one I know about. And why the hell would she need one anyway? I'm tempted to call out and ask what the hell she's doing, but my curiosity gets the best of me. I stay a few yards back but keep her in my line of sight. She's up to no good, but what exactly does that mean?

The day she moved into the clubhouse, I sensed something wasn't right. I couldn't put my finger on it, but in my gut, I knew something was wrong. I ran plenty of background checks on her and used all my dark web knowledge to research her past. According to all the records, she's a simple farm girl from a tiny town in Montana. I've got her report cards from first grade through high school. I know which sports she played. I know her hobbies. I even know who her friends are. But here's the weird part. Her social media seems off. I can't explain it, but it doesn't feel genuine. It's almost as if she's not real. However, this isn't the first time someone didn't feel real in my life, so I don't know what to think.

Wind whips swirling snow against my cheeks. My feet are nice and toasty because of the snow boots, but I'm freezing my balls off. Even though we're moving quickly, it's not like running, and my clothes aren't doing a damn thing to protect me. I may as well be naked. This isn't good. If she doesn't stop soon, I'll have to confront her. The last thing I need is frostbite on my dick.

After another ten minutes of trailing her, I'm about to call out when she abruptly stops. Dropping into a crouch, she slips her backpack off. I also squat. My head is on a swivel. It still feels like we're alone, but I can't drop my guard. If she's on high alert, then so am I.

She pulls binoculars out of her pack. Holding them up to her eyes, she scans the forest in front of her. God dammit, is she bird-watching or some bullshit? It's still dark as fuck. Is she insane? Maybe she's lost her mind. I've had about enough of this crap. I'm cold. I'm pissed off. I'm going to rip her head off for this.

As I stand and take a step toward her, she pulls a pistol out. Her back is still to me, giving me enough time to melt against the nearest tree trunk. She spins toward me, searching the darkness. I press against the bark, praying she doesn't distinguish the anomaly of my profile. She's as still as the eye of a hurricane. I wait for her to point the gun at me, but she doesn't. Instead, she turns back toward whatever caught her attention in the first place.

Relieved, I relax my muscles enough to take a deeper breath. In incremental movements, I slip my hand into my hoodie and pull the knife out of my pocket. Bringing a knife to a gunfight is stupid, but what other choice do I have? Until I know what the hell's happening, I won't know how to respond.

Sneaking up on her seems like an incredibly stupid plan, so I choose a different option. I need to see what she's seeing. Using every skill Talon taught me about moving silently through the forest, I circle around until I spot what has her attention. There's a campground about ten yards from her hiding spot. It's full of men holding M4 carbine rifles. Two white SUVs with extreme terrain snow tires sit in the center of the snow-covered clearing. The only tracks in lead to the SUVs. There aren't any tracks out. At least not yet.

At the sound of voices, I creep closer. A man in a black ski suit with feature-obscuring ski goggles is talking to another man wearing snow camo pants and a matching hooded jacket.

"The merchandise needs to leave Montana in the next twenty-four hours. Our mutual contact assured me you're aware of the stipulations."

"We are. The merchandise will be moved

tonight. We should be out of the state before sunrise."

"You have the money?" the man in snow camo asks.

"Fifty thousand in cash, small bills, as requested." The other guy signals to one of the rifle-carrying men to bring a silver suitcase. After opening it and showing the snow camo guy the contents, he snaps it closed. "I'd like to inspect the merchandise."

"Of course. Bring the girls." He signals to his men.

The rear door to one of the SUVs opens. Three girls, who can't be older than thirteen, get out. They're wide-eyed and trembling. I fucking know that look. Son of a bitch. These fuckers are human traffickers. How the hell is Daisy mixed up in this shit?

"Blackstone said they were young." The buyer's tone carries more than a hint of lust. "It's too bad they need to stay intact for the man who ordered them."

"If they don't arrive unharmed, it's your ass. When you need more, reach out to Blackstone."

Blackstone? An involuntary shiver slithers down my spine.

"Will do." The lecherous man points to his SUV. "Get in, girls. You're going to a new home in New Orleans. You won't have to deal with all this godforsaken snow any longer. Won't that be nice?"

The girls nod wordlessly before climbing into his vehicle. I glance at Daisy, who's slowly advancing. She's got her gun in one hand and a phone in the other. She keeps looking at the screen and frowning. Finally, she shoves the phone into her pocket and sprints toward the men.

"FBI! Drop your weapons and put your hands up!"

FBI?

What. The. Fuck?

I can't even process what just happened before all hell breaks loose. The buyer and seller rush to their SUVs while their bodyguards lay down cover fire. Daisy is pinned behind a tree. There's no way in hell she can take all of them on. She's insane.

The SUVs roar to life. All but two men get into the vehicles. The remaining pair stalk toward Daisy. It's clear they've been left behind to handle her. Well, I don't know what the fuck's happening, but I won't let her get killed. I need answers, and she's the only one who can give them to me.

"Daisy, run!"

Her head whips toward me. Her eyes go wide, and her mouth drops open. A second passes before she recovers. Gunshots crack in rapid succession. She ducks and scrambles off into the woods. I'm hot on her heels. It takes me a minute to catch up to her. I run beside her through the snow, fully aware of the huge trail we're leaving. Those men will be on us if we don't act fast.

"The river!"

I shoulder-check her to the right. To her credit, she picks up on my meaning and dashes toward the partially frozen river. When we hit the edge, I take the lead. Glancing behind me, I make sure she's following. She is. I race along the ice, praying we don't hit a thin patch. We're still leaving a trail, but it's not nearly as bad as before.

"Ahead. Log!" Daisy yells.

I leap up onto the fallen tree. Using my arms for balance, I walk as fast as I dare. If I lose my focus even for a second, I'll plunge into the rushing water in the center of the river and get dragged under the ice. Drowning isn't an option. I make it to the other side just as the men chasing us hit the riverbank.

"Hurry!"

I turn and watch in horror as Daisy runs across the log. Shots ring out. Wood explodes by her feet, but she makes it across unharmed.

"We need to lose them," she says between heavy breaths.

"Pin them down. I'll find a place to hide. How much ammo do you have?"

"Thirty-three round extended mag."

"Shots left?"

"Twenty-five."

"Extra mag?"

"Two."

"Hold them off."

I run into the woods. Snow blankets the ground. Staying on the forest floor won't work. We'll be too easy to track.

A shot rings out. It's hard to pinpoint the location, but I hope it came from Daisy and not the men in pursuit.

Fortunately, I know the area well. I've spent many hours exploring the woods, so I've got an idea that might save us. There's a large series of rock outcroppings up ahead. It's the most obvious hiding place, so we can't use it. But I can make it look like we're holed up somewhere in the area. There are enough small caves in the rocks that they'll waste a lot of time searching them. My plan should buy us enough time to find a better spot to take cover.

I drag my feet and make clear impressions in the snow and mud around the base of the rocks. I repeat the process while counting gunshots. It's not an exact science since I don't know who's shooting, but I hope Daisy's good enough to keep them at bay until I get back. If my count is accurate, she's about to run out of ammo. I've got to move fast.

The key to making my plan work is to erase any other trail we leave. I grab a huge pine bough and throw it onto the edge of the tracks. When we return, I'll use it to hide our real footprints in the snow.

I run back to her just as she's doing a tactical reload. Watching her in action shocks the fuck out of me. Her movements are so precise I realize she's done this at least a thousand times. She's no farm girl. She really is with the fucking FBI. What the hell is going on?

"Let's go!"

"Coming." She lays down a bunch of fire before rushing into the woods to join me.

"I've got a plan. Just do what I say."

"Yep."

As soon as we get to the rocks, I grab the pine bough. We slow our pace considerably because I need to make sure our tracks aren't visible. If these guys have any sense, they'll figure it out, but at least we'll be far ahead of them by then. Hopefully, we'll find a better place to hide.

I keep washing the pine bough over the snow until my arms ache. The rock wall is a solid twenty minutes behind us now, so I think it's safe to drop the branch.

"There's a rendezvous spot across the next stream. It's an old hunting cabin." Daisy glances at me.

"Is it full of FBI agents?"

"I don't … I don't know."

"Why the fuck not?"

"Something's wrong. I was supposed to have backup."

"They didn't come."

"No. And that *never* happens."

"We're not going to the cabin," I say firmly.

"We have to get out of this weather. Your pants are soaked through. You'll get hypothermia."

"Don't care. I'm not letting you take me in. I know a place we can go."

"Where?"

"Somewhere those guys won't find us. The FBI won't either."

She goes silent, which is good because one more word and I'll happily wring her lying little neck.

FBI. Un-fucking-believable.

I lead her through the forest for another hour. We crisscross the highway, which will effectively cover our tracks. It's almost six a.m., but the sun won't be up for two more hours. There's no one on the road, so we haven't been spotted. By the time we get to the club's secret cabin, I'm shivering. I punch in the code to deactivate the alarm and shove Daisy inside. Before she knows what's happening, I grab the gun from her hand.

"Hey!"

"Shut up and sit down."

"Matrix!"

"Sit." I stab my finger at the well-worn couch in front of the hearth. Seething, I throw logs into the fireplace before lighting the pile. I have about fifty-million questions to ask her, and she's going to answer every last one of them. I'm so damn mad I can hardly think. She's been lying to me for months. Months! I knew something wasn't right. Fuck!

I wait until the fire crackles and spits embers before facing her. I catch her fiddling with her phone, so I grab it and crush it beneath my boot. She's not calling anyone for backup. She's on her own now, and she's not leaving until I say she is.

Pointing her gun at her heart, I narrow my gaze and ask the question I've been dying to ask since the ambush at the campground. "Who the fuck are you?"

CHAPTER 2: DAISY

This isn't the first time someone's pointed a gun at me, but it might be the last. I've never seen Matrix this furious. Now that my cover's blown, I'm in a world of trouble. Underground Vengeance, Matrix's MC, is one of the most secretive and deadliest clubs in Montana. The only other club that comes even close is the Demon Riders. That group of thugs is covertly funded by Jonathan Blackstone, the Silicon Valley billionaire who was just elected governor of Montana. At least one of the men at the campground is affiliated with the Demon Riders. I've seen their FBI files. I'd recognize their faces anywhere. But they aren't my biggest problem right now; Matrix is. If I don't talk fast, he'll kill me and bury my body where no one will ever find it.

"Don't make me repeat myself." The darkness in his gaze sends shivers down my spine. He's not messing around. If I don't tell him who I am, he'll kill me. If I confess my secrets, he might murder me anyway. I'm screwed no matter what I do, so I might as well tell him the truth.

"I'm an undercover FBI agent."

"No shit. Why?"

"It's complicated."

"We've got all night. I'm going to take my pants off. If you move a fucking hair, I'll shoot."

He glares until I shift uncomfortably. He keeps the gun trained on me while sliding his soaked sweatpants down past his muscular thighs. Although he's wearing tan boxer briefs, he may as well be naked because the cloth is plastered to his skin. Everything is on display. *Everything.*

I tear my gaze away from his huge bulge, hoping he doesn't notice the flush hitting my cheeks. When I glance back, he's frowning. He saw it and clearly didn't like it. I shouldn't be looking at him like that anyway. He's not someone I could ever date, not just because he's pointing a gun at me but because he's a criminal. I'm supposed to uphold the law, not break it. But every time I look at this man, all I want to do is break the rules.

His pants pool by his ankles as he removes his boots with one hand. I'm tempted to take advantage of the distraction. I could try to push him over so I can regain control of the situation, but he still has the gun, which makes it too risky. I've seen him in action. He's faster than a hawk hunting a field mouse. I don't stand a chance.

After setting his boots and socks in front of the fire, he stands with his back to the flames. He's still wearing his black sweatshirt, probably because he'd have to set the gun down to remove it. That's good because I don't think I could handle him shirtless, too.

Our eyes lock. Heat rushes through me, pebbling my nipples before cascading to pool low and tight in my body. He has no idea what he does to me. Whenever he's around, I can't control myself. A single glance from him sets my body on fire. Frankly, it's humiliating. I've been good about hiding my reaction to him because it's my job to stay focused. It's been hard to ignore the electricity between us, but it has to be done. I've got to focus. I can't forget I'm a professional. This isn't the worst situation I've been in, not even close. I'll find a way out of this mess, too. I just need an escape plan.

"I am—*was*—part of a sting operation tasked with capturing local human traffickers." I pause, unsure of exactly how much information I'll need to disclose to gain his trust.

"Those girls at the campground."

"Yes. They're victims. We didn't have intel on how many would be involved with this trade. We just knew they'd be there. Our objective was to stop the handoff, rescue the girls, and take the traffickers into custody."

"But you didn't."

"No." I sigh and drop my chin to my chest.

"Why not?"

"I was supposed to have backup. This wasn't even my primary assignment."

"What was?" He leans against the wall while keeping the gun trained on me.

A dozen responses pop into my mind, but only one is the truth. "Infiltrate Underground Vengeance."

"For what purpose?"

"The official one?" When he nods, I continue, "We know Scar helped his wife, Julia, protect Max Curtis from his father. The field agent in charge of that case hasn't given up on finding the boy."

"Max is safe."

"Where is he?" There's no way he'll tell me, but I'm asking anyway. Maybe he'll let something slip that will lead us to the missing child.

"So, you lied to us so you could spy for the Feds?" he asks, ignoring my question.

"Yes." I look away quickly, hoping he won't see I'm still not telling him the full truth.

"How long were you planning on pretending to be a club girl?"

"There wasn't a specific timeframe. They left it open-ended."

"This wasn't just about Max, was it?"

"No. They also wanted me to report any illegal activities."

"You never witnessed any," he says

confidently.

"Not directly. You guys are too good. Also, I had certain limitations as a club girl."

"No wonder you never fucked anyone."

"What?" My face flames. I'm sure my cheeks are scarlet.

"You never fucked anyone."

"How do you know?"

"I know everything that happens in our clubhouse."

"Apparently not everything," I blurt.

"A fucking Fed. Un-fucking-believable."

He uses the butt of the gun to rub the muscle twitching over his eye. His dark gaze never leaves mine. When I can't take it anymore, I break the connection. I stare into the flames and try not to think about the way he's looking at me. It's predatory and carnal, and it's destroying my ability to focus.

"They'll start looking for me in the morning," I say, breaking the tense silence.

"They won't find you."

"Why not?" I whisper.

"Because you're mine now."

"What the fuck does that mean?"

"I haven't figured that out yet. I just know you belong to me."

"If I don't check in, they'll send a fleet of agents to the clubhouse to look for me." I press back into the couch and squeeze my thighs together. Is he planning on killing me? I told him some of the truth to save my ass, but it might not be enough.

"How do you usually communicate with the other Feds? Burner phone?"

"Email."

"Email?" He arches a brow like I just suggested I use carrier pigeons. "That's impossible. I see everything sent over the net."

"No, you don't." I can't help but feel a little smug. He's a damn good hacker, but I'm better.

"How?"

"If I tell you, will you let me go?"

"No."

"You're not good at bargaining," I say dryly.

"I don't need to. You're the one who's fucked." A slow, devilish grin spreads across his face. I'm struck by the feral look in his eyes. He's never looked at me quite like this. I don't know what to make of it.

"Why should I tell you anything?" I ask.

"I'll make your death painless?" He shrugs as if he couldn't care less either way.

"That's not good enough." Maybe he'll kill me anyway, but I'm not going down without a fight. I don't give up easily, and death isn't an option. No one's looking for my missing sister except for me. She's counting on me to stay alive long enough to find her. If I die, no one will be left to search for her. I'm not leaving her to suffer at the hands of a bunch of human traffickers. Even if it's the last thing I do, I'll find her.

"If you knew the lengths Reaper will go to in order to get a confession from someone, you'd be begging me for a merciful death. You'd spill your guts in a heartbeat."

"Reaper?" I swallow the lump forming in my throat. He's the only club member who truly terrifies me. A shroud of darkness covers each of the men in Underground Vengeance, but with Reaper, there's something more. It's as if the Devil himself is under Reaper's command.

"He should be here any minute now."

"What?" I jump to my feet.

"Sit the fuck down!" Matrix takes two long strides toward me, towering over me like a monster until I return to my spot on the couch. "First, you're going to tell me how the hell you're getting emails out without my knowledge. Second, I want to know what else you're doing at the clubhouse. It's not about Max, is it? Kids go missing all the time. If the case isn't solved in the first few months, the Feds give up because there's always another missing kid. And another. And another. Do you know how many children disappear each year?"

"Too many. Usually, a non-custodial parent kidnaps them. We know where to look and can find most of those kids."

"True, but that's not always the case. Like with those girls today. We don't even know who they are. Their parents might be looking for them, and we let them slip away. We could have intervened and saved those girls if you'd told us about your half-assed operation." He paces back and forth in front of the fireplace.

"I thought we had it under control."

"You fucking Feds never get shit right."

"We help recover over ninety percent of missing children, so don't start with that bullshit." I'm back on my feet. I don't give a crap about what he might do to me. Maybe we screwed up this operation, but something went wrong. There should have been at least twenty other agents there. As soon as I get away from Matrix, I'm going to demand answers from the team.

"They mentioned Blackstone." He stops in front of the fireplace. Without turning his back to me, he throws another log on the fire.

"Right. We don't know the details about how Blackstone's associated with them, but his name has come up several times in connection with this trafficking ring."

"There's an active group in the county?" He seems surprised.

"Yes. Based on our intel, this group is new to the area. We sent an agent to infiltrate them, but he went missing. We haven't heard from him in months. He's presumed dead."

"How's Blackstone connected to them?"

"He funds another MC, the Demon Riders."

"I know."

"They run drugs and guns, but we weren't

sure about human trafficking until recently. I mean, we don't have any evidence yet, but tonight's bust was going to change that. The Demon Riders are in league with the traffickers. I saw at least one of their members at the campground, solidifying the connection. We would have arrested them tonight, but something went wrong. Someone must have called off the raid."

"Why?"

"I don't know. I'm telling you the truth. If I don't check in, they'll come looking for me."

"You're holding something back. What is it?" He stares at me so intently it's almost as if he's trying to peer into my soul.

A slow tremble overtakes my body. I can't stop it. Every time I think about my sister and what might be happening to her, I can't control my reaction.

"Daisy. Sit," he says softly while guiding me back to the couch. Once I'm seated, he settles in beside me and places the gun on the side table next to the lamp. There's no way I can get to it, so I don't even consider it. Besides, even if I did manage to grab it, I'm shaking so hard I'd never get a solid shot before he grabbed it again. "Talk to me."

"You can't kill me. No one else is looking for her."

"Who?"

"My sister."

"What happened?" Concern replaces the fury in his gaze.

"She went missing almost a year ago."

"How do you know she didn't just run away? Lots of people disappear to escape from their lives."

"She was thirteen when she vanished from the mall."

"Old enough to be a runaway."

"No. Never. We pulled the CCTV footage. She was abducted in the parking lot. The video was too grainy to make out any details. We searched for months but didn't get any leads. Then suddenly, we got a hit on a wiretap."

"What wiretap?"

"Blackstone's."

"What? Are you investigating him?" He arches a brow.

"Yes. There were questions about where some of his campaign contribution money came from. Local politicians didn't like having an out-of-state candidate running for office. Someone pulled some strings with the local FBI office, and we got a warrant to listen in on Blackstone's calls. They were looking for any reason to stop him from being elected."

"That had to be a goldmine."

"Not really. We only had legal access to his calls originating in Montana."

"How is this related to your sister's abduction?"

"Blackstone's driver made a call from the ranch's landline."

"They still have those?" He snorts.

"Cell reception can be spotty in the mountains."

"True."

"Anyway, her name came up. One of the agents listening remembered my sister's case. He told me about the call. The driver didn't say anything incriminating, but Blackstone is connected. Her name wouldn't have popped up if he didn't have something to do with her kidnapping. We don't have any evidence yet, but I suspect he's connected to the trafficking ring." I take a breath before continuing. I've already told him so much. I may as well tell him everything. It might be my only shot at getting out of this cabin alive. "There's more …"

"Tell me."

"I know about Underground Vengeance's ability to skirt the law. I also know you're the best hacker in the state."

"In the country."

"Maybe so. And I know you guys have it out for Blackstone."

"What gives you that impression?" he asks cautiously.

"You're rivals with his unofficially-funded club, the Demon Riders."

"So?"

"You've also got twenty-four-hour

surveillance on his compound."

"How'd you figure that out?"

"We found your cameras when we went to set up our own. Instead of installing more and risk getting caught, we piggybacked onto your system."

"Who the fuck is working with you? Why haven't I detected any breaches?"

"Because I'm good at what I do."

"You?" He laughs for a second before realizing I'm serious. "Really? You?"

"I started taking computers apart before I could read. They fascinate me." I shrug.

He stares at me like he's never seen me before, and maybe that's true. I've never let him see the real me, only the fake persona I adopted to become part of the club. He has no clue who I am. Although I seem to be a simple country girl, I'm not. Watching the slow realization cross his face is almost amusing. It would be hilarious if he didn't still have my gun.

"I think we can work together. We both want to take down Blackstone but for different reasons."

"Do you know why we want him locked up or dead?" he asks slowly.

"No, but it doesn't matter to me. I want to find my sister. I took this undercover job when I heard you were watching Blackstone. You have information I can't access, and I have resources you could never dream of. If we work together—"

"We don't ride with Feds."

"I'm not asking you to ride with us. I'm asking you to help me find my sister. The FBI hasn't made any headway in months. I know you're the one who leaked the video of Blackstone and Senator McNash talking about trafficking kids."

"I have no idea what you're talking about."

"Liar."

His smirk makes my belly flip. I hate that my body reacts to him so viscerally. It's ridiculous. He's so disgustingly sexy that I cream the hell out of my panties every time he walks into the room, but I can't ever let him touch me. Not that he wants to. He's had every opportunity to make a move in the last few months, yet he never did. Going undercover as a club girl included the possibility that I'd have to seduce one of the members. I never could pull the trigger on that because the only guy who sets my body on fire also seems to hate me. Now that he knows I'm a Fed, Matrix probably despises me.

Outside, the sound of a truck cuts through the night. Matrix grabs my weapon and walks to the window. He pushes back the curtain with the barrel of the gun. "Boys are here."

"Yours?"

"Yeah."

"What are you going to tell them?"

"Don't know yet."

Footsteps pound up the porch. A hard knock

sounds on the door. When Matrix opens it, Scar, Nitro, Talon, and Reaper storm in with guns drawn. They encircle me with enough firepower to blow me into the next county.

"We got the distress signal," Scar says, not taking his eyes off me.

"Why the hell are we here at …" Nitro glances at his watch. "The ass-crack of dawn?"

"Because she's a Fed," Matrix says, pointing at me.

"The fuck?" Talon gasps.

"No way," Nitro says.

"Basement?" Reaper asks in that low, deadly tone that terrifies me to the core.

"Yep," Matrix says.

"Wait! I can explain!"

Reaper pulls a zip tie out of his cut while Talon grabs my arms and pulls them behind my back. I'm trussed up before I even have the chance to put up a fight. They're a lethal team, and I'm at their complete mercy.

As Reaper pushes me toward the door, Matrix grabs his semi-dry pants and pulls them on.

"Why's your ass hanging out anyway?" Talon asks.

"Long story." Matrix's silver eyes meet mine. "I'll tell you when we get back to the clubhouse."

"Can't wait to hear this shit," Scar grumbles.

Reaper opens the rear hatch of the SUV and pushes me inside. As I scramble to right myself, he gets in beside me and pulls the hatch closed, locking us in. The others get in, and soon, we're headed back toward the clubhouse. I don't know what Matrix will do with me. It might not even be up to him. Federal agents are usually killed when their cover is blown. Will that be my fate? If I die today, how will my sister ever be rescued?

I blink back tears because the last thing I want is to show any weakness. I can't worry about my sister until I get away from these men. That's priority number one. After I escape, I'll report back to the bureau and find out why backup didn't come. Then I'll get back to searching for my sister.

Today couldn't have gone any worse, but it's not over until I'm six feet under. Until that happens, I've still got a chance to make it out of this mess alive.

CHAPTER 3: MATRIX

As soon as we return to the clubhouse, Reaper takes Daisy to the basement, so Scar and the others can interrogate her. I take Scar aside and tell him that beating the shit out of her isn't a good idea. We need her in one piece because she may be an asset to the club. He's skeptical but agrees not to torture her. Not yet. However, if she doesn't give him useful information, there won't be any reason to keep her around. Reaper will be digging her grave in no time. I can't let that happen. I head straight to my room to change into something warm and dry so I can join everyone in the basement.

I throw on a jacket over my snow pants and hoodie. The basement's always freezing, even in the middle of summer. During the winter, it's positively frigid. I'm not looking forward to going down there, but then again, none of us ever are. The basement reminds us of Blackstone's dungeon, a hell we never want to revisit. If I weren't concerned about Daisy, I wouldn't bother joining the others. But for some reason, I've got a gut feeling that we need to keep her alive.

After heading outside, I open the door to the shed. The steps leading to the basement are concealed behind a huge shelf that looks solid but was built on a swivel. If you know how to move it, then it's lighter than a milk carton. I swing it open, descend several steps, then close the entrance behind me.

Cold gray concrete walls enclose the space. It's claustrophobic, especially when more than a few guys are down here. Right now, everyone's standing around while Scar fires questions at our prisoner. I still can't believe sweet little Daisy is a fucking FBI agent. How did she manage to slip under our radar? I'm worried we're getting too soft. No one should have been able to infiltrate the club like that. I'll give her one thing; she's a damn good actress.

"Tell me again exactly how the failed op went down." Scar towers over her seated form. It's his favorite, low-key intimidation tactic.

"We already went over this several times." Her gaze snaps to me. "Ask Matrix. He was there."

"What were you doing in the woods in the middle of the night?" Scar asks, directing his furious gaze at me.

"I was about to go for a run when I saw Daisy sneaking out of the clubhouse."

"We found an unopened beer on the kitchen

countertop," Nitro says.

"Yeah, that was mine."

"A beer before a run?" Talon raises a brow.

"Is that really the most important issue right now?" I snap.

"Okay, so you followed her. Then what?" Scar asks.

After relaying my version of the events leading up to and after the ambush, I tell him about how we escaped to the club's secret cabin. I hit the distress signal right after punching the code to get into the building. That's how they knew to come and get me.

"Did she tell you about her sister and Blackstone?" I ask.

"Her sister?" Scar returns his attention to her. "Talk."

Daisy sighs and glances at me with a look of betrayal. I didn't know her sister's case was supposed to be a secret. In our club, we don't keep things from each other. Whatever I know, they know. It's how it's always been. That's why we all trust each other implicitly.

"My thirteen-year-old sister was kidnapped from the mall almost a year ago. I've been trying to find her ever since." As Daisy explains the connection between her sister and Blackstone, defeat enters her voice. She's exhausted, broken down by her failure at the campground, and now, she's ready to give up everything. A small part of me hates seeing her so dejected, but she lied to us. She lied to me. I can't forget that, and I'll never be able to forgive her for it.

"What else do you know about our club?" Scar asks.

"Not much. You guys are good at covering your tracks and hiding evidence." She smirks. "We were starting to wonder if the undercover operation was worth it anymore. They were talking about pulling me out, but then I managed to hack Matrix's computer when he was in the hospital—"

"I knew it. I suspected my laptop had been compromised, but I couldn't figure out how you did it." I cross my arms over my chest.

"It wasn't that hard. I mean, for a normal person, maybe, but not for me." The hint of a smile tugs at her lips but dies before it can fully form.

"Get the Feds out of our shit," Scar tells me.

"I'll double-check everything."

"Today!"

"Yes, pres." I press my lips together and glare at Daisy. Because of her, Scar doesn't trust my capabilities completely anymore. She fucked that up for me. It's just one more reason I shouldn't want her around. However, there might be merit in keeping her. I need to talk to Scar about it privately. "Pres, I need a word."

"Church in ten. Matrix, you're with me. Reaper, make sure she's locked up nice and tight."

"Gladly." When Reaper's black eyes land on

her, she jolts. She should be afraid. One word from Scar and Reaper will kill her without hesitation.

As everyone except for Reaper files out of the basement, Scar motions for me to go with him. The sun's up when we step outside, but the air is just as chilly as last night. I zip my jacket to my chin and shove my hands in my pockets.

"Walk with me," Scar says, heading toward the partially frozen river. "What's your take on all of this?"

"Honestly, I don't know what to make of it. My first instinct is to kill her. She is a Fed."

"Right."

"But I don't know if that's the best course of action."

"Got any other ideas?"

"She knows more about Blackstone and his human trafficking connections than we do."

"True."

"And she's got access to resources we don't have, like a wiretap on Blackstone's landline. She could be useful to us."

"We can't trust her."

"Not even for a second," I agree.

"Reaper says the only good Fed is a dead Fed. I tend to agree."

"Normally, I would too, but she's not like the others. She's got more at stake than the usual government bullshit. Her sister's caught up in this. If you had a sister, wouldn't you do everything in your power to find her?"

"I would."

"Me too. I think we've got two issues here. One, she's a Fed who's using us to get intel on Blackstone. She's trying to take him down, and so are we. We're aligned on that front."

"We are." Scar nods.

"And two, she's looking for her sister. Protecting people is what we do. If her sister's caught up in trafficking, Fed or not, we have a duty to help find her."

"A duty?" Scar raises a brow. "This *duty* doesn't have anything to do with your dick, does it?"

"Asshole."

"It's a valid question. She's been living here for months. I see how you two look at each other. You think I don't notice, but I do. What's the deal with you and her?"

"Nothing. There's not a damn thing going on. And there never will be. You think I want to fuck a Fed?"

"She's hot."

"I'll make sure Julia knows you think Daisy's hot."

"Leave my wife out of this. I can objectively say a chick's hot even if I don't want to fuck her. There's only one woman in the world for me, and right now, she's at home, in my bed, waiting for me to come back. I've got more to protect than just this club. I've got a family. Nitro's got a family. We've got kids. If we don't get rid of Daisy, we're risking everyone's lives. You get that, right?"

"Understood."

"And you still think it's worth it? Will she bring enough to the table to make it worth keeping her alive?"

"If I didn't think so, I would've let Reaper kill her at the cabin."

"I just want to make sure you're thinking with your head and not your dick."

"She's not my type. Bringing down Blackstone is the only thing I care about. She's nothing to me, a means to an end. That's all." Even as I speak, I feel the shift in my body. When I lie, that disconnected, floaty feeling drags me away from reality. I become untethered, free from the consequences of deceit. Whenever it happens, I'm half-convinced we're living in a simulation. The world doesn't feel real. It becomes a waking dream, or a nightmare, depending on the circumstances.

"Matrix." Scar snaps his fingers in front of my face. "Get your ass back here."

"Sorry," I mutter.

"I need you here, not off in la-la land."

"We'll keep her alive while she's useful. The minute that changes, we'll make her disappear."

"I'm going to hold you to that."

"My loyalty will always be to the club, not a Fed. If the time comes and she's not helping us anymore, you have my word that I'll kill her myself."

"Good. She's your responsibility from here on out. I want you all over her. She's not even allowed to take a piss unless you say so. Move her into your room today. Don't let her out of your sight. Not even for a second. If shit goes south, it's on you."

"Got it."

"Let's go. The guys are waiting." Scar turns on his heel and walks back toward the clubhouse.

As I head into the house, I glance at the floor. I'm sure she can hear our footsteps overhead. She's probably terrified because she knows we're discussing her fate. Well, tough shit. Sympathy isn't something I can afford to feel. I understand her motives. If I had a missing sister, I'd lie, cheat, and steal to get any information that might help me find her. I'd do exactly what she did. For that reason, I can't really blame her. But Scar's right. Daisy's a huge liability. I have to keep her close because there's no way I can trust her.

We hold Church in a meeting room at the back of the ranch-style clubhouse. When I walk into the room, the others are already gathered around the huge wooden table Talon built out of old barn wood. The large, antique clock on the wall chimes nine times. My stomach growls. I haven't eaten since dinner, and I'm hungry as fuck. All that running around made me work up one hell of an appetite.

"Church is in session." Scar pounds the gavel. "I talked to Matrix, and here's the deal. We're keeping the Fed alive."

"What?" Reaper leans his elbows on the table.

"Why?" Talon asks.

"She knows things about Blackstone that we don't know. Somehow, we missed the fact that he started up his human trafficking ring again, but she caught it. She claims she's got intel that it's active, and I'm inclined to believe her. The connection between the men at the campground and Blackstone is tenuous, but still, there's some kind of association between them."

"And the Demon Riders were there. She mentioned it while you were changing," Nitro says to me.

"We thought we broke up their club while Max was hiding at Nina's, but they regrouped. Daisy knows more about that club and their dealings than we ever did." Scar looks around the room. "I think we can use her."

"How?" Reaper asks.

"For information. As far as the FBI knows, she hasn't been compromised. Somehow, she missed the fucking memo that the op wasn't going down the way she thought it was. I think we need to let her check in so she can find out why shit went south. She might learn something useful," Scar says.

"Or she might go running back to the Feds and bust us. We don't know what she knows about our club," Talon says.

"She would've passed on whatever she knows already. She wouldn't be sitting on information. We're good at what we do. We conceal shit, especially from club girls. After what happened with that bitch Crystal, we made sure we kept our business private. Even after I kicked her out of the clubhouse, we kept our mouths closed around Daisy. She doesn't know anything we don't want her to know," Scar says.

"She hacked Matrix's computer," Reaper says.

"Is she better than you at hacker shit?" Talon asks.

"No."

"It doesn't matter who's better. This isn't a dick-measuring contest," Scar says.

"That girl definitely doesn't have a dick." Talon whistles.

"Shut the fuck up." I glare.

"We'll vote. As always, if it's not unanimous, then it won't happen. All in favor of keeping her around, aye?" Scar raises his hand.

I thrust mine into the air. The others slowly follow until the only holdout is Reaper.

"Who's calling the shots if she fucks us?" he asks.

"Matrix has orders to kill her if she does," Scar says.

I nod solemnly. Although I don't look forward to that possibility, I can't hesitate to follow through if getting rid of her becomes necessary for the safety of the club. My brothers come first. Always.

"If she fucks us over, it's on you." Reaper raises his hand, indicating he agrees with the rest of us.

"Then it's settled. Move Daisy into your room right now. Talon, help him get her shit. Reaper, bring her upstairs. And Matrix?"

"Yeah?"

"She's your responsibility twenty-four-seven. We can't afford to fuck this up, so keep your dick in your pants. Meeting adjourned." Scar slams the gavel.

"This is gonna be good." Talon smirks.

"What is?" I ask as we head down the hall toward Daisy's bedroom.

"Watching you two trying not to fuck."

"What the hell are you talking about? I don't want her. Never did." My hands tingle like they're going numb. I shake them slightly to stop the sensation.

"Right. I'd let her suck my—"

I slam Talon into the wall just outside her room. "Shut the fuck up. Help me get her stuff, and then fuck off."

"Shit. Okay. Okay." He holds up his hands. "Jesus, you're touchy."

"I'm tired."

"Me too, bro. Your Fed bullshit woke me up from the best dream. Two chicks. Hot as fuck. They were …"

I stop listening as Talon launches into a detailed description of his dirty dream. I've had dreams like that too, and they seem to be getting worse. Only one woman ever appears in them. Daisy. She's like a curse I can't get rid of. I don't want her. I really don't. But those dreams keep tormenting me. I can't count how many times I've woken up, covered in sweat, my dick twitching out my release as her tight, fantasy pussy continues to milk my cock. Sometimes it feels so real that I get confused. I can't tell if I'm dreaming or if she's really riding my dick. I don't know why I have those dreams, but I wish they'd stop, especially now. She's completely off-limits. Even if I wanted her, which I don't, I couldn't have her.

"Lift the mattress higher," Talon says, interrupting my thoughts.

"I am." I angle her twin bed through the doorway. We carry it to the far wall and drop it on the floor. "Grab some of her clothes. We can get the rest later. I'll get sheets and shit."

"Make her do it."

"I should." I laugh, but I just want this to be over so I can finally get some sleep.

Talon comes back with an armful of clothes. A pair of embroidered pink panties sits atop the heap.

"Of course you went into her underwear drawer." I scowl, snatching the panties off the pile.

"If you'd prefer she wasn't wearing any, then give them back. I'll make sure they stay safe."

"You're such a fucking pervert."

"You know it." Talon's grin threatens to split his face.

"Asshole," I call as he leaves the room.

A second later, Reaper drags Daisy into my bedroom. "You belong to him now," he says to her before addressing me. "She's your problem, but if she becomes the club's, then she's mine. And you know what that means."

"I know."

He'll kill her. Viciously. Reaper's so loyal to the club that he'd do anything for it. Torture included. However, he's never executed anyone who didn't deserve it. I hope Daisy never compromises the club. If that happens, I'll be forced to kill her. But if I can't pull the trigger, Reaper won't hesitate to do it.

After he leaves the room and closes the door behind him, Daisy stands perfectly still. We stare at each other for a full minute before I finally break the silence.

"We should get some sleep. When we get up, we've got a lot of work to do, starting with your hacking skills. You're going to teach me everything you know. I want details on how you bypassed my code."

"But—"

"Get in bed." I point toward her bed. When she starts to balk, I add, "We dragged it in here. From now on, you're with me. Don't get any cute ideas, or I'll kill you myself. Are we clear?"

She nods meekly before climbing onto the sheets. I'm not fooled for a second. Although I should try to get some shut-eye, I can't trust her. I'll have to sleep with one eye open, but that's fine. She's been a pain in my ass for months. Now, she'll actually be useful.

I can't wait to get started.

CHAPTER 4: DAISY

Sleep eludes me. Although my eyes feel grainy, as if filled with sand, I don't dare close them. I don't know exactly what was said or who said it, but someone in this club saved my life. I think Matrix stuck his neck out for me. I can't imagine who else would have done it. The temptation to ask him keeps bouncing around in my head, but I stay silent because I can tell he's in one of his moods. He's not sleeping any more than I am. I've glanced over several times only to find him watching me.

"What?" I finally ask.

"You're still awake."

"Not tired."

"Me either." He swings his legs over the edge of his mattress. He's still wearing the clothes he changed into after we got back to the clubhouse. I haven't traded my winter gear for anything more appropriate. Running away in pajamas in the dead of winter isn't a good plan. I don't know when or if I'll get the chance to run, but if an opportunity presents itself, I want to be ready to bolt.

My stomach rumbles loud enough for him to hear it.

"It's lunchtime. You'll cook for the guys while I watch to make sure you don't try to poison us," Matrix says.

"I wouldn't dare," I say truthfully. There's no way I'd attempt something that stupid. Poisoning five grown men would be tricky. They wouldn't all go down at once. Someone would figure out what was happening, and then I'd be a dead woman.

"Let's go, then."

As we walk toward the kitchen, the muffled sound of a television carries from somewhere down the hall. The other guys must be in their bedrooms because the living room is empty.

"What do you want to eat?" I ask.

"Grilled cheese and tomato soup."

"Kid's food?"

"Yeah. So?" He leans against the counter, watching me gather the ingredients.

"Just an observation."

"Are you good at that, watching people?"

"I like to think so. I wouldn't be an effective agent if I didn't pay attention."

"You must have overheard some stuff over the last few months. Things you shouldn't know about."

I turn the knob on the gas stove. It clicks

twice before flames lick out. After setting a large pot on the burner, I dump several cans of tomato soup into it. Normally, I'd cook from scratch, but I can hardly see straight, let alone whip up something gourmet. It's a good thing he wanted a simple lunch because I don't think I could manage anything else right now.

"Well?" he prompts.

"I know a little bit. I don't know where Max is, but I've seen him at barbecues."

"Did you report it to your SAC?"

"No." I fire up a frying pan so I can cook the sandwiches.

"Why not?"

"He seemed happy. I know all about his case. You did the right thing." I butter several slices of bread before adding them to the pan to toast them.

"The Feds would have put him in foster care." The bitterness in his voice surprises me.

"Don't you trust the system?"

"It's failed too many kids."

"What makes you say that?"

"I'm right, and you know it."

"Were you ever in the system?" When he doesn't respond, I continue, "Your FBI files are tiny compared to most people's. The only thing we know for sure is that you all lived with Nina Grady for several years. We don't have any information before that."

"So?"

"So, it's weird. No school records. No birth certificates. We don't have a single document proving who you are before you popped up in some hospital medical records a few years after Nina took you in. Before that, there's no trace of you, of any of you. You're all ghosts."

"You didn't look hard enough." He walks to the kitchen table and pulls out a chair. After sitting, he leans his elbow on the table and rests his head on his hand.

"Were you in foster care? If you were, that would explain why I couldn't find you. Those records are sealed." He doesn't answer for so long that I look away from the sandwiches to make sure he heard me. A haunted look crosses his face. His jaw tightens, but he doesn't respond. "It's not a perfect system, but it works for a lot of children."

"If you say so."

"You must have been in the system." I pile the first batch of sandwiches on a serving tray. He watches me but doesn't confirm or deny my suspicion.

"We need you to check in with your team."

"What?" I'm confused for a second until I realize he's talking about my team at the FBI. He's right. I need to make contact before they send a bunch of agents to pull me out.

"In all the chaos, I forgot about it earlier. You said you had to email them to set up a meeting, right?"

"Yes."

"I'll grab a laptop. Don't even think about trying to leave. I have this place on lockdown."

"Wouldn't dream of it."

He scowls at my sarcasm before leaving to retrieve the laptop. I don't bother checking the doors. If he says he's got the clubhouse locked up tight, I believe him. He's got no reason to lie.

After returning, he motions toward me. "Come here." When I get close enough, he grabs me by the waist and drags me into his lap. I'm breathless as he types in his password. "I want you to set up a meeting with your SAC tonight. Tell him you want to meet at the campground."

"He'll never go for that. We don't meet in secluded places." I squirm in his lap.

"Do it anyway. See what he says." He tightens his grip on my waist. "I'll be watching, so no bullshit."

"Okay." My voice is barely a whisper because I suddenly can't breathe. Being this close to him awakens all the parts I shut off during this assignment. I'm not a woman; I'm an agent. If only my body would get the damn message.

After logging into a secret server I installed on Matrix's network, I compose an email to the SAC. There's no way he'll agree to meet me at the campground, but at least I tried.

"How long does he usually take to respond?"

"Typically, under an hour."

"Good."

"Can I get up now?" I ask, hating how my voice is thick with an emotion I don't dare acknowledge.

"Yeah."

When I slide off his lap, he gives my ass a little pat. "Good girl."

Oh, holy hell. No one's ever called me that before. Coming from his lips, it feels so deliciously naughty that I'm instantly wet. I'm tempted to crawl back into his lap or drag him into our bedroom, but that would be crazy. I'm not insane, just horny. I haven't gotten laid once since I've been on assignment. Dating is impossible when you're undercover. I've got needs, just like anyone else, but I can't use Matrix to fulfill them. Things are way too complicated between us. Besides, I don't think he's interested. He's only hard as steel because of the friction. That's enough to give any guy an erection, isn't it?

As I walk away from him, I shake my head. Obviously, I'm not thinking clearly. I've got sex on the brain, which makes zero sense, considering the situation. Maybe I should have tried harder to get some sleep because I clearly need it. I can't focus on what's important, and that could get me killed.

A door opens down the hall, and a few seconds later, Talon strolls into the kitchen. He grabs a chair, turns it around so the back is closest to the table, then straddles it. "I've been craving a good grilled cheese."

"Here." I carry the platter to the table. "The soup's almost ready. I'll get the others."

"I'll do it," Matrix says.

As soon as he leaves the room, Talon leans back to watch me. "Did they teach you how to cook at Club Fed?"

"What?"

"You know, Fed training school."

"The FBI Academy?"

"Yeah."

"No."

"It's hard to believe you're an agent. How the hell did you slip past us?"

"You're *guys*. You see a pretty girl who looks like a country bumpkin and don't question it. There's implied bias because I'm a woman. Most people think of men when they think of FBI agents."

"Aren't most of them dudes?"

"A lot, but definitely not all. There were several women in my class at Quantico."

"Hot as you?"

My face burns. I'm glad I've got my back to him while I stir the soup.

"Stop hitting on the Fed," Matrix says as he strolls back into the room. "Soup's probably warm enough. I'll get bowls."

We work together to portion it out, then carry the bowls to the table. Reaper's in the seat across from Talon. I didn't even hear him come in. Sometimes I think he's more ghost than human. It's fucking weird. I'm glad they didn't assign him to be my prison guard. I don't think I'd be able to handle his constant snarling and scowling.

Everyone's seated by the time Scar joins us. He sits at the head of the table. "Since everyone's still awake, let's move forward on having her contact her SAC."

"Done," Matrix says. "Waiting on a reply."

"Good." Scar drags his spoon through the soup but doesn't move to eat any of it.

"Talon and I watched her. She didn't poison it." Matrix eats a spoonful. "See, not dead."

"Not yet," Reaper growls.

A chime sounds on the laptop. Matrix pushes his food out of the way and drags the computer into its place. "Bingo. SAC Vale says he'll meet you at sunset at the campground."

"Really?" I'm surprised.

"That's what the email says."

"We need our men in place well before then," Scar says.

"Chow first. Work after," Talon says before cramming a whole sandwich into his mouth.

"Slow down. You're going to choke," I blurt.

Everyone turns to look at me. I shrink back in my chair. Maybe they don't realize it, but I don't hold any ill will toward any of these men. If anything, I admire them. Sure, they're consummate lawbreakers, but they usually do it for the right reasons. They aren't bad people, just horribly misguided. There are legal ways they could accomplish their goals, but they choose to circumvent the law. I don't fully understand why they do things their way, but it's fascinating. Maybe they're just impatient. Doing things legally takes time. In some cases, maybe they simply don't want to wait.

That said, if I knew my sister was being held at Blackstone's ranch, I wouldn't sit around waiting for a warrant. I'd storm the place and kill anyone who got between my sister and me. Maybe these men feel the same way about the people they're trying to protect. In some cases, waiting around isn't an option. I've seen plenty of cases where the justice system failed to protect a victim. They've probably seen it happen too, which is why they don't rely on the law to make things right.

"I want her wired up," Scar tells Matrix before turning to me. "Get all the info you can from Vale, and don't you dare try to signal him. I've got no problem making both of you disappear."

"Got it."

As the afternoon hours crawl by, I do my best to stay busy. Worrying about the meeting is pointless. Whatever happens, happens. I have very little control over this situation anymore. The minute my cover was blown, I became the club's property. My life is in their hands. I just have to play along until I figure out what to do next. Ultimately, I want to find my sister, but that will require multiple steps that can't happen until everyone calms down. Right now, I'm caught between the FBI and Underground Vengeance. I've got to play both sides without letting either know that the only side I'm on is my sister's.

After lunch, Matrix helps me clean the kitchen, which is really sweet of him. He could have sat on his ass and watched me work, but he didn't. He chipped in instead. Although he presents himself as a badass, and he is one, he's also got a softer side. I've seen it peek through from time to time. I can't help but wonder if that's how he is in bed. When he's naked and vulnerable, does that sweetness come out, or is he still the big, scary biker who takes complete control of his partner's pleasure?

A shiver of desire shimmies through my traitorous body. These random flashes of lust drive me crazy. I shouldn't feel like this. The only emotion I should be experiencing is fear. I'm in a terrible situation, stuck between a bunch of bikers who won't hesitate to kill me and an agency I've sworn to be loyal to. I'm screwed either way.

Matrix mercifully allows me to shower in the bathroom connected to his room. I could probably squeeze through the window, but escape is the farthest thing from my mind right now. I need to figure out how to get as much information as I can about the traffickers from last night without revealing the fact that I've been compromised. SAC Vale has been with the agency for over twenty years. He's sharp and can read people very well. I don't know if I'll be able to pull this off.

As I walk out of the bathroom wearing only a towel, Matrix's gaze locks with mine. Warmth pools low in my body, and tendrils of longing wrap around my belly. There's something raw and demanding in his eyes, yet he doesn't say a word. He simply watches me. It feels like a challenge, so instead of grabbing my clothes and retreating into the bathroom, I tighten my towel around my chest. I reach for a pair of panties and step into them. Sliding them up my thighs, I can't help but notice the hunger in Matrix's eyes. He's a man, so, of course, a half-naked woman turns him on, but I get the feeling there's more to it. Things have always been this way between us. There's this indescribable tension both repelling and attracting us. It's a huge distraction. I wish I knew what to do about it, but I don't.

The temptation to do a reverse striptease overcomes me. For a second, I'm sure I'll give in to the need to torment my warden. Then the sensation passes, and I finish dressing. There's no time for stupid games. My life depends on my ability to keep the truth about my situation from my SAC. I can't think about anything beyond this meeting. It's literally a matter of life or death.

"Ready?" Matrix asks gruffly.

"Let's go."

Since side roads are nearly impassable during the winter, we take one of the club's winterized trucks. I drive until we're a mile away from the campground. Pulling to the side of the road, I turn to face Matrix. "Here's your stop."

"We tested the wire earlier, so we know it works. We'll be listening. Reaper and Talon will have sniper rifles pointed directly at you and SAC Vale. Don't fuck this up." He hesitates. It looks like he wants to say something else, but he doesn't. After getting out of the truck, he silently closes the door.

My hands clench around the steering wheel. The sun's setting over the mountains, casting long shadows through the trees. The MC guys already did recon on this area of the forest. They know there aren't any agents hidden here, but there are some up ahead. Those men also have rifles. I'm surrounded by people who won't hesitate to shoot. The stakes couldn't be any higher, but I've got this. I'm a damn good agent. Being undercover requires a whole hell of a lot of lying. What's one more lie in a sea of them?

As soon as I pull into the campground, I spot SAC Vale's truck. I pull up beside it. He motions for me to get in, so I do.

"I was worried when you didn't check in last night. What happened?" he asks without preamble.

"I came here to the rendezvous point for the bust. The trade went down as expected, but you guys weren't here. I didn't have any backup. What the hell happened?" My anger is genuine. Without Matrix's help last night, I wouldn't have been able to escape those men.

"We called it off at the last minute. I sent the kill code."

"Nothing came through on my phone."

"I sent an email."

"Seriously? I didn't bring my damn laptop with me. There's no service in the middle of the forest. I needed to know well beforehand."

"It should have reached you before you left the clubhouse."

"Well, it didn't. I almost died."

"Tell me what happened."

I go through the details while leaving out Matrix's involvement. When I'm done, SAC Vale stares at me intently. "I can't believe you escaped."

"Me either." I'm exasperated, and it's not an act.

"You didn't run into anyone else? No one from the MC?"

"No. They didn't know I left last night. I had to sneak into my room this morning. I almost didn't make it back before breakfast."

"Do they suspect anything?"

"No. They still think I'm a stupid club girl."

"Good. At least your cover's intact. There's been talk about pulling you out."

"What?"

"But I shut that down."

"Good. We need more time."

"Agreed."

"Why was the op canceled?" I ask, redirecting him back to the events of last night.

"We decided to put surveillance on the traffickers instead. Last-minute intel says they're headed for Denver, Colorado."

"Denver?"

"We think it's the first stop to drop off one of the girls."

"Please tell me you've got a plan to rescue them at that meeting."

"We can't. This is the best lead we've had in months."

"Those girls were young. They couldn't have been more than thirteen."

"And I wish we could rescue all of them in Denver, but if we're going to take down the whole operation, we need a lot more evidence. Right now, all we have is conjecture and coincidence, neither of which holds up in court. You must trust me on this. Following them while they drop off girls is the only way to get what we need."

"Who's going to Denver?"

"Agents Wilcox and Viola."

"Only two?"

"They're not intercepting the traffickers.

They're being sent to follow them to see where they go next."

"To the second drop-off point for another girl, right?"

"Maybe. Or maybe these guys will lead us to the heart of whatever cartel, gang, or MC is running this operation. We still don't have shit about who is actually behind this. We suspect Blackstone's involved, but without anything solid, our hands are tied."

"What do you want me to do?" I ask because it's a question he'd expect from me.

"Sit tight with Underground Vengeance. See what else you can get from their servers. If anything comes up, contact me. I'll be close."

"Okay."

"Be careful, Daisy. You're a good agent, but these men are part of a violent, criminal enterprise. They seem to be doing the right thing on the surface, but you've got to ask yourself why. What's really going on in that club? No one rescues people the way they do without an ulterior motive. For all we know, they're human trafficking the people they supposedly rescue."

"I'll keep my eyes and ears open," I assure him.

After setting up our next scheduled check-in for a few days from now, I get back into my truck and wait until he's gone before driving toward the highway. The plan didn't involve me picking Matrix back up. He told me they were testing me. If I try to run, they'll hunt me down and kill me. By giving me the option to flee, they're trying to see where my loyalty lies. They don't get it yet, but I've only got one loyalty, and that's to my family. To my sister. Finding her is my reason for living. Eventually, they'll understand it, but for now, I have to play by their rules. With any luck, they'll help me find her. Maybe that's too hopeful, but hope is all I have right now. Anything else would just be a delusion.

CHAPTER 5: MATRIX

Daisy did everything according to plan. I'd be lying if I said I wasn't surprised. I expected her to jump at the chance to be sheltered by the Feds. It would be the sane thing to do. But she didn't take the opportunity to flee. Instead, she's heading back toward the clubhouse, just like we planned. This girl is full of surprises. I'm going to have to keep a close eye on her.

There isn't much traffic on the highway, but we picked up a tail. A black truck with darkened windows appeared in my rearview mirror a couple of minutes ago. It's two vehicles behind me. Daisy's three cars ahead. I can't tell if the tail is tracking her or if he's on my ass.

When Daisy blows past the offramp to the clubhouse, my gaze narrows. Maybe the guy following us is FBI. This could be part of some kind of plan to let her escape. I was listening in on the conversation between her and SAC Vale. Was there a secret signal I missed? Maybe she's not trustworthy after all.

The truck behind me picks up speed, passing me and heading straight for Daisy. I push the pedal to the metal to keep up. A gun pokes out of the driver's side window. Shots ring out.

"Fuck!"

I hit the gas and race toward them. Daisy swerves to avoid being shot at, but it's pointless. The guy's semi-auto shoots a barrage of bullets at the SUV. She's alone and unarmed, unable to fight back. I put her in this position by taking away her weapon. Since I discovered her secret, she hasn't shown any disloyalty, so there's no reason to think this is a setup. She's under attack.

Pulling my gun from my cut, I make an evasive maneuver around the last car between me and my target. I shove my gun out the window and fire. Hitting anything at this speed with a pistol will be nearly impossible, but I'm not worried about that. All I need is this asshole's attention.

The guy slams on the brakes. I'm still flying forward when I get parallel with his truck. I glance to the side. I'd recognize the guy's cut anywhere. He's a Demon Rider.

A sharp bend in the road catches my attention. Although I've got snow tires on this truck, black ice sends it skidding toward the side of the mountain. I turn the wheel to correct the slide and fishtail through a muddy snowbank on the side of the road until the wheels finally find purchase. I blast back onto the highway, but my momentum is gone. The Demon Rider pulls up beside me and shoots out my back windows. I hit the brakes and fire a shot through his passenger side window, which splinters into a million shards of glass.

The driver jerks the truck toward the opposite side of the highway. A steep drop looms. He narrowly misses plunging over the edge. Overcorrecting, he slams his truck into the side of mine. We're locked together as we speed around the next turn.

I've got a few shots left, so I must make them count. The first one pings off the road, but the second hits its mark. The front tire explodes. The truck loses control, crossing in front of me, clipping my bumper, and sending us straight into the side of the mountain. Metal screams as it scrapes against exposed granite. A jutting rock rips off my side mirror before shattering the windows.

When the Demon Rider's truck finally rolls to a stop in front of me, I jump out and run to the driver's door. I pull it open and grab the dazed man by his hair. Slamming his face into the side of the truck, I miss the sound of another vehicle's arrival.

"Stop! Stop! You're going to kill him!" I look up to find Daisy running toward us.

"He almost killed you. He almost killed us."

"We need to know why."

She's right, but the rage coursing through

my body fuels my fists. I throw several punches, then step back as the Demon Rider collapses.

Another truck parks behind mine. Scar jumps out. "Who the fuck is that guy?"

"Look at his cut." I spit out a mouthful of blood. I didn't even realize I had a busted lip until the metallic taste slid across my tongue.

"He tried to shoot me," Daisy says.

"And kill me," I add, wiping blood from my lips.

"Let's get him in the truck and take him back to the clubhouse. We need to know why he shot at you." Scar grabs the guy under the shoulders while I hoist him up by his knees. He's deadweight but easy enough to carry. All those hours in the clubhouse gym sure as fuck paid off. "Have Daisy drive you back. Your ride's shot. I'll send Reaper and Talon to clean this mess up. Meet me in the basement."

"Will do, pres."

Daisy rushes forward and wraps her arms around me. "Oh, God. I thought you were dead."

"You think they can send just one guy to attack you?" I snort. "Not a chance, babe." I hook my arm around her shoulders and walk her back to the SUV she was driving.

"You're in no condition to get us back to the clubhouse," she says as she slides into the driver's seat.

"Fine." I'm glad she offered because I need to be on the lookout for more Demon Riders.

Until we're safely back at the clubhouse, we're in danger.

As she heads down the mountain toward the clubhouse, I scan the trucks passing us. No one seems interested in us. We don't encounter any additional gunmen before making it home safely.

"We need to patch up your lip." Daisy parks in front of the clubhouse. "And change. There's blood everywhere."

"Don't worry. I'm as clean as a whistle. Nothing to catch. Also, there's no time to get pretty. We've got someone to interrogate."

"We?" She turns to look at me.

"Yeah. You're coming with me." I push open the door and get out of the SUV. When she doesn't immediately follow, I narrow my gaze. "Move!"

"I can't watch you break the law."

"What the fuck are you talking about?"

"You're going to torture him."

"Yeah? So?"

"That's illegal."

"No shit. Do you think we can ask nicely and expect to get an answer? Don't tell me you've never roughed up a suspect to get them talking."

"Never."

"Bullshit. You Feds are all the same. I'm sure you've looked the other way more than a few times. Try this; just pretend it's just another day at the office." I grab her hand and drag her toward the shed. She doesn't say another word as we walk down the steps into the basement.

Scar's testing the knots at the Demon Rider's feet. His hands are tied behind his back, and he's been stripped to his boxers. Men seem to talk faster when they're exposed like this. It's one of Reaper's tricks. He's not here yet, but Nitro walks in to join us.

"Back-to-back days in the basement. Perfect." The sarcasm in his voice isn't lost on me. I don't want to be down here either. The less I see of this place, the better. The only one of us who seems to like this place is Reaper. It's his playground.

"Let's wake this asshole up." Scar grabs a bucket of water and splashes the Demon Rider with it.

Coughing and sputtering, the man's swollen eyes crack open. "Fuck you."

Scar laughs before punching the guy in the face. When he lands another blow to the man's abdomen, the guy grunts in pain.

"What's your name?" I ask.

"Fuck you."

I grab his cut off the floor and hold it up. A patch bearing the name "Griller" gives us the information he's refusing to share. I show it to Scar.

"Why were you trying to kill our club girl, Daisy?" Scar asks.

"The Fed?" Griller spits at her but misses.

She backs up toward the nearest wall.

"Don't disrespect women." I slam my knuckles into his teeth. They cut through my flesh, but I welcome the pain.

"That your bitch?"

"This guy's an idiot." Scar does the honors, throat-punching the guy so fast that I almost miss it.

Doubled over with drool and blood dripping from his mouth, Griller looks like he's about to throw up. His eyes go blank. He's trying to do what I do, check out of the situation. That's not happening, not while I'm here.

I stomp on his bare foot, crushing the delicate bones in his feet, and he howls in pain.

"Matrix!" Daisy's horrified gaze meets mine.

"You think you can talk sense into this bastard?"

She shakes her head but doesn't respond. She knows there's only one way to get info out of this punk, and it will involve a lot of blood. I hate that she has to see this, but I'm not letting her leave. We can't risk it. She could run back to the FBI or rush into another ambush with the Demon Riders. Either way, she'd be in a whole hell of a lot of trouble, and I won't let that happen.

"Why were you trying to kill the Fed?" I stand in front of Griller, close enough to tower over him but not within head-butting range. Talon made that mistake once. I learned from it.

"There's a contract out on that bitch."

"Who ordered the hit?"

"Don't know."

"Lying will only make things worse for you." I jump and come down hard on his other foot. His piercing scream echoes through the basement.

"I swear I don't know. We were looking for her because she's got a price on her head. Figured we'd cash in. When we saw her with Vale a couple of weeks ago, we realized she was an undercover Fed. That got me real excited. Never killed a cop before."

"When did you see me with Vale?" Daisy askes, shocked.

"You met him at the Suds and Soap. One of our old ladies was there doing laundry. She recognized you from …" His voice trails off.

"From what?" I ask.

"Our Underground Vengeance kill board." He smiles through the blood. "One of our guys saw you last night at the campground. We figured you'd come back to look for clues, so we left a guy there. He radioed your location, and they sent me to get you. Capture or kill. Although I would have liked a little time with you before turning you in. You're one hot piece of ass."

"You're disgusting." Daisy turns her back on him.

I whip my piece out of my cut, but Scar grabs my wrist and pushes it down. "Not yet."

"I want to do it," I say through gritted teeth.

"He's yours. No argument there."

Footsteps sound on the stairs. Reaper and Talon show up at the same time.

"Taking away all my fun again?" Reaper grumbles.

"This one's Matrix's," Scar says in a tone that leaves no room for argument.

Reaper growls before crossing his arms over his chest. Normally, I let him do the dirty work down here, but this piece of shit belongs to me now.

"We know your crew has been watching our club. Why?" Scar asks.

"Someone's got a hard-on for you guys."

"Who?"

"Jonathan Blackstone. I hear you guys are intimately acquainted with him."

Daisy turns around and frowns at me. I ignore her.

"Why's he interested in the club?" I ask, not taking the bait.

"All I know is he was talking to our pres one day, and they were laughing at you shitheads."

"About what?"

"Something about stupid little boys who never put up much of a fight."

And just like that, I'm back in Blackstone's dungeon.

Pain. Pain so intense I can't breathe. They're kicking me in the ribs, and I can't get any air. I lift my throbbing head and search the other boys' faces. They're all watching. Some look terrified, while others don't even seem to be present. It's like they're somewhere else. I want to float away, too, to be anywhere but here.

"You think you deserve a piece of bread after what you did upstairs?" One of the guards laughs so hard he doubles over.

"The stupid shit couldn't make anyone happy today. Tough break, little dude." A second guard drives his steel-toed boot into my thigh.

I gasp as agony burns up my leg. From the moment I got here, I knew I would die. Never suspected it would be today, but now I'm sure I'm done. This is it. The end.

When the third guard begins to pummel me with his ruthless fists, I pray for death, for an end to years of suffering.

"Fight back," one of the boys yells. I recognize his voice. I don't know his name, but he's got scars all over his body. He's been here longer than me. Sometimes he gives me a bit of his bread and water. He's just as hungry as the rest of us, but he's stronger. I wish I could be more like him.

A guard grabs me by the throat and pins me to the wall. My thin legs kick as terror surges through my veins. I can't take a breath. The agony makes it impossible. And then the strangest thing happens.

Suddenly, there's nothing.

No pain. No suffering. Nothing but the sweet sensation of floating. I'm still in the room, but I'm not in my body. I'm standing beside it, looking at it like it belongs to someone else. It's not mine. It's not me.

Maybe I'm dreaming, or maybe the world isn't real. Yes. That's it. Nothing's real. It's all one big simulation. Just like those computer games they let me play when I'm a good boy. I bet this dungeon doesn't even exist. It's all in my mind. In my head. It's what they want me to believe. But it's not real.

Not real.

Not real.

"Fight!" the kid with scars yells, breaking through the fog. "Fight or die!"

When the guard drops me, I snap back into my body. I suck in two greedy breaths before joining the chaos of kicking and screaming kids. We outnumber them. We can get them back for what they did to us.

Swinging my fists, I blindly smash them into anything with flesh. I can't see through my swollen eyes, but they're all around me. Screaming something ... something ...

"Matrix, stop!"

I slam my fist into the man's face over and over and over while Scar and Reaper try to pull me off him. By the time they get me under control, I'm a bloody mess. But it's not my blood. It's Griller's.

"He's dead." Scar grabs my hands, but I pull them away and swing past him, trying to get at the lifeless body.

"Matrix, stop! What's wrong with you?"

Daisy covers her mouth with her hand and shakes her head. Her eyes have never been so wide or so filled with horror.

"Take her upstairs," Scar says to Talon.

"No! Mine!" I cross the room and grab her around the waist, pulling her hard against me.

Everyone's silent, staring at me like they've never seen me before.

"Stomp your feet, Matrix," Nitro says.

Out of habit, I stamp the ground with my boots.

Right. Left. Right. Left.

Oh, shit. I know what's going on now. I was gone again. I can't even remember what the hell just happened. One minute I was here. The next, I was back in Blackstone's dungeon, a place of unspeakable evil.

Right. Left. Right. Left.

The guys have seen me like this before. The first time it happened, we were still at Blackstone's. But it wasn't the last. In times of immense pain or stress, I get sucked out of my body. Doc calls it "disassociation." I call it freedom. It's the only time I ever feel free of this dark and terrible world.

"Reaper, take care of the body," Scar says.

Instead of complaining because he couldn't participate in the kill, Reaper unties the corpse and throws it over his shoulder. Talon grabs a shovel, and they leave together.

Daisy hasn't moved from my side, but her

body's rigid, ready to flee. She's probably afraid of me now. She doesn't understand what she just witnessed. I'm not a cold-blooded killer. Not usually. But today, something snapped.

"Should I call the girls to take Daisy for a few hours?" Scar asks.

"No."

"Are you back now?" He's asking because I've had trouble getting back into my body before. Sometimes I'll float for hours, and nothing they do will bring me home.

"Yeah."

"Take her upstairs and let her make you some food. Daisy." Scar turns to her. "When he has his ... episodes, he needs meat after. Something hearty to ground him again."

She nods.

"Are you okay staying with him?"

"Alone?" she asks softly.

"He won't hurt you."

"Are you sure?"

"I wouldn't leave you with him if I thought he would."

"Okay." She squeezes my waist. "How about steak and a big baked potato?"

The adrenaline is starting to wear off, leaving me exhausted. I sag against her, and Scar steps in and helps get me upstairs and into the kitchen. After settling me in a chair at the table, Scar motions for her to go with him into the pantry. He shuts the door, blocking my ability to hear whatever he's telling her.

I lean back and close my eyes. Killing a man doesn't bother me. The fucker deserved it. But now Daisy's looking at me like I'm a monster, and that's got me all messed up inside. Usually, I don't give a shit about what people think about me. Their assumptions don't matter. I shouldn't give a damn about her opinion either, but I do. And that pisses me off.

CHAPTER 6: DAISY

I can't stop shaking. Even though I shouldn't be showing any fear, I am. Being trapped in the pantry with Scar isn't helping. Although he isn't doing anything to intimidate me, his sheer size is terrifying. I can't forget how much danger I'm in. They claim they want to work with me, but once they get what they want, what will become of me then?

"He's never done that before," Scar says.

"Kill someone?"

"Not during one of his episodes."

"What happened down there? He totally lost it."

"Doc says it's 'dissociation.' It's a psychological coping mechanism where Matrix leaves his body—"

"Leaves?"

"Yeah. He doesn't realize where he's at or who he's with. It's like he's gone. He's still in the room, but he's not connected to his body anymore."

"I heard about cases like this at the academy. You wouldn't get that unless you went through intense trauma."

"Right." Scar looks at me carefully. "He had some shit happen to him, and that's how he survived."

"What happened?" Curiosity quickly replaces my fear. I'm not letting down my guard by much, but I need more information to know what I'm dealing with. If Matrix can snap and kill someone, then I need to know what might trigger it. I don't want to end up his next victim.

"That's not for me to say."

"Fine. I'll just ask him." I try to push past Scar to get out of the claustrophobic pantry, but he refuses to budge.

"That's not a good idea."

"Why? Because he'll freak out again? If I'm going to stay here, then I need to know I'm safe."

"The safest place you can be right now is in this clubhouse. If Blackstone puts a hit out on you, then the Demon Riders won't be the only club coming for you. There will be others. If the bounty is high enough, gangs and out-of-state clubs will come to Montana, looking to get a big score. I don't like the fact that you're a Fed. If I didn't think you could help us, I wouldn't have agreed to let you stay."

"What makes you think I can do anything for you?"

"You want to take down Blackstone as much

as we do. If he was involved in your sister's kidnapping, you'll want to make him pay for what he did."

"Exactly. But why are you guys so focused on him? What did he ever do to you?"

"We've got our reasons. You don't need the details."

"I'll find out eventually."

"Maybe. But right now, you need to cook dinner. We have to get Matrix grounded again so he can get back to work. Then we'll figure out what to do next."

"I'm not your club girl anymore. You can't order me around."

"If you want to leave, there's the door. But good luck to you. Once you walk off this property, you're not our problem anymore. You're a fool if you think the FBI can protect you from Blackstone. He's a monster who'll stop at nothing to get what he wants."

"You'd actually let me leave if I wanted to go?" I don't believe him for a second.

"I'll give you one chance to leave. Right now. If you stay, you're committing to working with us to take down Blackstone."

"And find my sister. That has to be part of our agreement."

"If that's all you want in exchange for Blackstone, consider it done. We'll help you rescue her once we find out where she's being held."

"That's all I want." My voice wavers even as I lift my chin.

"I know. If it weren't for your sister, I'd never consider keeping you around. Hell, I wouldn't have let you leave the basement if I didn't trust you at least a little bit. You've got one damn good reason not to fuck us over. You know the Feds haven't been able to find your sister, but we can. It might take a while—"

"We don't know how much time she's got left. She could be in terrible danger."

"Or she could already be dead."

"No." I back up a step.

"You can't discount that possibility."

"I would have felt it."

"How old is she? You're not twins, are you?"

"No. She's thirteen. Twelve years younger than me. Our parents didn't expect her. She's an 'oops' baby. But they love her so much. My mom won't even leave the house anymore because she's so distraught. Dad never drank a day in his life until after Angela went missing. We have to rescue her. Losing her will destroy my family."

"I don't make promises I'm not sure I can keep, but I'll tell you this, we'll do everything in our power to find her. But you'd better work your ass off to help us bring Blackstone to justice."

"I will."

"Good. Now, I know you're not our club girl anymore, but I do need your help. I'm going to call a few contacts I have in Denver to see if they know anything about the girls being transported there. While I'm working on that, I need you to cook the best steak dinner you've ever made. Give it to Matrix. Take care of him for a bit. I'm not asking you to do this as a club girl. I'm asking because that's what needs to be done right now. I can't do that while also making calls."

"Understood." I nod. "What about the other guys?"

"Don't worry about them. Matrix is our top priority right now. He's the only one who fully understands how all his computer stuff works. I know you can hack into the system without him, but you won't know where to start looking. I want you in his files, but I don't need you poking around in club business unrelated to Blackstone. Don't touch any of his shit until he's back to normal. Once he's himself again, then we can get to work."

"Okay."

Scar opens the door, and we walk back into the kitchen. Matrix hasn't moved from where Scar left him. He still looks dazed. According to Scar, all Matrix needs is some food. The sooner I can get that done, the better. I hate seeing him like this. He's usually so rational and analytical. I've never watched him lose control the way he did in the basement. I didn't even think he was capable of so much violence. He's a murderer. If I hadn't seen him do it, I wouldn't believe he could be so vicious. But I saw his explosive rage with my own eyes. It was so shocking that I'm questioning everything I thought I knew about him. From now on, I need to be cautious around him. Scar seems convinced Matrix won't snap, but how well can Scar really know him?

The familiar task of cooking dinner calms my nerves. Matrix hasn't said anything to me, but he's been watching me. His eyes follow me around the kitchen. It should be creepy, but it's not. There's nothing behind his gaze. I'm not even sure if he's still here with me. He seems like he's not really present. Maybe he's still disassociating.

"Steak and a baked potato," I announce, setting the plate in front of him. "I don't know what you take with it. Steak sauce? Sour cream? Butter?"

"Butter."

I open the fridge and take the butter tray out. After setting it in front of him, I grab a knife from the utensil drawer. Its blunt edge wouldn't make a good weapon; still, handing it to him feels dangerous. He takes it without incident. I back away and lean my hip against the counter.

"Where's your plate?" he asks.

"I'm not hungry." My stomach's still in turmoil. I'd throw up anything I attempted to eat right now.

"Are you just going to stand there then?"

"I'll make some tea." I set a kettle on the stove and wait for the water to boil. He glances at me between bites. I try not to look over at him, but it's impossible. Our strange connection is still there. It's an ever-present force, tying us together whenever we're in the same room.

"Sorry you had to see that." He slathers butter onto the potato. "I should have left you upstairs."

"You couldn't trust me to be alone."

"No," he agrees. "Still, wish you hadn't been there."

"What's done is done."

He stops chewing and looks at me for a long time before saying, "What did Scar tell you?"

"Not much. He said you can get really upset and disassociate."

"And?"

"That's all he said."

"If you're lying, I'll find out."

"I'm not. Is there more to it? Is there something you want to tell me about what happened?"

"No." He returns to eating his food.

Instead of trying to pry it out of him, I decide to let it go. For now. Eventually, I want to find out what happened to him, but I can't force him to tell me. I take a sip of mint tea. Its soothing warmth trickles through my body. I haven't really slept in two days, and I'm starting to crash. Scar wants us to get to work immediately, and I want that too, but I'm so tired.

"I need a nap," I mutter.

"Same." He grabs a napkin and wipes his mouth. "Thanks for dinner."

"I'm glad you liked it."

"Eating always helps keep me grounded. But it's not enough. I haven't slept in a few days. I need shut-eye before we get started."

"Me too." I grab his empty plate and carry it to the sink.

"Leave it. Let the others clean up for once."

"But I always—"

"Leave it."

He holds out his hand. I hesitate before taking it. We walk back to his bedroom and go inside. When he closes the door behind us, I tense. I'm alone with a man who just killed someone. This is crazy. I should be running for my life, but the weird thing is that I don't feel like I'm at risk. As long as I do what they say and help them with Blackstone, then they aren't a threat to me. Leaving the clubhouse is more dangerous. Scar's right. The FBI can't protect me from the men trying to hunt me down. Someone with Blackstone's reach will find a way to get to me. It would only be a matter of time before someone found me and captured or killed me. I can't tell my SAC what's going on, either. If the FBI finds out I've been compromised, they'll pull me off the case and throw me back on desk duty. I had to beg and plead to be allowed to take on this undercover assignment. If I fail, they'll never let me leave the office again. I'll be stuck hacking computers all day, far away from the action. Also, Underground Vengeance can get information I can't access legally. I know they can help me find my sister. Risking my life to save hers is worth it.

"I need a shower." Matrix heads into the bathroom, pulling the door closed behind him. A moment later, he tosses his bloodstained shirt out, and it lands on top of a pile of laundry. He does the same with his pants.

"I'll take these to the laundry room. If I don't get stain remover on them soon, we'll never get the blood out," I call through the crack in the door.

Matrix sticks his head out. His eyebrows draw together for a moment before he bursts out laughing. "You're worried about stains? Is that really your main concern right now?"

"Of course not. But I don't know what will make you freak out again, so until I figure that out, I'm sticking to neutral subjects," I snap.

"You're a little bit crazy, aren't you?"

I huff and leave the room. Jerk. Of course I'm not myself right now. The last two days have been completely insane. I'm exhausted, and I can't think clearly. He can't expect me to be rational. Also, he's one to talk. I'm not the one who basically had a psychotic break and killed a man. I'll be able to figure out what to do next once I've had some sleep.

After treating his clothes with stain

remover, I toss them into the washing machine. I turn it on, hoping the cold water being diverted here makes his shower hotter than hell. It's petty revenge, but it still feels good.

As I walk back to his room, Reaper steps into the hall. He glares at me, but I'm so angry that I scowl right back. If he thinks he can intimidate me, he's got another thing coming. As long as Scar wants me around, Reaper can't touch me. I know he's got it out for me, but too damn bad.

I brush past him, ignoring him. Once I'm back in Matrix's room, I slam the door behind me. I'm tired. I'm scared. I'm pissed off, and I need a nap.

After stripping down to my underwear, I put on the tank top I found in a pile of clothes beside my bed. I don't understand why I can't just stay in my room. I have no intention of running away. Scar's right. We need each other to achieve our goals. Until I get my sister back, I'm not leaving. I should be allowed some privacy.

I crawl into bed and close my eyes. Sleep drags me into a nightmarish abyss. My sister's cries for help fill a dark prison. Demons dance around her in a spiral, moving closer and closer, closing in with sickening intent. Depraved and indifferent to her suffering, they taunt her while she sobs uncontrollably. And who's there to console her? No one. Especially not me.

A scream wakes me. It's my own. Before I can stop hollering, Matrix is out of his bed, hovering over mine. "Hey, wake up. It's just a bad dream." His silvery gray eyes are all I can see. They're filled with concern. "Move over."

Without thinking, I slide over in the tiny bed to make room for him. Someone knocks on the door.

"Everything okay in there?" Talon yells.

"Yeah, we're good," Matrix says.

"Daisy?"

"I'm okay. I just had a nightmare."

"If you need anything, I'm right down the hall," Talon says.

"She said she's fine." Matrix glares at the door.

"Can you blame me for checking after what you did to that Demon Rider?"

"No. But she's fine."

"I am, really."

"Okay. But like I said, I'm two doors away if you need me. You know where to find me."

"Asshole," Matrix mutters.

"He's just trying to make sure I'm all right. That's really sweet of him."

"I'll take care of you." Matrix pulls me into his arms and cradles me against his chest. His warmth soothes me, so I relax against his body. Maybe I'm a fool, but I'm not afraid of him. He's never done anything to frighten me. Although he's been gruff from time to time, he's always treated me with care and respect. I trust him not to hurt me.

"Tell me about the nightmare." When his lips graze my temple, a shiver of desire shimmies through me.

"I've had that same dream before. There are a bunch of demons circling my sister, and I can't get to her. I can't save her."

"Nightmares suck."

"Do you ever have them?"

"All the time."

"What are they about?" I wind my arms around him and hold him as tightly as he clings to me.

"The past."

"Scar told me." I don't elaborate further. I learned this common interrogation tactic in one of my academy classes. I got the highest score out of everyone in my class; however, I've never actually used this method in the field before. Trying to trick Matrix into telling me more is risky, but I need to know what happened to make him disassociate the way he does.

"What did Scar say?"

Well, that didn't work. Of course, he's too smart to fall for it. "He told me about Blackstone."

"What about him?"

"Honestly, not much. I know you guys think he's evil."

"He's the Devil."

"Right, but why? What makes you think that?" I ask.

He rests his chin on the top of my head and sighs. "If you knew the details, you'd agree."

"Tell me what happened."

"It's bad, Daisy. If I told you about the things he did, you couldn't handle it."

"I'm an FBI agent. I may look like a sweet girl, but I assure you, I've seen the depths of depravity a person can go to. Before I became a field agent, I spent all my time searching computers for evidence. I've helped to put away some truly disgusting perps."

"What kind of things did you see?"

"Unbelievably vile stuff. A lot of porn. Videos. Sick, perverted, absolutely criminal acts committed by warped people. Men and women who shouldn't be allowed to take another breath on this earth." I shudder as images I'll never unsee flash before my eyes like stills from an old 8mm film.

"Anything from Blackstone?" His entire body goes rigid.

"Just the video you leaked to the press. How did you get that anyway?"

He relaxes slightly. "I have my ways."

"What happened to you, Matrix? How's Blackstone involved in it? There's a connection, isn't there?"

"Yes, but I don't want to talk about it. Not with you."

"Why not?"

"Some things are impossible to put into

words."

"Try." I adjust my position so that I'm half-facing him. "Talk to me."

He stares into my eyes for what feels like an eternity before his gaze finally drops to my lips. I suck in a breath because I know what he's going to do even before he moves. The magnetism drawing us together is inescapable. I'm pulled to him, unable to resist. Unwilling to do anything but succumb to this burning attraction.

When his lips meet mine, it's not sweet or gentle or even affectionate. His kiss is hard, rough, and demanding. It scalds my soul and makes me want more. I push my tongue past his lips, taking control of the kiss. I've wanted to do this since the first day we met. Denying it is pointless. The fire burning between us was destined to explode into an inferno; it was just a matter of time before it happened.

"Daisy," he groans.

"Shut up and kiss me."

He glides his tongue across mine, stealing my breath and making me want to shred every bit of clothing between us. In the back of my mind, I know he's only kissing me so I'll stop asking him questions, but I don't care. After all the stress and tension of the last forty-eight hours, I need this. I want him. And now, I'm going to have him.

CHAPTER 7: MATRIX

I've wanted Daisy for months. Trying to resist her has been slowly driving me insane, but relationships are fucking terrifying. I prefer to avoid them. I'm happy to live in my virtual world without the complications of reality. Also, I'm still not entirely convinced I'm not living in a simulation. For all I know, Daisy's an NPC, a non-player character, in a sick world designed by some cruel entity for its perverse pleasure. Maybe none of this is real.

"Stay with me," Daisy whispers.

The fact that she realizes I'm drifting away shocks me to the core. I'm usually so good at hiding what's going on inside me, but when she's around, I seem to lose control. That's why I beat that Demon Rider to death. He was talking shit about Daisy, and I couldn't stand it. The thought of some lowlife piece of shit getting his hands on her pushed me into the worst dissociative episode I've ever had. Killing isn't new to me, but being unable to control my blind rage is a new experience. I hate it.

"If you don't stop thinking, I'm going to send you back to your bed," she murmurs before nibbling on my earlobe.

Desire floods my body. My cock swells with every kiss and wanton caress. As she glides her tongue down the curve of my neck, I force myself to stay present. I can't black out during this. I've wanted her since the day we met. She was so fucking cute in her little cut-off shorts and crop-top shirt, and those ribbons she wears in her hair have inspired more than one bondage fantasy. Visions of tying her down and licking her until she screamed quickly became my favorite way to get off. She'd probably be revolted to know how many times I wrapped my hand around my cock and stroked it while my fantasy version of her lay bound on my bed.

"Okay, I warned you." She pushes at my chest, but I don't budge. "If you're not going to participate, I'm going to—" I flip her onto her back, grab her wrists, and pin them over her head. "Ah!"

"You're playing a dangerous game, babe. Once I get started, I don't stop."

"Prove it."

The challenge in her eyes makes my cock jerk. Trying to maneuver on this shitty little bed isn't going to work for me. I slide off the mattress and stand beside it. She props up on her elbows, frowning. I smirk before grabbing her around the waist and hoisting her over my shoulder.

"Matrix! Put me down!"

"Gladly." I throw her onto my king-sized bed. "Much better. Now, tell me, Ms. FBI Agent, what kinds of sex games do you like to play?"

"Sex games?" Her breath is heavy and deep, making her breasts rise and fall most tantalizingly. I could watch her all night.

"Whips? Chains? Butt plugs?" I raise a brow.

"Oh, I've never …" She blushes.

"Never what?" I straddle her, hovering without putting any weight on her body.

"I haven't done anything like that."

"Really?" Maybe she's as sweet as she was pretending to be, after all. "Not once?"

"No."

"You're not a virgin, are you?" The thought is so horrifying that I wish I'd never had it. But if she hasn't been touched, I need to know. It wouldn't stop me entirely, but I'd have to think things through. Adding a lovesick virgin to my ever-growing list of problems isn't a good idea. Personally, I've never had to deal with one, but I've seen it go down, and it's a disaster every time.

"I've had sex." She turns even redder, as if that's even possible, and looks away.

"When?" I can't stop the Cheshire Cat-like grin from spreading across my face. Thank fucking hell she's not a virgin.

"That's none of your business," she bristles.

"You haven't gotten laid since you moved into the clubhouse. I would have heard about it if you were fucking someone else."

"I've never touched anyone here."

"Why not?"

"Because …" She bites her bottom lip.

"Tell me."

"You're the only one I wanted, but you didn't seem interested."

"That's where you're wrong. For an FBI agent, you're not very good at reading people. I've wanted to get between your sexy little thighs for a long damn time."

"Why didn't you?"

Her emerald-green eyes meet mine, sending a stab of lust through my belly. I don't know how to answer her question without spilling my guts, so I kiss her instead. I palm her cheeks and press my lips against her luscious mouth. For months, I dreamed about kissing her like this. The real thing is so much better than my fantasies.

She tastes like mint and forbidden passion. Everything I've kept caged since she arrived at the clubhouse finally breaks free. I'm wild with my need to possess her. Sitting back, I pull my shirt over my head. When her gaze lands on my nipples, she gasps.

"What is that?" She traces her finger over the barbell ring through my right nipple.

"A piercing."

"I can see that," she says wryly. "But what—

is that a skull and cross bones on one side and red lips on the other?"

"Yeah, it's called the 'Kiss of Death'." I grin. "You like it?"

"It's ... interesting."

"I bet you've never fucked a guy with piercings before."

"No. Can't say that I have. I can't believe you got both of them pierced." As she scrapes her thumb over my left nipple, I shiver. Precum leaks from my cock, and all I can think about is shoving it between her lips. "Did it hurt?"

"What?" I'm confused for a second because I'm too busy thinking about all the places I want to bury my cock. "Oh, yeah. The piercing. It hurt like hell, but I'm into that, so no big deal."

"What do you mean you're into it?"

"I love pain."

"Is that why you did this?" She brushes the backs of her knuckles over the scars running up and down my arms.

"Yeah." I can't keep the disappointment out of my voice. Although I've cut myself hundreds of times, it's never been enough. After the cuts heal, the pain stops, and the nightmares return. Cutting only causes temporary relief. I wish there were a way to make it last longer.

"I'm glad you stopped."

"Scar made me."

"He's just watching out for you."

"I guess."

"Is anything else pierced?" She playfully slips her fingers into my boxers and tugs.

"Oh, yeah. Wanna see?"

The way she's smiling up at me makes my chest hurt. She's so innocent and so trusting. Although she's an FBI agent, I get the sense she doesn't have a ton of experience with men. She says she's not a virgin, so I have to believe her on that, but can she handle a man like me, someone who loves pain more than pleasure?

Slowly dragging my boxers down, I reveal myself inch by inch. When my cock finally pops free, she scrambles back against the headboard. "Oh, holy shit."

"I know it looks scary."

"It's at least nine inches!"

"A blessing or a curse, depending on how you look at it."

"It's huge!"

"And ribbed for her pleasure." I hold up the shaft so she can see the underside. A series of small barbels form a ladder down my frenulum. "It's called a Jacob's Ladder."

"Because it leads to heaven?"

"Only a good church-going girl would know that one."

"Not necessarily. I'm well-read."

"You can read about a lot of things, but experience will always be a better teacher."

"I want it." She wraps her fingers around my cock before stroking down each rung on the ladder. Her big green eyes widen as she looks up at me. The way she glances from my face to my dick then back is so fucking hot. It's like she can't wait to go on her first rollercoaster ride. "Show me what you can do with it."

Her enthusiasm is unbelievable. "Fuck, Daisy."

"That's the idea."

"I'm not a hearts and rainbows and happily ever after kind of guy. You get that, right?"

"You want me. I want you. Seems simple enough."

"How do I know you won't catch feelings later?"

"You have a high opinion of yourself. Maybe I just want to have some fun and blow off steam."

"Me too."

"Then shut up and fuck me."

"You have a dirty fucking mouth."

"And I know how to use it."

"Prove it." I lace my fingers through her hair and tug her forward. "Be a good girl, and don't choke on my cock."

She licks her lips before sucking me deep. The piercings clang against her teeth, but she takes it all, swallowing every inch until I'm balls deep in her scorching hot mouth. Pleasure rips up my spine. My ass clenches as I threaten to lose my balance. She's curling her tongue around each barbell, tickling and teasing as she goes. Never in a million years would I have guessed she'd be this damn good at sucking cock. As soon as I get close, she pulls back just enough to keep me teetering on the edge. She's masterful with her lips. The best I've ever had. Ever. They can't possibly teach Cockteasing 101 at the academy, can they?

My eyes roll back as she finds the perfect rhythm. Sucking and licking and slobbering all over my dick, she seems determined to kill me with her mouth. She brings me to the brink of oblivion before backing off just enough to let me regain some semblance of control. Then just when I think I'm good, she does something magical with her tongue, and I'm right back on the ledge. I want to come so bad. It's taking every bit of what little concentration I've got left to stop myself from exploding.

"Daisy, slow down." I pull back, freeing my cock from her greedy little mouth.

"I want more."

Her seductive purr awakens every demon I've got trapped in my body. The urge to possess her overcomes me. Pushing her thighs apart with my knees, I glare down at her panties and tank top. They're in my way, so I grab a fistful of panties and tear them off.

"Oh!" She blinks up at me.

"This has to go too." I grab the front of her flimsy shirt and rip it open, exposing her voluptuous breasts. She's not wearing a bra, so they spill into my hands. Scraping the rough pads of my thumbs over her nipples, I revel in how she writhes beneath me.

"Touch me all over," she moans.

"That's the plan." I lower my head to capture one plump nipple between my teeth. Giving it a little tug, I check her reaction to make sure she's good with it. Some girls don't like pain, but it's firing her up. She grinds her wet pussy against my thigh. I know what she really wants, and I'm going to give it to her. Eventually.

It's my turn to tease the naughty minx. She's not the only one who's good with their tongue. Sliding between her thighs, I wrap my hands around them and yank them open. Her glistening pussy is the most beautiful thing I've ever seen. It's so pink and perfect. And it's all mine.

Rasping my tongue across her pussy, I drag her closer to my mouth. I press into her sex, spreading her and tasting her for the first time. I've wondered what she would taste like, and now, I know. Salty but sweet, like a mix of nuts and candy. And tart like a lemon cream pie. There's an idea, a creampie.

"What are you grinning about?" Her tone is thick, sexy, and filled with desire.

"After I make you come on my face, I'm going to make you come on my cock."

"Oh, shit." She arches her back as I claim her clit. The tiny little nub belongs to me now, and I'm going to play with it until she's shrieking.

Unlike her, I don't plan on edging her over and over the way she did with me. No, I'm going to take her from zero to sixty and shock her with how fast I can make her orgasm.

With quick flicks of my tongue, I drive her higher and higher until the only parts of her touching the bed are her ass and her head. She's arching so hard she almost looks possessed. I glance up to find her eyes rolled back in her head. She's grunting the most unladylike sounds, and it's so hot I'm about to come too. I wish I could record her because I could listen to this for hours.

"Oh, God. Matrix, wait!"

There's no goddamn way I'm going to stop now. She's mine, and I want her to realize it right now. I suck her clit with the perfect amount of pressure. I know it's exactly right because she screams as an orgasm rips through her body. Her legs shake. Her pussy pulses on my tongue. Every muscle in her body contracts at once. She tries to curl to the side, but I pin her hips and make her ride my face until the last twitch of pleasure leaves her limp.

"Mm." I lick her juices off my lips. "Much tastier than that steak."

"I thought you liked it." Her voice is dazed and dreamy.

"It was excellent. But you're better."

"I might be dead."

"Not a chance. I'm not done playing with you yet."

"And after that?"

"Who knows. Don't worry about tomorrow. Worry about how you're going to ride my dick until I say you can stop."

"Until you say I can stop?" She arches a brow, but that playful smile is still on her lips.

"You're a farm girl. You've ridden before, haven't you?" I smirk while lying next to her. "Show me what you can do."

Grinning, she straddles me. "Hang on, cowboy. I like to ride hard."

"Do you, now?"

"Oh, yeah."

As she slides down my cock, her eyelids flutter each time she passes over another one of my piercings. I wasn't kidding when I told her it was ribbed for her pleasure. In addition to loving the pain of being pierced, I love how it feels when I'm fucking. The barbells tug just a bit, adding a layer of friction I wouldn't get without them. It's good for her and me.

"You're so fucking sexy," I murmur, grabbing her hips and guiding her up and down. "Just like that, babe."

"Like this?" she asks in a thready voice.

"Exactly."

She bounces and rolls her hips, then grinds her pussy against my shaft. I can tell she's close when she stops breathing. A low, animalistic sound rumbles in her chest. She sits down hard, taking me so deep I see stars. My balls tighten, and the tingling in my spine reaches a crescendo. Our moans and cries of pleasure fill the room as we reach mind-blowing climaxes together.

When she's finally done shuddering, and I've given her every last ounce of my pleasure, I roll her onto her side and cuddle her against my body. She's the little spoon, and I'm the big spoon. I've never done this before. Usually, I don't stick around after sex, but with Daisy, it's different. It wasn't just amazing and perfect; there was an element of fun and playfulness that I've never had before. Women are usually too clingy and needy, but with Daisy, I don't get that from her. She knows tonight wasn't about love and promises. It was hard, hot, dirty sex, and that's it. Not having the added pressure of explaining that to her made it so much better. I'm glad we're on the same page because it would be awkward as fuck if she let her heart get involved.

After several minutes, she rolls over to face me. She smiles as I brush a lock of hair out of her eyes. Grabbing my hand, she drapes it over her hip. Her gaze roams over my body as if trying to memorize it. Eventually, she traces her finger over the tattoo on my shoulder. It's an image of a phoenix rising out of the ashes with the words "Free Yourself" written below it. "What does this mean?"

"The only time I feel free is when I'm behind my keyboard." I don't know why I'm telling her this, but after what we just shared, I feel comfortable opening up a little.

"But the phoenix? Why did you pick that creature?"

"Because it doesn't exist."

"Okay …"

"And because it rises out of the ashes to be reborn."

"Is that something you did?"

"No. I never rose."

"But you were reduced to ashes?"

"Yeah."

"When?"

"Years ago."

"What happened?"

"Daisy, I can't. I don't talk about that with anyone." I pull the blankets over us, hoping she'll take the hint and go to sleep. I don't have the will to kick her out of my bed. She's so warm and cuddly that I want to keep her here. If I tell her about Blackstone, she'll leave. How could she possibly stay after finding out what he did to me? I can't tell her about him. I can't reveal anything from that time. It's done. It's over.

I won't be able to rise from the ashes of my past until I get my revenge. Until that happens, I'll never truly be free. I can't explain this to her without going into a bunch of details I'm not willing to share.

For now, she'll just have to accept that there are things I won't ever tell her. Since we're not in a relationship, it shouldn't matter. But I'll have to watch out because I can tell she's trying to get closer to me. I don't want her to think that's an option because it's not. We had some fun in bed, that's it. If she wants anything more, she'd better be ready to be disappointed because I can't give her anything other than sex. I've got nothing else to give.

CHAPTER 8: DAISY

I wake up and stretch like a cat—a very satisfied, extremely sore cat. Matrix let me sleep for a few hours before he pawed at me again. Don't get me wrong, I'm not complaining by any means, but damn, my body's out of shape. I really need to use the clubhouse's gym so I can keep up with him. He's a total animal in bed, almost a monster, but not quite. I'm not afraid of him at all. If he wanted to kill me, he would have done it already. After spending the night in his arms, I'm convinced I'm safe.

The shower's running. I slide out of bed and pad across the room. When I open the bathroom door, steam curls out. He must love his showers hot because the water is scalding as I step in to join him.

"Morning." I stand behind him and wrap my arms around his chest. I give those sexy nipple piercings a little tweak.

"Ouch!" He growls before turning to face me. "Next time, do it harder."

I grin because that means there'll be another hot sex session sometime in the future. Although I don't expect this to go anywhere, he'll be a fun distraction while I'm looking for my sister. I haven't forgotten her, but I needed this break. Searching for her has taken a toll on me. I didn't realize how bad I felt until after my first orgasm. The tension in my body vanished for the first time in months and hasn't returned. I hope it stays away so we can concentrate on what we need to do today.

"Don't drop the soap, babe." He grins while handing it to me.

"Or what?" I intentionally let it slip through my fingers.

"Now you're going to have to bend over and get it."

"You'd better behave." As I lean forward, I know he's going to do something. I'm not surprised when he grabs my hips and rubs his semi-erect cock against my ass.

"I already want you again." His husky tone tightens my nipples. I'm wet, both inside and out, and I need him too.

"Then what's stopping you?" I ask coyly.

He rubs his cock against my slippery folds before sliding deep inside. I brace my hands on the tiled wall to keep from falling over. There's nothing slow or sensual about how he's taking me. My breasts bounce as he pummels me with savage thrusts. I spread my legs wider, giving him everything he wants. He takes it all and more. Circling his fingers over my clit, he plays with me until my toes curl.

"Oh, God. Matrix!"

"Be a good girl, and come on my cock." He bites the side of my neck before licking away the pain. The added sensation isn't anything I've ever experienced. Who the hell knew that pain could lead to even more pleasure? I don't understand how that's possible, but it is.

"Fuck," I moan as I grind back, rubbing his shaft against that spot that always sends me into the stratosphere.

"You're so tight." He buries his cock deep before flicking his thumb back and forth over my clit. He's not moving anymore, and it's driving me completely insane.

"Matrix, please," I beg.

"You want this?" He pulls back before slamming his hips against my ass.

"More."

He keeps the hand teasing my pussy in place while using the other to grab a fistful of my hair. Treating me like his own personal fuck toy, he plunges into me over and over until my knees shake, and I can't take it anymore.

"Oh, God. Yes!"

I lose my footing as my legs buckle. He grips me tightly, holding me up while still fucking me from behind. The intensity of my orgasm is too much. I try to escape his powerful arms, but it's impossible. I'm coming so hard I'm sure I'm going to black out.

"You're so fucking hot," he moans.

His cock spurts as he fills me with his release. Last night we talked about protection but found out we don't need it. We're both clean, and I'm on birth control. With nothing between us, the sex is so incredible I don't know how I'll ever be able to walk away from it. Eventually, I will, but not anytime soon.

We take turns soaping each other up before rinsing off. He gets out first and then hands me a towel. We dry off in comfortable silence. Part of me wonders why I didn't try to seduce him before, but I know the answer to that. I'm an undercover agent. He's a criminal. It would never work between us.

"Breakfast, then let's get to work." He pulls on a pair of tight-fitting jeans and a long-sleeved shirt. I do the same.

After devouring pancakes, eggs, sausage, bacon, and waffles, I'm sure my pants will burst at the seams. At least I'm not hungry anymore.

"Let's set up in my office."

"Okay."

We head into his newly remodeled office. After he almost died on the floor, they had one of the prospects, Tucker, tear out the carpet and replace it with wood. It's a deep mahogany, and it suits him. Two large windows overlook the river below. Floor-to-ceiling bookshelves cover the wall behind his desk. His chair looks very modern and extremely expensive. Two French-inspired fabric-covered chairs give visitors a soft place to sit. I drag one of them next to his chair to watch him work.

"I'm going to cast my computer to the TV on the wall, so it'll be easier to see." After a few keystrokes, his desktop appears on the large screen, which takes up most of one wall.

"Where should we start?" I ask.

"I'll show you everything we've got on Blackstone. With a fresh set of eyes, you might see something we missed."

"Let's do it."

We spend the next several hours pouring over video footage from Blackstone's ranch. He sends photos of everyone coming and going from the property to my email so I can send them through facial recognition software. Our FBI file on Blackstone already contains most of this information, but we may have missed one of these people.

"What else do you have on him?" I ask.

"How much of the Blackstone/McNash tape did you see? We gave Reynolds the entire recording, but he only aired part of it."

"We got the whole thing. I think. Let's watch it again." As he pulls it up, my stomach curdles. Listening to Blackstone talk about choosing children from binders full of them is just as disgusting as it was the first time I heard it.

"Wait. Rewind it a little."

"What?" Matrix backs up the recording.

"He mentions cartels. We know they're going to Denver. What's the biggest cartel operating in Denver right now?"

"I don't know. Would you have that info in one of your databases?"

"Yes. Give me a laptop. I need to use a VPN, so they won't know I'm accessing the files."

"Won't they recognize your username and password?"

"Oh, baby. You have no idea what kind of skills I have."

He leans over my shoulder to watch me work my magic. Since I helped to set up the security system, I'm able to pop in a back door and get in without detection, but once I'm in, I'll leave a trail. As far as I know, we don't have anyone at the agency double-checking my security measures. That's my job. But I want to be extra cautious, just in case.

"Bingo. Los Serpientes de Cristal." I sit back in my chair.

"The Crystal Snakes."

"You know Spanish?"

"A little bit, but I'm not fluent. The only languages I have mastery over are computer related."

"Same." I glance up to find him watching me. "What?"

"I just never figured you were that …"

"Smart?"

"We assumed you were a country girl who only knew how to cook and clean. You surprise me."

"Thanks." I grin.

"What else can you do on this thing?"

"Let's see what the cartel has been up to in Denver." I type a quick search string to pull up recent arrests in the Denver area. "Lots of little meth trafficking busts. Oh, here's one. An OCDETF task force took down a major cocaine trafficking network three months ago. They picked up ten men and two women in connection with the illegal drug trade. It looks like the charges were dropped due to mishandled evidence."

"Of course." The sarcasm in his tone rubs me the wrong way.

"Law enforcement does everything they can to make sure these people are convicted of their crimes."

"Not in this case."

"Sometimes someone fucks up, and criminals go free. I hate it as much as you do."

"If the Feds would do their jobs, we wouldn't have to clean up after them. I know you must think we're renegades with no regard for the law, but you're wrong. We encourage people to take the legal route whenever possible, but sometimes it fails. That's where we come in."

"I understand that. I just wish you didn't do

things illegally to help people."

"By the time someone comes to us for help, the law has failed. The victims we help are out of options, so they need us to do what you guys couldn't do. We made it happen. I won't apologize for doing what's right, even if you think it's wrong."

"I don't approve of your methods, but I understand why you feel the need to take the law into your own hands. There are times I wish I could have thrown the book away and done things my way, but I swore an oath to protect the Constitution of the United States and defend it to the best of my ability. I take that oath seriously. I can't circumvent the law."

Tense silence fills the room. I break away from his searching look and refocus my attention on my screen. After clicking through several files, I find the one we need.

"Check this out. Two months ago, an informant in the Denver area told one of our agents that the cartel was moving into a new operation. You'll never guess what it is."

"Human trafficking."

"Exactly. Running drugs got too hot, so they decided to switch up their cargo. It's people, now."

"Your sister went missing almost a year ago, so she couldn't have come through this cartel."

"Unless they've been trafficking people this whole time, and we didn't know it. The agency could have been too busy following the drugs to realize they were also smuggling people."

"Good point."

"Cartels are crafty. They're very good at making a lot of noise in one area while distracting us from their other businesses. Maybe trafficking wasn't their main source of income, but after the drug bust, they had to ramp things up to cover their losses."

"It makes sense."

A knock sounds on the door. Scar pokes his head in a second later. "Got something for you."

"Come in."

"I heard back from the president of our Denver chapter. You remember Acid?"

"That crazy motherfucker's the president now?"

"They had to make a change in leadership."

"No shit."

"He's got eyes and ears all over the city. He heard about the girls coming in. Got the intel a few days ago before we ever knew about it. He and his guys are planning to intercept the traffickers and rescue the girls tonight. If they capture any of the traffickers, they'll interrogate them to find out what they know about the operation. He'll call me tomorrow to pass on any information he gets from them."

"I want to go down there." I'm on my feet, pacing around the room like a caged animal. "I need to ask them about my sister. They may have seen her."

"That's a long shot," Matrix says. "We don't know that she was trafficked through Denver. Blackstone could have sent her anywhere in the world."

"But we know he's connected to the men trafficking those three girls through Denver. It's the only lead we have. I'm going to follow it whether you like it or not." I head toward the door, but Matrix catches up. He grabs my upper arm to stop me. "Let go. Now!"

"I know enough about you to realize I can't talk you out of this. If you're going, then I'm going too."

"No," Scar says.

"Why not?" I jerk my arm free and turn to face Scar. "I'm not going to sit around and wait while someone else interrogates the men who may have helped traffic my sister. If you want to stop me, then you're going to have to kill me."

"Matrix?" Scar arches a brow.

"Don't look at me, pres." He grins. "She's a firecracker just waiting to pop off. The only way I can stop her involves tying her to my bed, which I won't do."

"Why not?" Scar asks, smirking.

"Because when I do eventually use those ribbons of hers to tie her up, I want her begging me to do it." Matrix's silver eyes glitter with carnal desire.

Scar rolls his eyes. "Fine. We're not going to

hold her prisoner."

"Thank you." I flash a sarcastic smile his way.

"I guess you're both going to Denver then."

"Yep." I nod.

"I'll set it up with Acid, but while you're there, you're a guest of that club. Whatever Acid says, goes. Got it?"

"Absolutely."

"Will do, pres."

"Don't make me regret greenlighting this," Scar says as he walks out.

As soon as he's gone, I throw myself into Matrix's arms. "This is closer than I've ever gotten since I started searching for her."

"It might be a wild goose chase," he warns.

"Maybe. But at least I'll be able to take this cartel off my list of possible suspects. Narrowing down the options isn't as good as being handed a dossier of possible perps, but it's better than nothing."

"I hope we find something when we get there." Stroking his hand down my back, he holds me close.

"Me too."

I kiss him softly at first, but the passion simmering between us can't be contained. Although I must have felt his lips on mine dozens of times last night, I can't seem to get enough. If I weren't so focused on getting to Denver, I'd drag him back to bed immediately.

Scar returns several minutes later. "We're all set. Acid's looking forward to meeting the Fed smart enough to sneak into our club."

"Daisy will be safe, right?" Matrix asks.

"Acid assured me he'd look the other way. He doesn't have any interest in bringing a bunch of heat down on his club. As far as he's concerned, she's your old lady."

"Uh, that's not ..." Matrix slides his gaze down to me.

"Don't worry," I tell him. "I don't expect hearts and rainbows or happily ever afters. I know what's up."

"Consider it your cover," Scar says. "I told him you'd be there by morning. I figured you wouldn't want to wait."

"We'll take turns driving. It's only eleven hours," Matrix says.

"I don't plan on sleeping any time soon." My racing heart will make it impossible to sleep.

We're so close to a possible lead that I wish we could fly to Denver. However, by the time we book flights and arrange everything, we may as well just drive. I can use the time to figure out what to do once we arrive. If Acid's club manages to capture some of the traffickers, we'll be able to interrogate them. If they die while the club tries to rescue the girls, I can talk to them instead. Either way, I'm going to get information I didn't have before. It's a long shot, but it's one worth pursuing.

CHAPTER 9: MATRIX

I want Daisy in my lap, but she refuses, claiming I won't be able to drive if I'm trying to fuck her too. Well, she's not wrong. I'd love to be able to pull over and give it to her hard on the side of the road. Unfortunately, I'll have to wait. She'll kill me if I stop driving before we get to the clubhouse in Denver. Hopefully, the interrogation won't take long once we arrive. I can't wait to have her naked and riding my cock again.

Shifting in my seat, I check the GPS navigation map. We've still got another twenty miles before we'll roll in. The clubhouse is located northwest of Denver near Coal Creek Canyon. I haven't been there in years, but I should try to visit these guys more often. Their parties are legendary. I vaguely remember the last one I attended. The booze flowed like a river that night. Hopefully, we'll have time to enjoy another party while we're here.

"How much longer is it?" Daisy asks.

"Almost there, babe. Have you thought about the questions you want to ask them?"

"That's all I've been doing. I can't think about anything else."

"I know you're anxious about this meeting, but don't get too far ahead of yourself. We don't even know if they picked up those guys. I don't want you to be disappointed if we get there and they've got nothing for us."

"Based on what Scar said, these guys don't fail. They'll have the men who kidnapped those girls. The kids will be safe, and we'll be able to take them home."

"We?"

"How else are they going to get back to Montana?"

"You're assuming they all live there or that they'll want to go home. Some of the kids who get trafficked are running away from even worse situations. I've rescued children from parents who didn't deserve kids after the way they mistreated them."

"If any of the girls don't want to go home, then what?" The concern in her voice warms my heart. She's just as worried about helping people as I am.

"We'll know more when we meet them. Speculating is pointless. We'll be able to handle whatever we find once we're there. Remember what Scar said, we're guests. Let Acid take the lead. He's the club pres in Denver, so he has authority there."

"How does that work within the hierarchy? Wouldn't Scar be above him since he's the president of the founder's chapter?"

"No. Each pres is the ultimate authority in their area. The club pres' are all equals, even Scar."

"Interesting. I thought he'd be the head of everything."

"Our structure isn't about hierarchies. Sure, within each club, there's a difference between a fully patched member, a prospect, and an associate or friend of the club, but once you're patched, everyone's equal. When we visit another chapter, we're well-respected, but we don't have any authority over that chapter."

"I see."

"When we get to the clubhouse, let me talk. I know all the unspoken rules. Follow my lead. Acid and I got along great the last time I saw him. I don't think we'll have any issues gaining access to the kidnappers."

I keep a close eye on the map because it's easy to miss the dirt turnoff, especially since we're arriving in the middle of the night. There aren't any streetlights in the mountains, so I've got to stay alert. I spot the Underground Vengeance symbol on a wooden post tucked back from the road. Anyone who wasn't looking for it would miss it. I'm glad I found it on the first pass.

Pulling off the road, I drive onto the paved

parking area that spans the length of the long, single-story clubhouse. In addition to the main living space, the club has a large barn, which I've never been invited into. There's also a greenhouse and a big shed for tools. During their parties, a patched member mans the grill in the gazebo next to the house. I ate my fill of steak the last time I was here, and damn, it was tasty. Man, I wish we were coming for a party and not a funeral.

"We're here." I open the door and jog around to Daisy's side to help her out.

"This is their clubhouse?" She eyes the very nondescript wood building, clearly not impressed.

"It doesn't look like much from the outside, but you'll see." I grin.

"Lead the way."

I rest my hand on the small of her back as we walk up to the front door, which opens before I can knock. The name on the club member's patch is Moose. He's the club's sergeant at arms and he looks like the animal he's nicknamed after. The guy's six foot five with a long nose and thin face. One of the girls said he looked like a giraffe and Adrien Brody fucked and made a hot kid. I don't rate guys, but he got plenty of pussy during that party, so the chick must've been right.

"Matrix! I heard you were coming by." Moose pulls me into an embrace and slaps my back hard enough to knock the wind out of me.

"Long time no see, brother."

"No shit! How the hell have you been? How's Scar?"

"Good. He's married now."

"I heard. Sorry we couldn't make it to the wedding. We had some shit go down at the club that had to be dealt with."

"Understood. Is everything good now?"

"Peachy. And speaking of peaches, who's this fine woman?"

"This is Daisy, my old lady." I don't know how I manage to get the words past my lips without biting my tongue off. The thought of being tied down to one woman is about as appealing as being stabbed under my fingernails with tiny needles.

"Hello." She flashes a smile so enchanting it leaves me bristling. She shouldn't be looking at other guys like that. Even though she's not really mine, it pisses me off to see her being so flirty with him.

"Can I get you a drink?" Moose asks her.

"No, thank you. Did you capture the kidnappers?"

"Yeah. Piece of cake. Fucking idiots didn't even see us coming. We only had to shoot one out of three. We've got the other two over in the barn. They're having a little chat with Acid and Fender."

"I need to talk to them." Daisy's tone is

too demanding. She needs to tone it down and remember who's in charge here. It's not us.

Moose raises a brow before looking at me. "Stay put while I talk to Acid."

"Will do." When Daisy starts after him, I grab her arm. "Stop, babe. Remember what I told you, we're guests here. Don't push it. They don't have any obligation to keep either of us alive. We'll get some leeway since I'm a patched member of Underground Vengeance, but Acid knows you're a Fed. He won't hesitate to find a reason to kill you."

"Ugh!" she huffs and crosses her arms.

"Just be patient. These guys want what we want. They don't like having trafficking scum in their backyards any more than we do. Our mission is the same."

"You're right. It's just hard to hold back another minute when I've had to wait months for any viable leads."

"I know, which is why you need to stay calm. We need to get invited into that barn so we can at least watch the interrogation."

"But I want to talk to them myself."

"Of course. However, that might not happen right away."

"I understand."

"Good." I gently pry her arms loose before pulling her close. She slides her hands down my back and rests them on my waist. Having her wrapped around me like this feels right. I don't know why I like her so damn much, but it's impossible to ignore our connection.

"Okay, lovebirds. Acid says you can come in." Moose waves us over to the barn.

"Remember what I said," I whisper so only she can hear me.

"I will. If things get crazy in there, will you freak out and kill someone again?" she asks softly.

"No. I don't know what the hell happened to make me disassociate like that, but it's not going to be a problem tonight."

"Glad to hear it." She softly squeezes my hand as we walk past Moose into the barn.

Inside, it's dim, lit only by a single, naked lightbulb hanging over two trussed-up men. It's hard to tell they're guys anymore because their faces are bloody pulps. Unfortunately, they're also completely exposed, so there's no question we're dealing with a couple of dickheads.

"Welcome to the party," Acid says, holding up his bloody hands. "I'd shake, but I'm in the middle of something."

"I can see that. I'd like you to meet Daisy, my old lady."

Acid smirks at me because he knows I'm lying. Scar told me that Acid's the only member of the Denver chapter in on Daisy's secret. It was Acid's idea to keep it quiet.

"Stay back, and you won't get blood on you," he tells her.

"I'm not afraid of a few stains," she counters.

"Spunky. I like it." Acid cracks his neck before returning his attention to the traffickers. "These two fucks were just telling us about their gang, Los Serpientes de Cristal. That's who you're working for, right?"

The guy on the left nods but doesn't bother opening his swollen, blood-crusted eyes.

"Where are the girls?" Daisy asks.

"Safe. Our club girls are getting them cleaned up and fed. They'll never have to see these fuckers' faces again." Acid spits on the guy on the right.

"No one's ever going to see their ugly mugs after tonight," Moose says.

"We suspected they were part of the cartel, but what else have they told you?" Daisy asks.

Acid arches a brow, but I keep my face neutral. So far, he hasn't told her to keep her mouth shut, so I'm not going to step in.

"A local politician bought one of the girls. She won't be joining that piece of shit tonight." Acid grabs a bottle of water and dumps it over his head. Grime and blood trickle down his square face before dripping off his long beard. He takes a long swig of what's left before tossing the bottle aside.

"Acid, would it be possible if I asked them a question?" The meek, sweet tone in Daisy's voice catches me by surprise.

"What is it?"

"I want to know if they've ever seen this girl." She opens the photo app on her phone to a picture of her sister. In the photo, the girl is smiling and happy, and it breaks my heart to know she may be caught up in Blackstone's sick world of perversion.

"Go ahead and show them," Acid says.

"Thank you." She gives him a soft smile before approaching the men. "Have you guys seen this girl before? It might have been last year."

"Open your fucking eyes and look, motherfuckers!" Acid kicks one guy in the ribs before punching the other in the kidney. Both men scream in pain, but no one else in the barn gives a single shit about their agony.

"Her name's Angela. She might go by Angie too." Daisy sounds so young and vulnerable, completely unlike her FBI-agent self. She's not an agent right now; she's a civilian worried about her sister. All I want to do is protect her from scumbags like this, but I can't. Daisy chose to become a member of law enforcement. She had to realize she might end up in a situation like this. Although, I doubt she thought her innocent sister would be the victim.

"Angie? Yeah," the guy on the right mumbles.

"You saw her? Where?" Daisy asks.

"Grabbed her from a mall in Montana."

"When?" She glances at me with so much hope and pain in her eyes that I can't stay away. I walk up beside her and wrap an arm around her waist to offer my support.

"A year ago," the other kidnapper says. "That little bitch fought like hell, but we got her anyway."

"You bastard!" Daisy launches herself at him, throwing a solid right hook into the man's jaw. When several teeth land on the dirt floor, I make a mental note not to piss her off. She's stronger than she looks, that's for sure.

"Damn." Acid folds his arms over his chest and regards her as if seeing her for the first time. There's admiration in his gaze. Too much for my liking, but I keep my mouth shut. Instead, I haul her back and tighten my arm around her again.

"Where did you take her?" Daisy asks.

"New Orleans."

"I need details. Where did you go in the city?" When neither responds, she kicks one guy in the nuts. All the men in the room groan and turn away. "Tell me, or I'll rip your fucking dicks off."

"Daisy." I release her and step between her and the men.

"Shut up! These motherfuckers know where my sister's at. Tell me, or I'm going to fucking kill you!" She pushes past me and gets right in their faces.

"We go there all the time," one guy finally

says.

"Address," she snaps.

He rattles off an easy to remember address.

"That's in the Garden District," Daisy says after consulting the map app on her phone.

"They keep the girls there until they can be moved out of the country." The man slurs his words, but they're still understandable.

"Shut up, Javier. Don't give them any details," the other man growls.

"They're going to kill us no matter what. We're fucked. There's no way out of this. If they're going to murder us, I want a quick death." Javier lifts his head and addresses Daisy. "What else do you want to know?"

"Tell me about the house. How many rooms does it have? How many girls do they keep there at a time? How many guards do they have, and what's their schedule?"

As the man confesses everything he knows, Acid pulls me aside, out of earshot of everyone else. "I know she's a Fed, but she's tough. You seem to like her a lot."

"You see everything, don't you?" I ask.

"Wouldn't be president if I didn't. What's the plan once she finishes with these guys?"

"She wants to talk to the girls next."

"Done."

"If they want to go home and they live in Montana, then we'd like to take them back with us. With your permission, of course."

"That would save my club a trip. We can make that happen."

"Great." My gaze slides over to where Daisy's still interrogating the men. "Can we crash here for a bit first? I don't think I can drive eleven more hours without at least a couple of hours of shut-eye."

"You're our guests for as long as you want to stay. I'll get you and Daisy set up in one of the rooms. Since she's supposedly your old lady, you can't be in different ones without everyone getting suspicious."

"I appreciate that." Returning my attention to him, I add, "I'm surprised you let her come here."

"If anyone else had asked, I would have told them to go fuck themselves. Scar knows who he can and can't trust. If he thinks this Fed's one of the few good ones, then I believe him."

"He'll be happy to hear that."

"Don't tell him that shit." Acid laughs. "His head's already too big now that he's a dad. But you know what? I'm glad he's happy. He deserves it. One of these days, I need to take my club up to Montana for a visit."

"Our doors are always open to you and your men. I'm sure Scar agrees."

"I'll take you up on that. Maybe this summer."

"Let Scar know when you're coming. He'll try to out-party your ass. I don't think it's possible, but I'd love to see him try."

"Sounds like a plan." Acid grins.

A gunshot goes off. We both grab our pieces and turn to find one of the strung-up men hanging lifeless. The other guy's screaming and begging for his life. He's the jackass who refused to cooperate.

"I'm done," Daisy says.

"You gave her a gun?" Acid side-eyes me.

"I didn't give her anything. Woman!"

"I left the other guy for Acid and his guys," she says sweetly. "Thank you for letting me talk to them. One was very helpful. The other is going to enjoy a long, agonizing death."

"You got that shit right. Carbon's in the clubhouse. Go find him, and he'll give you a room."

"Thanks, Acid." Daisy hugs him before grabbing my hand and practically skipping out of the barn.

When we get outside, I pull her to a stop and grab the gun out of her hand. "What the fuck?"

"I grabbed it on the way out of our clubhouse. It's the one you guys keep hidden under the coffee table."

"Daisy!"

"You wouldn't give mine back, and I wasn't about to walk into another club without protection."

"Next time, ask."

"Fine." She rubs her forehead with her

fingers.

"Are you okay?"

"They kidnapped my sister and trafficked her to New Orleans. No, I'm not fucking okay." Her bottom lip quivers.

"Babe, we've got a lead now. We're going to find her. I promise."

"Don't make promises you can't keep." She buries her face in my chest while I hold her.

"I try not to, but I've got a feeling we're going to get her back."

"Please, God. Let that be true."

As we walk toward the clubhouse, my jaw tightens. Even though Daisy's not my old lady, I want to kill anyone who makes her cry like this. It's not right. No woman should ever have to feel this way. I'm going to help get her sister back. It won't be easy. We have no idea where she was moved after New Orleans, but at least we have another breadcrumb to follow. Once we get some rest, we'll be able to figure out our next steps.

CHAPTER 10: DAISY

The inside of the clubhouse is much nicer than I expected. Several people, including a few scantily clad women, mill around. Some are playing pool, while others sit at the bar drinking. The bartender finishes cleaning the glass she's working on and then looks up. As soon as she spots us, she puts the glass on a rack and wipes her hands. Tossing the towel aside, she circles the bar. Her legs are a mile long, and her eight-inch stilettos don't do a damn thing to slow her down. Her huge, braless chest sways wantonly as she approaches.

"Baby, you're back." She wraps her arms around Matrix's waist and kisses him on the mouth. With tongue. I already want to kill her.

"Fuck off, Maggie." He pries himself loose from the hussy's grip and wraps his hand around my waist.

"Who's this?" the girl demands.

"Daisy. She's my old lady." The way Matrix says it sounds so unrehearsed that I almost believe him. I know the truth. I'm nothing to him, but he's very convincing. If I didn't know better, I wouldn't question our relationship. Unfortunately, this chick doesn't feel the same way.

"No way." Her fiery red nails, more like talons, dig into her fists as she clenches her hands.

"Yep." He leans down and gives me a passionate kiss. "As you can see, I'm taken. Where's Carbon?"

Maggie doesn't seem to believe him. She's sizing me up, trying to assess something about me. I don't know what she's attempting to see, but whatever it is, she doesn't like it.

"How'd you get your claws into him?" she asks.

"Claws?" I toss my hair over my shoulder and laugh.

"Unlike you, Daisy doesn't have those. She's as sweet as summer rain," Matrix says, and the look of pure adoration in his eyes sends butterflies flitting through my belly. He's a damn good actor. Maybe he missed his calling as an undercover agent. He'd make a good one.

"I'll bet. Matrix, I really need to talk to you in private," Maggie says.

"Anything you have to say can be said in front of my woman."

She huffs before narrowing her gaze. "It's just that there's something I have to tell you.

Something I don't want anyone else to know."

"Are you in some kind of trouble?" Matrix asks.

"Not exactly. I just thought that we could catch up for a while. Alone." She slides her vicious gaze toward me. I'm sure I know exactly why she wants to get him away from me. This bitch is crazy. She can't seem to take no for an answer.

"I really don't have time for that. Go get Carbon for me." His tone is firm.

"But *Matrix*."

Her whiney tone sets me off. We don't have the luxury of being nice anymore. She can't seem to take a hint, so now *I've* got to deal with her stupid ass.

"Look, he's not interested. He's with me. I'm sure you're someone's favorite fuck-of-the-month, but Matrix is past that now. Right, babe?" I give him a look that says he'd better agree with me, or heads will roll.

"Of course, honey bunny." He smirks.

"So, go fetch Carbon and stay the fuck out of our way. Got it?" I didn't intend to raise my voice, but she brought this on herself.

"What a cunt," Maggie mutters under her breath.

"What did you say?" Matrix towers over her. Even in those ridiculous heels, she's nowhere near his height. He could squash her like a bug.

"You're an asshole." She turns on her

stilettos and stomps off.

"She's not wrong about that." Matrix grins at me before lowering his voice. "Babe, that was hot. I can't wait to strip you down and show you how hard you just made me."

"Sounds fun, but I'm tired, and we still need to talk to the girls."

An older woman, probably in her fifties, walks into the room. "Carbon sent me to show you to your rooms. I'm Alicia."

"I don't know if you remember me from the big Fourth of July party a few years ago—"

"Do I remember you? Ha!" She laughs. "You were running around the backyard naked as the day you were born. If you weren't young enough to be one of my kids, I would have dragged you into the woods for a wild ride on the MILF train."

"Oh, boy." Matrix blushes. He actually turns redder than a firetruck. It's hilarious.

"I like you already," I tell her.

"Well, don't get too comfy. I know what you are." Her smile falls. "Acid told me. I was against letting you come here, but he insisted. Don't poke your nose anywhere it doesn't belong."

"I'm not here for anything but the girls. Are they settled yet? Can I speak with them?"

"They were so stressed out I had to give them a sedative."

"What?" I'm appalled.

"Not like that. Just some tea I brewed up. They haven't slept in days. You can talk to them tomorrow."

"But I need—"

"I don't give a fuck what you need. Those girls take priority over everyone else in this clubhouse tonight. Tomorrow, you can ask them anything you want. Tonight, they're mine. And if you try to bother them, you'll have to deal with me. If you thought Maggie was a bitch, by the time you're done with me, you'll think she's a fucking fairy princess."

"Okay. Jeez." I scrunch up my face and glance at Matrix. He's got bags under his eyes because he did most of the driving. He needs to sleep, and so do I. "Acid mentioned we could stay here tonight."

"Right. Room's down here. Come on." As she walks away, I can't help but be envious of her curvy figure. She's probably twice my age, but she looks amazing. I hope I'm half as sexy when I get older.

She shows us to a room that looks surprisingly similar to Matrix's. In addition to a king-sized bed, there's a dresser, a television on the wall, and an adjoining bathroom.

"Carbon will come by in an hour to check on you. He's currently ... occupied." Her smirk makes me think he's probably entertaining one of their club girls in his room.

"Thank you," Matrix says.

"Anytime, hon. Make sure the Fed doesn't sneak out when you're not looking. You can't trust them for a second."

"I'll tie her up if I have to." Matrix grins before closing the door. "Well, you heard the lady. Time to put those little ribbons of yours to use."

"Not now. Seriously, I'm about to faceplant; I'm so tired."

"Shower first. Then bed."

"Okay, but one at a time. I don't have the energy for anything else."

He lets me use the bathroom first before heading in to get himself cleaned up. By the time he's done, I'm snuggled up in bed. Although I've tried closing my eyes several times, I can't stand the images that immediately pop into my head. It's a series of vile snapshots of what my sister might be enduring at the hands of men like the ones we interrogated today.

"What's going on, babe?" Matrix slides under the sheets and pulls me across his body. I rest my head on his chest, listening to his heartbeat. The sound is so soothing. It's exactly what I need right now.

"I'm worried about my sister. I'm afraid we're too late. She might not be at the house in New Orleans. If they're still trafficking her, she could be anywhere in the world. She could be dead already."

"Don't think like that." He strokes my hair. "She could still be there. Those guys were low-level thugs in the supply chain. They might be wrong about what happens at that house. She could still be in the US."

"I hope so. God, we have to find her."

"We will." He kisses my head so sweetly that my heart melts.

"I can't imagine doing this without you," I confess.

"Then don't. I'm right here, and I'm not going anywhere. We're in this together until the end. Okay?"

"Thank you."

"Don't thank me now. Wait until after we bring Angie home." He strokes my back in lazy circles. "Tell me about her."

"She's so much smarter than I was at that age."

"I'm sure you were just as bright. They don't typically take stupid people into the FBI academy."

"True."

"Don't sell yourself short. You managed to slide under the radar and infiltrate my club. You hacked my computer, which I'm still planning on punishing you for."

"Punishing me?"

"I can't let something like that go." He flashes a wicked grin.

"How do you plan on doing that?" I'm dying to know what diabolical ideas he has flitting around in his dirty mind.

"I can't tell you that."

"Why not?"

"It's classified."

I burst out laughing. He has no idea how much his playful attitude soothes my soul. I don't know if he even realizes what a great man he is. Someone as intelligent and kind as Matrix should realize his worth. But the scars on his arms tell a different story. I wish I knew more about why he did that to himself.

"One day, will you tell me about this?" I trace a finger over his scars.

"Go to sleep. We'll figure out what to do with the girls in the morning."

"I'm going to get it out of you eventually." It's a mystery I need to solve. I won't give up until he explains why he hates himself enough to inflict that kind of pain on his body.

"Goodnight, babe."

A moment later, he's snoring softly. I've never heard him do that before, so he must be exhausted. I also try to sleep, but I can't stop thinking about my sister. Until we find her, I'm not going to be able to relax enough to get any rest.

When morning comes, I've managed to get a few hours of sleep, but that's it. Well, it will have to be enough because we've got work to do.

"Carbon stopped by a few minutes ago. Breakfast is in the kitchen, but what I really want to eat is right here." Matrix rolls on top of me and kisses me.

"Stop that." I giggle before trying to push

him off.

"Come on, babe. How about a quickie before we go?"

"I doubt you'll ever be a one-minute man."

"Got that right." His smile turns feral. "But, babe, I *could* be a five-minute man if that's all the time we have."

I laugh because that's not nearly enough time for us to enjoy each other. But after the tension of the last few days, I happily let him slide his wicked tongue down my body. By the time he's done making me come, I'm famished. However, I won't ask him to take a raincheck for his pleasure.

Licking and sucking and taking him deep into my mouth, I give him every reason never to get out of this bed. If it were up to us, we'd stay here forever, but other people are counting on us to help them. We can't play all day.

After bringing him to a very satisfying climax, we get dressed. I'm almost ready to go when I realize where the kitchen's located.

"What's wrong?" he asks, easily reading my apprehension.

"Is that girl from last night going to be out there?"

"Maggie? No. Acid heard what she did. He sent her to Denver to do some shopping for the club. She won't be back until we're gone."

"Were you two dating?"

"No. I slept with her once, but that was

during a party a few years ago. It didn't mean anything, and I haven't seen her since. Don't get jealous. I'm not interested in her."

I want to ask if that's because he wants more than just sex from me, but I keep my mouth shut because I might not like his answer.

"The girls are eating breakfast, but you can talk with them afterward. Be gentle with them," he says.

"I will. I've interviewed victims before."

"You have?"

"Well, not directly, but I've watched other agents do it. That was part of my training."

"I'm glad you're with me. After what they've been through, talking to a woman will be a lot easier than speaking with a man. I won't jump in unless you give me the signal."

"Thank you." His faith in me silences my fears about making a mistake. I don't want to do anything to traumatize these girls further.

"You got this, babe." He slaps my ass playfully as we leave the bedroom.

When we get to the kitchen, it's packed with club members. Several guys are hanging out around the stove and sink, while others are seated at a long, wooden table. All three girls are sitting between two huge bikers. The kids look slightly nervous, but they're eating, so that's a good sign.

"Hello." I smile at them.

"Hey," one of the girls mumbles.

"My name's Daisy. I was wondering if I could chat with you after breakfast."

"Okay."

"Great. What are we having?"

"I'll fix you a plate," Matrix says, leaving me with them as I take a seat opposite the girls.

"Can't believe Matrix finally settled down." Fender's name is on his patch. That's the only real introduction we get. I also saw him last night in the barn, but he didn't say much.

"Yep." Talking about my nonexistent relationship with him isn't a good idea. The less we have to lie, the better.

"Here you go, babe." Matrix slides a plate filled with waffles and scrambled eggs in front of me. His plate is twice as laden with food. He digs into it, making quick work of the meal.

After we're done eating, I take the girls into the club's library. Unlike the rest of the house, this room is opulent. Expensive, high-end wood covers every surface. A coffered ceiling is just one of the many details added to make the room magnificent. I want to read the titles of all the books lining the shelves, but that will have to wait.

The girls sit in various plush reading chairs, and I chose a blue velvet settee across from them. We're alone with the door closed. Earlier, Matrix and I debated telling the girls I'm an FBI agent. Ultimately, we decided not to say anything yet. We don't want to take any chances that they might tell someone in the club before we leave.

"Matrix and I are here to take you home. If you want to go back. I know you've been through a lot, but I can help girls like you."

"I want to go home," one girl sobs.

"Where do you live?"

"Billings."

"Okay. We're heading back to Montana today. We can take you home." I look at the other girls. "Are either of you from Montana too?"

"I am," the brown-haired girl says quietly.

"Do you want to go back?"

"No."

"Can I ask you why not?"

"My stepfather …" Her face drops as her voice trails off. I don't even have to ask her why she's afraid of him. It's all over her face.

"You don't have to go home. We can help you find a safe place to live instead."

"Really?" Light flows back into her eyes.

"Yes."

"Why? How do we know we can trust you?" the third girl asks.

"You can," I say in a reassuring tone. "Matrix and I work with girls like you. We put bad people, like the men who kidnapped you, in jail." Technically, Matrix puts men like them six feet under, but I don't want to scare the girls.

"I don't want to go home either." She grabs the girl sitting beside her's hand. "Can we stay together?"

"We'll do everything we can to make that happen, but I don't want to make any promises we might not be able to keep. We can definitely take you to a safe place, but it may not be the same house."

"Anything's better than home," the second girl says.

"We'll go together." The third girl squeezes her friend's hand, almost as if to reassure her.

"Great. We want to leave soon, so pack anything you brought, and we'll leave in an hour."

"We don't need that much time. All we have are the clothes we're wearing," the first girl says.

"All right. I'll tell Matrix. We can get on the road right away."

"Thank you."

"Yeah. Thanks."

The third girl doesn't say anything but gives me a sharp nod.

After saying goodbye to the Denver club members, we get the girls into the SUV. We're back on the road with eleven hours to go. I reach over and gently grasp Matrix's hand in mine. He insisted on driving, but I want him to know I'm here to support him if he needs it.

He's been so sweet to me since we left Montana. Going on this trip together changed things between us. The lingering animosity is gone. We're working together now. It feels like this is how it's always been, but that's not true.

It's all still so new to me, but I like it. Matrix isn't just a big, sexy biker. He's a good man too. I like seeing this side of him.

That said, the newfound intimacy between us makes me a bit nervous. I can't afford to get emotionally involved with him. Being with him is supposed to be part of my assignment to infiltrate the club, but is that what I'm still doing? It feels more like the other way around. I'm not slipping into his life. He's sneaking into mine, and if I'm not careful, he might find his way into my heart too.

CHAPTER 11: MATRIX

By the time we get back to Montana, I'm dead tired. After all that driving, I could sleep for a week. Daisy offered to take over several times, but I didn't let her. She needed rest as much as I did but stayed awake, quietly talking with me while the girls dozed in the back seat. They went through one hell of an ordeal, so I expected them to be out for the whole trip, and they were.

"I'm so glad to be home," Daisy says when we pull up to the clubhouse's front door. "I'll get the girls settled in my old room. Do you still have those extra cots we set up in the living room last summer?"

"Yeah. They're in Reaper's closet. I'll get them."

"Girls, we're home. Wake up," Daisy says.

"Where are we?" Carrie, the girl eager to go home, rubs her eyes while the others yawn.

"We're at our house," I say. "Daisy will show you where the bathroom is while I get your beds ready."

"I can sleep on the floor. I don't care where you put me as long as I don't have to go back." Tina, one of the two girls who doesn't want to return home, looks around with wide eyes.

"Me too." Kim, the girl who was being abused by her stepfather, grabs Tina's hand as if to reassure her that they're safe.

"Carrie, your parents are already on their way. It's going to take them a few hours to get here, so you can rest until then," Daisy says.

"What about us?" Kim asks.

"We're looking into several options. If we can keep you together, we will," I say. "Tomorrow morning, I'll have more information. Until then, just know you're safe now. Okay?"

"Yeah," Kim says. Her tone isn't very convincing, but I don't blame her for not trusting us. If I were in her shoes, I wouldn't believe myself either.

While Daisy ushers them into her old bedroom, I go to Reaper's room and knock. "It's Matrix."

"Come in!"

"You decent?" I ask, cracking the door open.

"No. My dick's out. I'm banging three women at once. How was Denver?"

I push open the door to find him lounging on his bed. Fortunately, he's fully clothed. He's reading the latest issue of the *Journal of Forensic Sciences*.

"The trip was long but good. We found out

a lot while we were there. I'll tell you everything when Scar calls Church. I just drove eleven hours, and I'm tired as fuck. I need to grab cots for the three girls we rescued. Anything good in that magazine?" I walk past him and open his closet. It's as neat and orderly as a morgue.

"I've been reading a paper about the effects of crime scene contaminants of surface-enhanced Raman hair analysis."

"Sounds like some light nighttime reading." I smirk.

"It's about how saliva, blood, dirt, and, my personal favorite, bleach can alter the accuracy of surface-enhanced Raman spectroscopy. It's interesting stuff."

"I'll take your word for it."

He reads that journal religiously, always on the lookout for new law enforcement techniques. Once he figures out how the technology works, he can find ways to keep our crime scenes clean. The last thing we need is a bunch of science nerds beating us at our own game. Reaper says bleach is still the best way to wipe down a place. I trust him. He knows his shit.

I drag the cots to Daisy's old room and get them lined up. The girls are with her in the bathroom. I don't know how the hell they all fit, but whatever. It's like there's some unspoken female rule that if one of them goes in, they all have to go. I leave before they come out.

Scar steps into the hallway. "Hey, I wanted to be here when you returned, but Julia wouldn't let me out of bed. You know how she is."

"Please stop rubbing it in." I chuckle.

"I'm calling Church so we can all hear what happened in Denver. Nitro's on his way. He should be here soon."

"Sounds good. I'll let Reaper and Talon know."

After rounding up the guys, we meet in the conference room. Nitro arrives a minute later. "Got here as soon as I could."

"Let me guess. Holly wouldn't let you out of bed either?" I ask.

"How did you—Do you have our place bugged?"

"Why would I want to see or hear that shit? Been there, done that. The day you two moved out of the clubhouse was the first time any of us got more than a few hours of sleep without having to listen to you two fucking like animals." I shake my head, but really, I'm just giving him a hard time because it's funny as hell.

"You're just jealous." Nitro sticks his tongue out.

"Okay, children, now that we're all here, let's get to work." Scar bangs the gavel. "Matrix, tell us what went down in Denver."

I recount the trip, including the details about the cartel smuggling the girls to the house in New Orleans. That piques everyone's interest.

Unfortunately, I don't know anything about the place beside the address and what little info the cartel thugs told us before they died. I'm about to tell them about the girls when someone knocks on the door.

"Who the fuck is it?" Scar demands.

Daisy pokes her head in. "I'm so sorry to interrupt, but I need to talk to Matrix for a second. It's really important."

"So is Church," Scar says.

"I realize that, but it will only take a minute."

I look at Scar and wait. No one interrupts Church without a fight.

"Meeting adjourned for five minutes. Grab beers or piss or whatever. Back in five." Scar pounds the gavel.

"What's up?" I ask her, gently grasping her elbow between my fingers before steering her toward the living room.

"The girls are settled."

"Thank you, but that's not important enough to justify interrupting Church." I hate scolding her, but she should understand how things work around here. She's been living at the clubhouse long enough to know better.

"I know. Don't kill me for this, but I just wanted a kiss before I go to bed."

"A kiss?" I grin and slide my hands around her waist. "Babe, you couldn't wait?"

"I can hardly keep my eyes open." She

yawns.

"Scar's going to have my ass for this," I murmur before brushing my lips across hers. One sweet taste isn't enough. I return for a second, deeper kiss. This time, she melts against me, matching my passion with her own until we're both left breathless and wanting more. "Damn, woman. You know I can't follow you to bed right now."

"Which is why I wanted a kiss." She smiles seductively. "Don't wake me when you come in."

"I won't, but you might feel a little poke," I tease.

"There's nothing little about it." She smirks before sashaying down the hall.

I watch her perfect ass sway until she disappears into my room. When I turn toward the kitchen, I find everyone staring. Scar's holding a beer an inch from his mouth as if he'd stopped mid-sip.

"What?" I ask.

"Guys, head back to the meeting room. I'm going to have a quick word with Matrix," Scar says.

"Busted," Nitro whispers as he walks past me.

"He's hot for the Fed," Reaper mutters.

"Why not? She's smokin'," Talon says. His comment earns him a glare from me, which only makes him grin harder.

As soon as they're gone, Scar hands me

a freshly opened beer. I take a long pull. Even though we're all adults here, I know I'm in trouble. It wasn't my fault she interrupted Church, but I've got a feeling I'm going to be the one paying for it.

"What's up, pres?" I ask.

"You and the Fed got close while you two were in Denver."

"We had to share a room because Acid didn't tell anyone who she really is."

"And you're shacked up here too."

"You were the one who made her move into my room. Did you really expect me to babysit her sexy ass without something happening?" I finish off the beer and toss the bottle into the recycling bin.

"Where's your head at?"

"What do you mean?"

"Are you falling for her?"

"No!" Maybe I'm a bit too defensive, but I blame the beer and lack of sleep.

"Don't forget for one second that she's an FBI agent. For all we know, she could be playing you. She infiltrated the club and set up shop right under our noses. Don't underestimate her. She's smart, resourceful, and cunning. Women like that are trouble."

"You could say the same thing about Julia, and you made her your old lady."

"It's not the same thing. Julia was an elementary school nurse. She wasn't a sworn enemy of the club."

"Daisy's not like other FBI agents. She's trying to do the right thing. Her hatred of Blackstone is equal to ours. The guy had her sister snatched and sold her into a trafficking ring. She's with us, pres. You have to trust me on this."

"I know I can count on you, but she's a wildcard. We don't know what she'll do once we help her find her sister. She could turn on us. You need to be aware of this possibility. Don't let your dick blind you to all the *other* ways she could fuck you."

"Got it." I clench my jaw, so I won't say anything I'll regret. He means well, but he doesn't know a damn thing about her. He didn't get to see how sweet she was with the girls. During the entire ride home, she kept checking to make sure they didn't need food or a restroom. She's going to make one hell of a mom if she ever decides to have kids. Scar just hasn't seen that side of her.

"Don't drop your guard. Ever." He gives me a long, piercing look before walking down the hall.

Inhaling deeply, I take a second to calm my racing heart. My gut says I can trust Daisy, but what if he's right? What if she's just fucking me to get as much information as possible to make a case against Blackstone? Maybe Scar's right, and I need to be more cautious. I'm not turning my back on her, but I've got to keep my eyes open.

The sex is hot, but it's not worth any potential damage she could cause to the club. My brothers will always come first. Going forward, I need to keep this at the forefront of my mind, so I don't get caught off guard.

When everyone's settled in their chairs, Scar restarts the meeting. "Earlier today, I called our contacts at the UV Washington State chapter. They have a family willing and able to take in the two girls who don't want to return home."

"Did anyone verify the kids' stories?" Talon asks.

"Yeah." Nitro scowls. "Tina's family is a frequent flier with Child Protective Services. They have a way of skirting the line so CPS can't take their kids away, but it's bad. If I were her, I wouldn't want to go back either."

"What about the other girl?" Reaper asks.

"Kim's stepfather is a royal piece of shit. He's got multiple convictions for sexual assault, but like a lot of those pieces of shit, he's on probation now. As far as I could tell, Kim never reported him for anything. That doesn't mean she hasn't been abused, though."

"Lots of kids are too afraid to speak up," Reaper says.

"Yeah." I nod. We're all silent for a moment. "Which one of us is taking them to Washington?"

"Nitro and Holly volunteered to go. They'll

leave tomorrow morning," Scar says.

"It's eleven hours each way," Talon says.

"Been there, done that. Glad I don't have to do it again right away," I say.

"Back to Denver. Tell me more about this house in NOLA. Do you think there's a chance Daisy's sister could still be there?" Scar asks.

"It's not likely, but she's going to check it out. I think we should go with her. Blackstone's connected to this operation somehow. We don't know the details, but we might be able to find evidence of his involvement. This could be the break we need to bring him to justice finally."

"Are you confident he's affiliated with this trafficking ring?"

"Yes. The guy at the campsite said his name, the Demon Rider we interrogated here confirmed it, and then the cartel member in Denver mentioned it. I'm sure Blackstone's using the cartels to move people. If we can find a solid connection between him and the traffickers, he's done. Daisy can take the evidence to the Feds and make sure he spends the rest of his life in prison."

"It's not enough," Reaper grumbles.

"I want him strung up by the balls as much as you do, but if we can put him behind bars while proving he's a child predator, he won't last long. Inmates don't like dudes who mess with kids. He'll be a dead man walking."

"Sounds like we're going to New Orleans," Scar says.

"We are?" I arch a brow.

"If her sister's linked to Blackstone and we find her, we've got a witness. That's worth more than anything we've ever had on him. The tape we leaked didn't work because there wasn't a victim to parade across the television. That's what we need. If it bleeds, it leads."

I don't like how Scar's talking about Angela, but I need him on board. Going to New Orleans with the whole club is much better than going alone with Daisy. She and I might be able to make some progress, but these guys will have our backs. Even though she's a Fed, she's part of the family. Maybe she's the ugly stepchild right now, but she's still our club girl. Scar never kicked her out. He'd never turn his back on a woman in trouble. Daisy needs us to help her find Angela. In exchange, we want whatever she can get us on Blackstone. As far as I can tell, it's a win-win for everyone.

"Another winter storm is blowing in tomorrow night. I want us on the road to NOLA after Nitro and Holly leave for Washington. Carrie's parents are on their way from Billings. They should be here soon." Scar looks around the table. "Get some sleep tonight. Tomorrow, we've got a long road ahead of us. Adjourned."

"I can't wait to get on my bike again," Reaper says.

"Me either. How far down do you think we'll have to go with the trailers before we can pull them out?" I ask.

"Arkansas. Maybe. Weather's been nuts this year. It was snowing in Texas last week."

"True. I was hoping we could get the bikes out sooner, but at least we know we can ride in Louisiana."

"As long as it's not flooding."

"True. But that's more of a summer/fall issue." As I stop outside my bedroom door, Reaper grunts in agreement. "See you tomorrow."

He nods before plodding down the hall.

After taking a long, hot shower, I crawl into bed beside my woman. Damn, I can't think about her like that. I want her more than anything, but Scar's right. She's a Fed. I don't really know where her loyalties lie. I want to believe it's with the club and me, but she's still in touch with the Feds. For all I know, she could be feeding them details about everything we discuss. I should be more careful about what I say to her in the future, at least until I know if she's with or against us.

As she coils around me like a sexy little snake, I will my cock to stand down. It's impossible not to react to her soft, warm breasts or her slowly stroking my ass. She's not even conscious, and she's got the power to make me hard as hell. I want her so badly it worries me. I'm becoming addicted to her. The only thing that's ever had that kind of hold over me was cutting.

I brush my thumb over the scars on my wrist. I haven't picked up a knife to cut myself since I left the hospital. The desire to do it is gone. Is that because Daisy has become my new obsession? Is she taking away my pain instead of the knife? And when this is all over, will she hurt me worse than the sharpest blade in the world?

These unsettling thoughts keep me awake far into the night.

CHAPTER 12: DAISY

Sitting on the back of Matrix's bike is making me so horny. I can't wait to get to the NOLA chapter's clubhouse. As soon as I have him to myself, I'm going to jump on his huge cock and ride him harder than ever before. It's going to be amazing. Sex with him is incredible, and I swear it keeps getting better. Every time we get together, we learn a bit more about what the other person likes in bed. He's into rough stuff. I haven't done much of that before, but it's exciting and feels so dangerous. I love it.

We pull up to Café Du Monde and park outside. The New Orleans landmark has been in the French Quarter since 1862. The open-air coffee shop has plenty of outdoor seating under a green canopy, and a couple of dozen small tables fill the space. We timed our ride to get here just after sundown.

I'm super excited because I've never been to this city before. Matrix hasn't either, so we'll be exploring it for the first time together. I don't know how much time we'll actually have to look around, but I hope we'll get a chance to see the St. Louis Cathedral in Jackson Square.

As we get off our bikes, everyone in the café turns to stare. The guys are wearing their leathers and cuts, proudly representing Underground Vengeance. One lady cowers and pulls her toddler into her lap. Another woman whispers to her friend, and based on his reaction, he's not impressed with the club.

If these people knew how much good the club does, they wouldn't feel the way they do. But looks are deceiving, and not all clubs are dedicated to doing the right thing. In fact, many of them thrive on being criminals, so it's no wonder people are afraid of them.

"Grab some chairs. I'll go order," Scar says.

"He didn't ask what we want," I whisper to Matrix.

"That's because there's only one thing you order here."

"Two," Reaper interjects.

"Right. Coffee and beignets."

"The little powdered French-style doughnuts? I've never actually had one." I sit beside Matrix while Reaper pulls an extra table over for the other guys.

"You're in for a treat." He takes my hand under the table. I smile at him, and our gazes lock. "The coffee's good too."

"You'll be on the biggest sugar high ever by

the time you're done. Back in a second." Talon heads toward Scar to help him carry plates filled with beignets. After setting them down on the table, they go back to get coffee for everyone.

"Be careful. They're fresh and hot." Matrix leans over to whisper in my ear. "Like you, babe."

I giggle and kiss him on the cheek. Reaper gives me the side-eye, but I ignore him. He can judge all he wants. He's probably wondering why I'm not freaking out about my sister and demanding we find her immediately. I would be, except Scar pulled me aside at the last rest stop and told me the local chapter is well aware of the Garden District house and has a plan. His confidence helped quell my nerves. So, until we get to the NOLA clubhouse, I'm going to enjoy myself. We're meeting them in an hour, so it's not like I have to wait too long.

The first bite of sugary goodness melts on my tongue. The beignet is still very hot, but it's just cool enough that I won't burn the roof of my mouth.

"Well?" Matrix asks.

"Better than sex," I mumble through a mouthful.

"Really?" He scowls. "No doughnut in the world will outdo me. I'll have to change that as soon as we get a room."

"Wish they had a room right now," Reaper grumbles.

Scar's phone beeps. He pulls it out and looks

at a text message. "They're ready for us. Take your time. I'm going to order a few bags to go so we can bring them to the clubhouse."

"Make sure there's extra for me," Talon says.

As I sip my drink, I can't help but wonder why it tastes slightly off compared to regular coffee. "Do they brew this differently? It has a strange aftertaste."

"It has chicory in it," Matrix says.

"I hate to say it," I whisper, "but I'm not a fan."

"That's okay, babe. I'm sure the club will have real coffee too. Personally, I like the taste of chicory, but maybe that's because I'm also bitter." His tone is playful, but I wonder if there's something darker hiding behind his self-depreciation.

"The weather's perfect." I'm wearing jeans and a T-shirt. It's funny to watch tourists pulling their jackets tighter. Clearly, they don't live in the frozen north the way we do. The temperature is in the mid-sixties, which is shorts weather in Montana. I'd be wearing a pair if we weren't riding.

"Sometimes I think about moving back," Talon says softly.

"Really?" Matrix asks.

"Were you born here?" I ask.

"Yeah, and yeah. But the club's the only home I ever had, so I'm not leaving any time soon." He slaps Matrix on the back.

"Good to hear it, brother." Matrix gives Talon's shoulder a rough squeeze. "Because if you ever thought about leaving for real, I'd have to send you to the basement with Reaper so he could talk some sense into you."

"Wouldn't need to talk," Reaper says in a dark tone that sends shivers down my spine.

"Hey now," Talon holds up his hands in surrender. "I said I'm good."

"Better be." Reaper sips his coffee, but his eyes never leave Talon's face.

"You guys remind me of my brothers," I murmur.

"Brothers?" Matrix sits up. "You've got other siblings?"

"Three brothers and one sister, Angie."

"No shit," Talon says. "Where are they?"

"Montana. They're scattered around the state. I don't get to see them much because I'm working all the time." I shrug. It is what it is.

"I imagine it would be hard to see them, especially when you're undercover. That would make it nearly impossible." The sharp edge in Matrix's tone catches me off-guard. Obviously, he doesn't like the line of work I'm in, but it's all I ever wanted to do. He should know that by now.

"It's my job. You know that. I'm going to find a restroom." I push back from the table just as Scar returns with several packed white pastry bags.

"We ride in five," he says. "Eat up. Drink

up. Enjoy the treats because once we get to the clubhouse, it's back to work."

"Got it," Matrix says.

Reaper nods while Talon shoves an entire beignet into his mouth. Powdered sugar dusts the front of his vest. In fact, everyone has a fine layer of it on their clothes.

"I'll be back by then," I say before leaving.

"Where's she going?" Scar asks Matrix.

"Bathroom."

"Okay."

I wait until I'm out of sight to pick up my pace. The SAC running my office will be furious I went to New Orleans without his permission, but I didn't have time to ask. I pull out a burner phone I've kept hidden from the guys and use it to make the call.

He answers immediately. "Thank God you called. I was about to send in an extraction team."

"I'm fine. In fact, I just had my first beignet."

"You what?" He's furious. Crap.

"We've got a lead on my sister. We're here to check it out."

"What lead? Where are you?"

"New Orleans. She was spotted in the city a few months ago."

"By whom?"

"A man I talked to in Denver."

"Look, I'm getting sick of this vague shit. If you don't start giving me names and places, I'm pulling you off this case."

"You can't do that." I raise my voice so much that several tourists turn to stare at me. "When I have details, I'll pass them along."

I end the call before he can respond. Who the hell does he think he is? I'm following the first real lead in my sister's case since it was opened. The FBI hadn't made any progress until I joined Underground Vengeance. I've learned more about what happened to her since going undercover than the FBI ever did. Right now, my relationship with the club is far more important than the one I have with my boss. He's going to yank me off this case for sure, but I don't care. I'm staying with the club for as long as it takes to find my sister. If that means going rogue, then so be it.

After stopping in the bathroom to wash the rage off my face, I stare into the mirror. I'm exhausted, angry, and ready to rip someone's head off. Not a good combination.

By the time I get back to the guys, they're on their bikes, ready to ride. "Sorry. The line was huge."

"I was about to go looking for you," Matrix says.

"Good thing I'm here now, so you don't have to." I give him the sweetest smile I can manage, but my anger toward my SAC is pulling my lips too taut. I'm sure he can see it. Yanking on my helmet, I hope I can cover my expression before he asks me about it. I need to get myself under control. I don't want Matrix to get suspicious.

The clubhouse isn't more than a couple of miles from the edge of the French Quarter. We cross a canal before entering the Lower 9th Ward. During Hurricane Katrina, the entire area flooded. The water went as high as the rooftops and destroyed most of the houses. Those not ripped from their foundations ended up with extensive water damage. Many of the homes were condemned. Eventually, people were able to rebuild, but it's still an economically impoverished area. I'm glad Matrix let me keep one of the club's guns. I wouldn't want to be out after dark in this neighborhood without it.

As we rumble over streets filled with potholes, I grip Matrix's waist a little tighter. People sitting on porches watch us drive by. Clearly, we're outsiders. Because of that, we might have a target on our backs. I hope the clubhouse has plenty of extra security.

We arrive at a two-story row house made of stone. According to Matrix, the house survived Katrina, barely. It was completely underwater and infested with all kinds of vermin by the time officials let the club return to assess the damage. Members from surrounding chapters of UV chipped in with their time or other resources. Eventually, they returned the house to its previous condition. They even repainted it with an alabaster hue to make it non-descript compared to the other vibrantly painted houses in the neighborhood.

We park the bikes in a diagonal row in front of the house and store the trailers behind it. Several men in cut-off vests and shorts mill around the first and second-floor patios. Two huge glass windows flank the front door. As we walk up the steps, the guys stand to greet us.

After a lot of back-slapping and bro-hugs, they introduce themselves to me. Vapor, the club's president, is the tallest of the men. He's easily six and a half feet tall with enough muscle to be on a football team. His sharp blue eyes miss nothing.

"Scar says you've been a real asset to the club." He strokes his hand through his slicked-back hair. It's as black as a raven's.

"I do what I can," I say cautiously, unsure of how much Scar shared with the man.

"I'm Ice." The man standing next to Vapor is wearing the VP patch. Ice's long, platinum hair is so pale he resembles a vampire. He has an otherworldly aura, with piercing silver-blue eyes that seem to glow in the darkness. His hypnotic voice lingers in my mind, almost as if he's in my head.

"Nice to meet you."

"That's Diablo." Ice points to another man with an Enforcer patch on his cut. He has a ruggedly handsome face that is accentuated by a prominent jawline. His intense brown eyes seem to smolder with a hint of danger. He has short, tousled black hair that falls over his forehead, giving him a brooding, mysterious look. His physique is muscular and toned, with broad shoulders and a chest that exudes raw power. He stands tall and confident, with an imposing presence that commands attention. Yet, he never says a word.

"I'm Bones, the Sgt at Arms." He's a tall man with broad shoulders and a muscular build. His skin is a deep shade of bronze, and he has rugged, angular features. His hair is dark and thick, and he wears it short in a low-maintenance style. His eyes are chocolate brown, and they're just as warm as his smile.

Fang is the last man to introduce himself. He's the secretary/tech guru of the club. His impressive muscles are in sharp contrast to his nerdy demeanor. He's wearing a geeky graphic tee, cargo shorts, and sneakers. A pair of thick, black-rimmed glasses accentuate dazzling green eyes. I immediately like him because he reminds me of Matrix.

After finishing the introductions, Vapor leads us into the clubhouse. Several women wearing shorts and tank tops lounge around the living room. They're watching a reality TV show and seem completely uninterested in what's happening in the clubhouse until they spot me. Several of them narrow their gazes. I do my best not to roll my eyes. I'm not here to swipe one of their men. There's only one guy in this house that I have any interest in, and that's Matrix.

"Ladies, how about making a big batch of jambalaya," Vapor says. It sounds like a casual suggestion, but I can tell it's an order. Two women get to their feet and head into a kitchen toward the rear of the house. "The bedrooms are all upstairs. Fang will show you where to put your stuff down. Church in ten. We meet in the library. It's the door on the right just before you get to the kitchen."

"Come on, babe." Matrix grabs my hand, and we follow the others to our assigned room. After he pushes open the door, we walk in. It's small, with only a full-sized bed and a dresser. A French door leads to the balcony. "Well, it's not big, but it's got a bed. That's all we'll need."

"Can I come to the meeting?" I ask.

"No. Scar told them you're FBI. He didn't want you to have to walk around on eggshells the way you did in Denver. The guys don't like it, as expected, but they're willing to work with you."

"So, why can't I go to Church, then?" As I sit on the edge of the bed, the box springs creak slightly.

"Hmm, going to have to fuck slowly so we don't make a ton of noise." He grins, totally avoiding my question.

"Matrix..."

"After we meet, I'll tell you everything I'm allowed to talk about. Scar isn't in charge here.

It's Vapor's club, so we must follow his rules. Even if Scar had authority, I don't think he'd let you join us. It's just how we operate. We don't share club business with non-members."

"I know. I just hate sitting around waiting."

"You can watch TV with the other club girls."

"God, no. Did you see how they looked at me? If looks could kill, I'd be dead right now."

"They've got nothing to fear from you."

"Exactly. Wait, why do you say that?"

"Because you're here with me. As long as we're still ... a team, then they can fuck off."

"A team?"

"Yeah." He averts his eyes. "Back in a bit, babe."

My heart drops, but I don't say anything as he leaves. We've never talked about what's happening between us. At first, it was just sex, but over the last few days, it feels like it's something more. I want to ask him about it, but I'm afraid of what he'll say. I can't let my heart get tangled up in a relationship with him. It's been hard, *really hard*, especially after we have sex. My hormones go out of control, and all I want to do is cuddle with him forever.

It's a ridiculous reaction because I can't fall in love with him. If I did, I'd be the worst undercover agent ever. Maybe I am. With how things are going, I might not be employed by the FBI for much longer. If the SAC decides to fire me, he has every right to do so. Hell, he may have cut me loose already. I won't know until I contact him again.

I glance at my bag, which holds the hidden phone. Calling my boss would be the wise thing to do. I could placate him, buy myself a few more days so he doesn't fire me. That would be the smart thing to do. But it could also speed things up. He could officially pull me off this case. I can't risk that possibility.

I stare at my bag for a long time before finally lying on my back on the bed. There's no way I'm calling in. I'm so close to possibly finding my sister that I can't risk further entanglement with the agency. Once I find out more about her situation, I'll check in. Until then, I guess I've gone rogue.

CHAPTER 13: MATRIX

Daisy's a huge distraction. I can't stop thinking about what I told her about us being a team. There isn't a second that goes by that I don't want more. It's crazy and totally impossible to imagine a future with her, but that's all I could do on the ride down to New Orleans. I need to focus on the task ahead and stop picturing what life would be like with her by my side. It can't happen, so why go there?

I join Scar, Talon, and Reaper at the conference table in the center of the club's library. Mint green bookshelves line the walls. In addition to the books, a variety of knickknacks decorate the shelves. A tiny ceramic clown dressed in New Orleans Saints colors sits in the center of a collection of creepy dolls. On another shelf, a steamboat trinket box and a wooden toy mandolin share the space. A shrunken head, which I hope is fake, props up a large, leather-bound book.

If that's not strange enough, Mardi Gras

beads dangle from an altar in the corner by the window. The sacred space contains everything from a two-foot-tall statue of the Virgin Mary to an unopened bottle of spiced rum to a voodoo doll. Dollar bills and loose change are strewn across the shiny red altar cloth. Partially melted candles in glass jars add extra color to the space.

Glancing at Scar, I raise an eyebrow. He shrugs as Vapor and his men file into the room to take their seats.

"Church is in session." Vapor bangs the gavel. "First, I want to welcome everyone from the Montana chapter. You guys have been a huge inspiration to my crew and me. Based on several conversations I've had with Scar, we've been able to strategize ways to take down some of the local corrupt cops. They spring up like weeds, though, so our job is never done."

"Glad we could be of assistance," Scar says.

"We'd like to return the favor. I understand you're interested in Lulu's."

"That's the name of the Garden District house, right?"

"Yes. It was named after Lulu White, a brothel madam during the Storyville period. Storyville was the red-light district in New Orleans from 1897 to 1917. It was the city's attempt to regulate prostitution."

"Is it legal here?" Talon asks.

"Not since 1917. When World War I started, Secretary of War Newton Baker didn't want soldiers to be drawn to 'houses of ill repute'," he says with air quotes. "The Navy has troops stationed in NOLA, so Storyville and its madams had to go."

"This city is full of history."

"That it is. It's sort of a hobby of mine," Vapor says.

"He's a huge history nerd." Ice laughs.

Vapor punches him in the shoulder before continuing, "Lulu was an interesting woman. She was born in Selma, Alabama, but claimed to be from the West Indies. She was mixed race, which made it even harder for her to run a successful business, but she did. Her house was called Mahogany Hall, and it was big. Forty women worked there. There were five parlors for entertaining guests and fifteen private bedrooms upstairs. It was the only interracial brothel in New Orleans at that time, and it was high-class all the way. Lulu bought expensive shit like Tiffany-stained glass windows and French furniture. The works."

"Were the girls there of their own free will?" Scar asks.

"As far as we know, yes. She hired both black and white prostitutes, which wasn't done at the time. She thumbed her nose at racial segregation laws."

"Did she ever run into trouble with cops?" Reaper asks.

"Many times. A woman after my own

heart." Vapor chuckles. "But eventually, she had financial problems, so she moved to California. Historians haven't been able to trace her after that, and details aren't very clear, but in her heyday, she was one of the only mixed-race self-made millionaires."

"Why would the local cartel choose to name their place after her?"

"Who knows? Maybe they wanted to keep her memory alive. It's unfortunate, though, because what they're doing isn't legal or ethical. She'd probably roll over in her grave if she knew they were using her name like this." Vapor makes a fist. "Anyway, we know all about those fucks who hold girls there."

"Who's running the house?" Scar asks.

"A cartel. Los Serpientes de Cristal."

"That's the same group out of Denver."

"They're all over the US now, taking over the bigger cities. They fought a bloody turf war here a few years back, during which they forced out a Mexican cartel. Bodies lined the streets. The local cops made a big show of arresting some of the Cristal members, but as soon as the media moved onto a new story, they were released. I don't have proof, but I suspect they're giving local cops kickbacks to look the other way."

"I hate that shit," Reaper says.

"Agreed." Diablo nods at his counterpart.

"We have reason to believe Daisy's sister was taken by the cartel. It's been months, but we have intel they took her to Lulu's. How long do they keep the girls at the house?" Scar asks.

"Sometimes a few days. Sometimes years. Depends on the girl." Fang types on his computer. A bookshelf drops to reveal a hidden television screen. It flicks on to display his computer screen. A chart with names and dates pops up.

"Cool," I whisper.

"This is the local cartel's organizational chart. We've spent years gathering data, and this is as far as we've gotten. We've got some names, but Blackstone was never mentioned. We didn't realize he was involved in this trafficking ring until Scar called us. I know you guys want Blackstone to go to prison. We'd love to help you put him there."

"First, we need to find out if Daisy's sister, Angela, is still being held at the house," I say. "Do you have any information on the girls?"

"We haven't been able to get anything other than names and sometimes ages. They have armed guards with metal detectors at the door. We can't bring guns or any type of recording device inside. Sometimes, they'll pat you down too, so you can't carry any weapons, even plastic ones."

"That sucks," Talon says.

"When was the last time you sent someone in?" I ask.

"It's been a couple of weeks. Since the cartel

is onto us, we only send in our prospects. The cartel knows who all our members are, and they've got orders to shoot us on sight. If you want to find out if Angela's there, you'll have to send one of your guys in. They don't know you," Vapor says.

"I'll go," I volunteer.

"No." Scar shakes his head. "You're too emotionally involved in the situation."

"Are you saying I can't be objective?"

"Not when it comes to Daisy's sister. If she's in there, we can't just walk her out of a house like that. We need a plan. Whoever we send in will have to find a way to check all the girls, then report back without alerting Angela."

"We can't send Reaper. He'll shoot up the place."

"Yeah." Reaper grins. "And I'd enjoy it too."

"Guess that leaves Scar or me," Talon says. "I'll go."

"Good. The objective is simple: get in, search for Angela, get out," Scar says. "If she's inside, then we'll regroup and find a way to get her out."

"I've got a full schematic of the house. Guard schedules. Whatever you need to make this thing happen," Fang says.

"Directions to the front door should just about do it." Talon leans back in his chair and laces his fingers behind his head.

"You can't just waltz in. It's by invitation only," Ice says.

"How do I get one of those?"

"You have to go to one of the local strip clubs and flash a whole lot of cash. Fortunately, we've got stacks of twenties in the safe." Vapor grins.

"Twenties?" I'm surprised.

"Inflation's a bitch. No one bats an eye when you make it rain with ones anymore. Twenties are the new minimum to get attention," Ice says.

"You sound like an expert on the local stripper scene."

"Research." Ice smirks.

"I'll bet. When do we go?" I ask.

"We?" Scar turns in his chair to face me.

"You can't send one guy into a club run by the cartel." I lean toward Vapor. "I'm assuming they run the clubs, too?"

"Yes."

"Then we need a group."

"Why? One guy is less suspicious," Bones says.

"Not really. Here's the play. We all go in like we're a group of dudes out partying for the night. Around one a.m., we start talking about going to one of the jazz clubs, but Talon doesn't want to go. We make a big scene about leaving him behind. That will draw attention to him. Then, he'll try to pay one of the strippers for sex. That should put him on their radar." I pause to see what they think.

"I actually like it," Vapor says. "It's the perfect way to get them to take the bait."

"Agreed," Scar says.

"Are we going tonight? I need a shower first. I smell like ass," Talon says.

"The clubs don't really get going until after ten anyway. Eleven is better. Who's going tonight?" Vapor asks Scar.

"Talon, Reaper, and Matrix. I'll stay behind."

"Julia would have his ass if he found out he was getting lap dances from naked women," Talon says.

"Wait until Daisy finds out." Reaper smirks.

"So, you and the Fed, hmm?" Vapor eyes me in a way that suggests he disapproves of our … whatever we are.

"Maybe we skip telling her the details." I don't want to lie to her, but if I tell her the truth, she might stop me from going. I can't risk it. Talon will need backup, at least until he gets an invite to Lulu's.

"It's your call," Vapor says to Scar.

"Don't tell her."

"Thanks, pres." I release the breath I've been holding.

"As long as you look but don't touch, it shouldn't matter," Talon says.

"Right. I'll let you explain that to her." I roll my eyes.

"Be ready to leave at quarter to ten," Scar says.

"Is there anything else we need to discuss while we're all here?" Vapor asks.

"No."

"Nope."

"The girls made jambalaya. It's in the kitchen. Feel free to eat up before you go," Vapor says before adjourning the meeting.

I'm dreading going upstairs and lying to Daisy. With each step, my feet seem to turn into lead. By the time I arrive at our bedroom door, my heart's beating a mile a minute. I can't lie to her. It wouldn't be right. Telling her what's really going on is the only way to avoid a guilty conscience. I'll have to convince her that I'm going for club business, nothing else, which is the truth.

I open the door and walk in to find her sleeping. Well, that solves that problem. I breathe a sigh of relief. She's probably wiped out from the ride since she's not used to being on a bike for so long. Waking her up to piss her off isn't a good idea. Besides, I'll be back before she even realizes I'm gone. Problem solved.

Backing out, I softly close the door behind me. I find Talon down in the living room sitting between two club girls. His hair's still wet from a shower, and he smells less like ass and more like magnolias. It's a huge improvement.

I sit in a recliner off to one side. They're watching a ridiculous show about a bachelor dating a bunch of women at once. It's so dumb that I can't help but be sucked into it. An hour later, I'm on Team Amber. I don't even know the chick, but I'm rooting for her to get the final rose.

"It's time to roll," Reaper says, interrupting the show.

"No. He's about to talk to Brittany and crush her soul," Talon says.

"He's going to pick Amber for sure," I say in agreement.

"Why choose?" Reaper asks. "They're both hot pieces of ass."

"You're crude," one of the club girls says. She scowls at him until he growls. Quickly looking away, she lets out a disgruntled huff.

Talon and I stall by taking our sweet time pulling out the keys to our bikes. I continue to buy time by pointing out that we can't wear our cuts to the club.

"I fucking knew it." I fist pump as Amber gets the final red rose.

"He picked the right one," Talon says.

"You guys are so fucked up." Reaper shakes his head as he walks out and fires up his bike. Talon and I laugh as we get ready to ride.

The trip to the club only takes ten minutes. It's situated in the middle of the French Quarter. A scantily clad girl and a hype man stand outside, trying to lure people in. He doesn't have to work hard to hook us. After all, we look like three drunk guys out on the town looking for pussy. We're his target market.

Inside, the club is full of other guys, and women in barely-there outfits flit from patron to patron, trying to score lap dances. Some of the ladies sit in their mark's lap while making their pitch. It's been a long time since I stepped foot in one of these places, but I immediately know why I stopped going. The scent of lust and desperation fills the air. The women are experts at teasing, but they don't actually fuck the men. At least, most of them don't. All a guy can hope for is a cock tease and a lonely, solo hand job when he gets home. Oh, and an empty wallet.

"Let's sit at the bar. We'll be the most visible there," Talon says.

"Shit, did you bring the money?" I ask.

"I did. You dumbasses were too busy hanging out with the club girls." Reaper pulls stacks of twenties out of his pockets and hands them to us. "Don't blow it all before one a.m."

"Yes, Dad," Talon says.

"Is he really your dad, baby? He doesn't look that old," a stripper coos as she wraps her arms around his shoulders.

"He thinks he is." Talon laughs.

"Want a dance?"

"Not yet ... but find me later."

"What about your friends?" She turns her attention to Reaper and me. "You boys looking to have some fun?"

"Just killing time before going to a jazz bar. He's the one who wanted to come in here." I jerk my head toward Talon.

"Those places are no fun. This is much

better." She flashes a seductive smile, but all I can think about is Daisy. She's so beautiful; this girl couldn't even hope to compete with her.

"Come on," Reaper says, ignoring her.

We snake our way through the tables, moving toward the huge stage in the center of the room. A gold-colored rail runs around the bottom of the stage, separating the dancers from the men tossing money at them. Several men drape dollar bills over the rail while gawking at the dancers. I start throwing twenties at the stripper on the stage. That gets her attention. She's on her back with her legs splayed, but I couldn't care less. She's also not my type at all. I remind myself that I only have to play the game for a few hours. Or at least until someone from the cartel invites Talon to Lulu's.

Discretely looking around the room, I spot several armed men. They blend into the darkness, but they don't fool me. They're definitely watching everyone. We need to catch their attention.

When a new girl gets on stage, I whisper to Talon, "Get a lap dance and ask for *extras*. That should tip her off that you want to pay for sex."

"Got it." Talon waits until the second song ends, and the girl is picking up her tips before making his move. "Can we go somewhere private?"

"You want a lap dance?"

"Yeah."

"Come with me." She grabs his hand and leads him to a booth near the back of the club.

"Don't watch them," I warn Reaper.

"Wasn't born yesterday," he growls.

Out of the corner of my eye, I keep an eye on Talon. He's definitely enjoying the dancer, but he hasn't lost focus. I can tell the minute he makes his move because the girl glances at the cartel members. She leans over and whispers something into Talon's ear before walking away. She briefly stops to have a conversation with one of them. He glances at Talon before looking over at us.

"Shit. Don't look," I tell Reaper. "We're on their radar. We need to tell Talon we're leaving without him. Ready?"

"Let's go."

We walk over to where Talon's sitting. In loud, drunken voices, we inform him the club sucks, and we're going to leave. He tells us to go fuck ourselves and that he's not leaving until he gets his dick sucked.

His flawless performance worked. As we're walking out, I glance at the mirror behind the stage. A cartel member hands Talon a white business card. Talon's grinning like an absolute fool because he got what he came for. Our work here is done. Now we just have to wait for the results of his trip to Lulu's.

CHAPTER 14: DAISY

"You did what?" I sit up in bed and stare at Matrix like he has two heads. He just informed me that he spent the last few hours in a strip club. Without me. Not that I would want to go to one of those places, but he should've let me know before he left.

"I didn't want to wake you," he says sheepishly. Oh, he knows he's in trouble. Good thing I'm more interested in their interaction with the cartel than I am in what he did at the strip club. He doesn't seem like the type of guy who indulges in lap dances, but that's an assumption I have zero interest in challenging.

"Well? What happened?"

"I didn't touch any of the strippers."

"Okay. And?" I slide out of bed and pull on my shirt and pants. If he thinks he's getting any tonight, he's dead wrong. I check my watch. It's two a.m.

"Talon's at Lulu's right now looking for your sister."

After he explains the plan in detail, including what did or didn't happen at the strip club, anxiety replaces my anger. "Have you heard anything yet?"

"No. But he's only been inside for a few hours."

"How do you know he's safe? Maybe they made him and killed him."

"Not a chance. You're not the only one who's good at undercover work. One time, we sent Talon to work at the Motor Vehicle Department because we needed a certain person's address."

"You couldn't hack their system and get it?"

"I mean, I could, but breaking into anything related to the government isn't the best idea. They've got fairly good tracking abilities. Getting a job at the MVD was much easier."

"I see."

"Are you going to stay mad all night?" he asks in an exasperated tone.

"Maybe." I look away and cross my arms.

"Babe, there isn't another woman in the world who could hold a candle to your beauty. And you're intelligent as hell, which turns me on so damn much." He gently grasps my folded arms and pulls them open. "Don't be pissed off about something I didn't do. It's a waste of energy."

"Fine."

He brushes his lips across mine so softly that it leaves me wanting more. I hate how much my body yearns for him. No matter how many times we have sex, it's never enough.

I give in far too easily and wind my arms around his neck. He returns to kiss me again, this time harder. His tongue slides across the seam of my lips, opening me to him. Sitting around waiting for news will drive me crazy, so I may as well enjoy being in his arms.

With a sigh, I surrender to the passion burning between us, and my desire for him explodes. Maybe I want to mark my territory, which is a concerning thought, or maybe I just want him. Either way, I pull his shirt off and toss it across the room. His nipple piercings catch in the low light from a single lamp. With the curtains drawn, it's the only illumination in the space. It's enough. A glorious play of light and shadow dances across his abs as he moves.

I lean down to capture one barbell between my teeth. When I give it a gentle tug, he groans and pulls away until his nipple is stretched taut. I'm sure it aches, but I know he loves it. The heavy length of his cock pokes at my belly, making me desperate to have him between my thighs. Releasing him from my mouth, I drift lower to unbutton his jeans. I pull them to his ankles so he can step out of them. He stumbles back before falling onto the bed.

When the springs creak wildly, we grin at each other. I'm sure this isn't the first time someone's made this bed squeak. I just hope we don't break it.

"We'd better keep it down," he whispers.

"Why? I want those club girls to know you're mine."

"Is that what I am? Yours?"

"Aren't you?"

I push him down on the bed and rid him of the rest of his clothes. His cock stands at attention, just waiting for me to wrap my lips around it. I strip faster than any exotic dancer ever could and climb onto the bed. Straddling him, I brush my wet sex along his shaft.

"You're so fucking hot," he murmurs. His hands slide up from my waist to close around my breasts. Tweaking my nipples, he tugs and pinches them before sitting up to lick away the pain.

I'm overwhelmed by my desire to claim him. I slide down between his thighs before brushing my lips across his shaft. There's nothing soft or sweet about the way I devour his cock. His hips jerk off the mattress while he curses loud enough to wake the dead.

"Shh," I moan around the head of his cock.

"Fuck, babe."

"Is that what you want?" I give him a coy smile before forcing him deep into my mouth. I never break eye contact, not even when his eyes roll back and his thighs quiver. Seeing him so turned on makes me even hotter. My pussy's dripping with need and so ready, but I delay my gratification because tormenting him is so much fun.

"I'm going to come," he growls, grabbing a fistful of my hair and dragging me off his cock. It slides out of my mouth with an audible pop.

He manhandles me onto my hands and knees before getting in behind me. There's nothing gentle about how he forces his cock deep inside me. I let out a cry I can't contain. Burying my face in the sheets, I try to stifle my screams of pleasure, but the way he's fucking me is so raw, so intense that I'm sure I'm going to die before it's over.

"Matrix, please," I moan.

"All I want is your sweet pussy. Every night. You're mine." He hammers me with rough thrusts until my weakened muscles give way. Then, he flattens me onto the bed without missing a single stroke.

Plunging into my pussy, he grinds me into the mattress. My clit pushes against a fold in the sheets, hitting me in just the right spot. The intensity of it flings me over the edge into the most violent orgasm I've ever had. I'm kicking and screaming and coming so hard everyone in the house must think he's murdering me.

Footsteps pound from somewhere down the hall. To my absolute horror, the door bursts open, and someone runs in. I try to get away, but Matrix has a death-grip on my hips.

"Get the fuck out. She's fine," he growls.

"I can see that." I recognize Fang's voice and

want to crawl under the bed. I'm so embarrassed that I make a silent vow never to leave the room again.

After the door shuts, Matrix laughs. He's still fucking me like a demon, stroking my cream again and again until I'm dripping wet. The tension in my body spirals tighter as I rush toward another peak. Ecstasy crashes over me, leaving me limp and breathless.

"I want to fuck you in the ass." He pulls me onto my knees and wraps an arm around my chest to hold me in place. His teeth capture my earlobe, and he bites until I'm a shivering mess.

"Yes," I whisper.

I'd agree to anything right now. Feral passion, unlike anything I've ever experienced, turns me into a beast. The second he releases my breasts, I fall forward. I grab the cheeks of my ass and spread them wide. No one's ever taken me there, but I trust him not to hurt me … too much. Since we began sleeping together, he has taught me an important lesson about sex. A little pain enhances my pleasure, and I'm starting to really love it.

"No yelling. Your pussy's so juicy, babe. I'm stealing some for lube." He pushes his fingers into me and waits until they're sopping wet before he pulls them out. Rubbing my tight little hole, he works his digits in me slowly.

"Oh, God!"

"You're shrieking again." There's playful

admonishment in his tone. "If you want this dick in your ass, you'd better keep quiet."

"I will," I gasp.

"Good."

He pushes the head of his cock against my puckered hole. The steady pressure makes me throb with twisted yearning. I don't know how much more I can take. It's so big. I'm so full. He's stuffing me with so much dick that I'm sure he's going to split me in two. What he's doing to me is so depraved, so obscene, and so erotic that I'm sure my heart's going to beat right out of my chest.

"Be a good girl and take it all. Yeah, just like that." His low, demanding voice makes me obey. I relax my muscles slightly, enough to give him access to all of me. He surges forward, impaling himself in my ass.

"Oh, Matrix," I whimper.

"What a good fucking girl you are." He sighs as he settles his hips against my butt.

"I don't know if I can—" He cuts me off with a wave of rhythmic thrusts. He owns me now. I'd do anything to make this ecstasy last forever. My mind's completely blank. I can't form a coherent thought. I don't have to do anything because he's doing everything.

"Let's make that pussy come again," he whispers.

His deft, evil little fingers stroke my clit without mercy. He's playing me better than any jazz musician ever could. Even if I could slow him down, I wouldn't. He's turning me into a wanton harlot, and I love every minute of this debauchery.

"Fuck, you're so tight." His smooth thrusts become erratic. I know he's close, so I give in to the storm breaking inside me.

I can't hold back my cries as I come so hard that I almost black out. He brutalizes my ass, slamming into me until he suddenly goes rigid. Grunting like a savage, he spills his seed into my quaking hole. Everything's trembling at once. My whole body is one shaky mess.

"Fuck, that was amazing," he whispers.

I whimper as he slowly pulls his cock free from my tender ass.

"Lay down, babe." He holds his arms open, and I shiver uncontrollably as I collapse into them. He pulls the sheets over us, but I can't stop quivering. Everything's still clenching and flexing. My pussy. My ass. Everything.

"Shh," he murmurs as he smooths his hand down my back. "Have you ever done that before?"

"No."

"I'm glad I was your first."

I try to respond, but the sound is unintelligible. I don't have the energy to be coherent, so I give up. My body's floating on a cloud of pure satisfaction. I never want to come down from it.

"Just relax. You'll be back soon."

I want to ask him what he means, but it seems irrelevant. I think I understand his obsession with cutting. He told me he goes to a floaty place. I'm positive that I'm in that place right now. It's so peaceful and disconnected from anything that matters. All my worries are gone. I don't care about anything. Not one damn thing.

Eventually, the sensation fades, and I'm solidly back in my body, but I'm so tired that I don't want to do anything but lay by his side. He hasn't stopped cuddling me since we finished together. We still haven't talked about what's happening between us, but I don't have the strength to deal with that right now. All I want to do is be with him.

"Tell me more about you." He pushes my hair behind my shoulders. "How did you get into computers?"

"When I was really little, I liked taking things apart. My dad had an old Compaq Presario desktop sitting in the garage. I got a hold of it when I was three. I hadn't quite figured out how to use a screwdriver, but I knew how to use a hammer."

"Oh, boy."

"Yep. Smashed it open so I could look inside. Dad was pissed until he asked me why I did it. I told him I was just trying to see in the box. After that, he encouraged me to learn a variety of electronics. He bought me a robotics kit when I was ten. By then, I could take apart and reassemble most of the items in the house."

"That's impressive."

"It was all I did. School was boring. It was too easy, especially math."

"I know what you mean. I see numbers and formulas in my head, but not how you're supposed to. Trying to show my work was impossible. My teachers hated me. I failed math even though I could get the right answers."

"The way they teach some kids is stupid. Not everyone has the same thought process."

"Some schools have great programs to help neurodiverse kids learn. If I ever had a kid who wasn't like the other children, I'd try to get them into one of those places."

"Do you want kids?" I ask.

"I don't know. For a long time, I didn't think I did. But recently …"

"What changed?"

"Seeing Scar and Nitro with their kids. We never thought we'd be good dads, but they're amazing fathers."

"Why did you think you'd be bad at it?" I turn so I can look at his face. It's dark and clouded over with pain. I wish he would share his secrets with me.

"If you didn't have the right role models, then it's harder to be an effective parent."

"I disagree. Terrible parents show you what *not* to do."

"Maybe."

"Tell me about your parents." I rest my cheek against his chest. It might be easier for him to talk about it if I'm not watching him.

"I don't remember them."

"Why not?"

"When I was a baby, they'd leave me in my crib for hours on end, starving and dirty. One of the neighbors heard me screaming and called the cops. I was removed from the house because I was suffering from extreme neglect."

"Oh, honey. I'm so sorry that happened to you."

"Thanks, babe. After child services took me away, I went through a series of foster homes, but none of them wanted me." The pain in his voice breaks my heart.

"There are many good foster families out there, but it sounds like you never found one."

"Nope. Never had friends either, not until I met Scar."

"Where did you two meet?"

"Hell."

"What do you mean by that?"

"It's a very long story. Someday, maybe I'll tell you everything."

"Why not now? I'm a good listener."

"You mentioned you have brothers, too, but you're not close to them. Why's that?"

"A lot of it's related to the work I do. I get busy, and I'm distracted a lot of the time. Also, I just haven't made the effort. Relationships die if you don't put some work into them. They don't seem to care, either. I've gotten a few calls since Angie went missing, but it feels like it's more out of obligation than actual interest."

"That sucks, but attachments aren't forever. I learned that when I was a kid."

"It's hard to form them when you're getting bounced around in the system."

"I learned how to be alone. I couldn't count on anyone, so I learned to rely on myself. In a weird way, I wouldn't be so capable if I hadn't gone through a rough upbringing. Growing up, if I wanted something, I had to figure out how to get it. I stole a lot. Food. Clothes."

"How old were you when you ran away from the last home?"

"You're assuming I decided to run. That's a big assumption."

"When a kid is forced to fend for himself, there's no point in staying with the family who isn't taking care of him. A lot of foster kids leave before they turn eighteen."

"I was ten."

"Oh, God."

"I wish I'd stayed. The family sucked, but if I'd known what was waiting for me, I would have happily eaten scraps. Starvation isn't the worst thing that can happen to you when you're a kid."

"Not by a mile. I've seen videos of what happens to runaways. The worst part of my desk job at the FBI involved sex crimes prosecutions.

I'd have to dig through the most disgusting videos to look for evidence. Crimes you wouldn't believe crossed my desk every week. It almost made me give up trying to make a difference because there were so many. So damn many."

"But you didn't quit. You kept at it."

"Yes. Not just because of my sister's kidnapping. That just added fuel to the fire. But before then, I'd already committed to the job. I knew I'd never be able to save every kid, but I could help stop as many perpetrators as possible."

"You love your job, don't you?"

"Yes."

"Then you shouldn't do anything to put it in jeopardy." He moves me out of his arms and rolls away.

I want to pull him back, but I hesitate because I finally realize what's happening between us. It hits me like a rock. I'm falling in love with him. And if he's warning me to be careful, then he must see it too. He understands something I don't want to admit. As long as I'm an FBI agent, we can't ever be together. To stay with him, I'd have to leave the agency and give up everything I've worked for. I don't know if I can do that. Love is a powerful feeling, but so is making a difference in the world. If I had to choose between him and my job, I don't know what I'd do. I hope I never have to make that decision.

CHAPTER 15: MATRIX

The fluorescent lighting in the gas station mini-mart feels wrong. It's too bright, yet it also flickers off, casting darkness over the aisles. My stomach rumbles, reminding me why I'm here. I only need a little food. Just enough to get me through another night.

As I walk down the row of snacks, I glance at the round mirror near the ceiling in the corner. The guy at the register hasn't stopped reading the magazine with the naked lady on the cover. He's not paying any attention to me, so I shouldn't have any trouble taking enough to last a few extra days. Stealing every night is risky. The less I have to do it, the better.

I stuff the biggest bag of potato chips I can find down my shirt. My stomach bulges out like a pregnant lady's. I consider putting it back, but the cash register guy hasn't looked up once. He'll never know. Also, he's not going to miss these candy bars. There are so many, and I only need a few. I grab a Snickers, a package of peanut butter cups, and a roll of six chocolate doughnuts.

By the time I've got it all stowed away, I'm slobbering. I want to rip into everything and stuff it in my face, but I'll have to wait until I get back to the park.

I walk past jugs of water but leave them alone. Water's not hard to get. There are drinking fountains in the park where I'm living. I wait until after dark to go out, so no one messes with me. I'd really like a soda to wash this all down. I haven't had one in days. Besides, one can won't change anything. I can swipe it from the refrigerated case. It'll be easy since no one's watching me.

Making my way toward the back of the store, a man who looks like a ghost steps into the aisle, blocking my path. I look up and up and up until I see his face. It's mean.

"Boy, are you going to pay for all that stuff?" His voice is angry and reminds me of my last foster dad. He was a bad man. This guy might be one too. He's got wild, black hair sticking up all over, just like that kid who stuck a knife into a light socket at my last house.

"Yeah." I back up a step.

"Where are your parents?" he demands.

"They're in here. Over there." I point, hoping he'll believe my lie and leave me alone.

"No one else is in the store. See that mirror? I can see everything. We're the only people shopping ... or stealing."

"I'm going to pay for it."

"Do you have money?"

"Yeah." I want to turn and run away. I'm tempted to drop the snacks so I can escape.

"I can buy those for you." The man's voice goes soft. He squats down so I can see his face better. It's puffy and very white.

"No, thanks," I mumble. I glance at the guy behind the counter. He's still not looking our way. So far, I'm still safe. I haven't really been caught.

"I can help you. I won't tell anyone you're stealing. You can come live with me. I have a whole room full of candy and soda. You can have as much as you want."

"Really?" I may only be ten years old, but I know grown-ups lie. "Why do you want to help me?"

"I have other kids your age who live with me."

"Are they yours?"

"They are now."

I don't understand what he means, but it doesn't matter. Maybe he's not like the other dads. If he has a lot of candy for kids, then he can't be a bad man. None of the other dads had sweets. I never got any until after I started stealing stuff.

"Where do you live?" I ask.

"On a big ranch in the mountains."

"What if I don't like it there?"

"Don't worry about that. It's your choice. Either you come with me, or I tell that man up there to call the police. Stealing is against the law. They put kids who steal in jail. You know what that is, right?"

"Uh huh." I nod while my eyes go wide. I've seen those cop shows on TV. Bad men go there. I can't go too.

"It's really a simple decision. Once you get to my house, you'll have so much candy your teeth will fall out."

"I don't know ..." My stomach hurts so much that I can't figure out what to do.

"Give me the stuff you hid in your clothes so I can pay for it." The man holds out his hands.

I check to make sure we're still alone before passing everything I stole over to him. If he's a bad man, I can always run away the way I did before ...

We're not in the store anymore. I don't know where I am. It's dark. Someone's crying in the corner. The floor's cold and damp.

Oh, no! Oh, no! It's the dungeon!

"Help!" I scream.

"Shh. They'll come down here if you don't shut up," one of the boys says in a hushed tone.

It all comes rushing back. The man. The way he tricked me into walking down the basement stairs. The sound of the lock clicking into place behind me, leaving me in the dark. I must get away. I have to run.

Someone shakes me, but I push them away. Then I'm on my feet, running down a long, dark tunnel that never seems to end. Finally, a light appears at the end. A wooden door creaks open. I can't go in. I can't. Because the man's in there, and he won't let me leave until he's done hurting me.

Screams fill the room.

They're mine.

I wake up disoriented and shaking.

"Matrix, it's me. It's Daisy. Honey, you had a nightmare."

"Fuck!" I drag my hand down my face. Sweat covers my palm. I wipe it away on the sheets.

"It's okay. I'll get you some water." She leaves the room, returning a few minutes later with a full glass. She hands it to me. "Drink that. You'll feel better."

"Thank you." I want to die of embarrassment. No one's ever caught me in the middle of a nightmare before. I can't believe Daisy heard me screaming. What else did I say? How much does she know? Did I yell out his name?

Slowly sipping the cool liquid, I avert my eyes so she can't read the turmoil in them.

"Do you have a lot of bad dreams?" she asks softly.

"Sometimes." I really don't want to get into this with her.

"I used to have them until I figured out what was causing them. If I got too warm, I'd have one, which would force me to wake up. My body was trying to protect me from becoming overheated."

"Sounds like it."

"It's not hot in here, so that couldn't have caused this."

"No." I set the empty glass on the nightstand. Sitting on the edge of the bed, I rest my elbows on my knees and rub my forehead with my fingers. Tension headaches tend to sneak up on me. I have to calm down before I end up with another one.

Daisy gets on her knees behind me and starts rubbing my shoulders. Her hands are so warm and soothing. "Do you want to tell me about it? Sometimes that helps."

"It won't."

"Matrix, I know something terrible happened to you a long time ago. I want to get to know you better, but I can't do that if you keep shutting me out."

"Daisy, you have no fucking idea what you're asking me to do." The muscles in my jaw twitch. I'm tempted to push her hands away, but they're working magic on my knotted shoulders. I can't bring myself to make her stop.

"You're right. I don't know anything because you won't talk to me. If you're afraid I'll judge you, don't worry about it. I've seen the worst of humanity. Anything you tell me won't be shocking. I've witnessed horror beyond your wildest nightmares."

"No dream could ever compare to the truth," I say bitterly.

"Is it really that bad?"

"Yes."

She sighs and pulls me back against her and

into a warm embrace. I place my hands over hers and hold her too. She's the balm I need right now. If she wants to offer comfort, then I'm going to take it. The alternative isn't good. I've woken up from nightmares before and ended up in a dissociative state for days. This time, I didn't, and I think it's because of her.

"If you're embarrassed or ashamed, don't be. Whatever happened to you wasn't your fault. I care about you a lot. Maybe too much." She releases me and then slides over to sit beside me. When she slips her hand into mine, I instinctively squeeze hers. "I don't know what *we* are, but I'm sure we're at least friends."

"Do you sleep with all your pals?" I ask in a gruff tone.

"No. Don't be a dick to me to cover up your pain. I won't put up with it."

"Sorry." I hang my head.

"I know it's not easy to talk about these things. I've seen plenty of kids take the stand to help put their abusers in jail. I know it's rough. If you really don't want to tell me, then I'll respect your wishes."

"Daisy, it's so fucked up."

"Did it happen after you left your last foster home? Or was the incident the reason you ran away?"

"After."

"Someone else hurt you. A man?"

"Isn't it always?"

"No. Some women are a thousand times more vicious than men. Those were the worst cases, mothers who tortured their children for their own perverse pleasure. I get sick just thinking about it." She rubs her stomach.

"This will make you want to vomit."

"I can take it, honey. I promise."

"The last family I lived with treated me like a dog. They even made me eat on my hands and knees like a mutt."

She shakes her head but doesn't interrupt.

"Their house was close to a big park. Homeless people lived in it, so I figured I could stay there too. I found a bunch of trees all smashed together. They formed a canopy overhead, and a few bushes covered a little den in the ground. At first, I thought another animal lived in the hole, but it was empty. So, I decided to move into it."

"Was this in Montana?"

"Yeah."

"I'm assuming you left during the summer?"

"Yes. It was right after the last snow in June."

"It still gets close to freezing at night, even during the hottest months."

"Yeah, but I learned how to stay warm from the homeless guys. They all slept on newspaper, so I did too. It insulates you from the ground, so you won't be cold."

"I've heard that before."

"It's true. During the day, I'd stay in the den unless I needed clothes. I hated stealing, but I didn't have money. A lot of the guys in the park panhandled, but they were much older. I couldn't do it without drawing too much attention. Cops patrolled the park sometimes, so I had to stay hidden when they were around."

"How long did you live like that?"

"Five months."

"You were ten years old, right?"

"Yeah."

"That's a lot to deal with as a kid."

"I spent my whole life hungry and fighting over scraps. This wasn't much different. At the very least, I wouldn't have to avoid the older foster kids who liked to beat me up. I didn't have a ridiculously huge list of chores to do. Honestly, it was heaven while it lasted."

"How did it end?" She snuggles closer before laying me down beside her.

Staring at the ceiling, I fight the urge to stop talking. She can take it. I know she can. But telling her the awful truth will change things between us. How could it not?

"That's what the nightmare was about," I finally say.

"Okay."

"I was in a convenience store one night, trying to steal dinner, when a man stopped me. He told me that if I didn't go with him, I'd go to jail because he knew I had a bunch of candy hidden in my clothes."

"Oh, God." She shakes her head. "He gave you an impossible choice."

"I wish I'd gone to jail instead. It wouldn't have been the end of the world. I would have been sent to a youth detention center. I know that now, but back then, I didn't have a clue about how the justice system worked."

"So, you went with him."

"Yeah. That was the biggest mistake of my life. You don't know how many times I've wished I could go back. I would have told myself to run away as fast and as far as possible."

"If only we could change the past."

"Yeah, but we can't. So here we are."

"What happened after he took you from the store?"

"He drove me to his ranch. As soon as we arrived, he tricked me into entering the basement. He said all the candy was down there."

"But it wasn't."

"No. Not even close."

"What was in the basement?"

"A dungeon."

"Holy shit."

"And other kids. A lot of other kids."

"Ones he kidnapped?"

"Some, yes. But others were literally handed to him by the system. He was a foster parent too."

"Was he married?"

"No."

"That's unusual. Usually, they try to place kids with married couples."

"If you have enough money, they don't give a fuck."

"He was rich?"

"Filthy rich. He has more money than God."

"He's still alive?"

I nod because I can't bring myself to say his name.

"Who is it? If you tell me, I can check the statute of limitations. We can prosecute him."

"It's probably too late. And even if you could, you wouldn't."

"Why the hell not?" Her eyebrows draw together.

"He's untouchable."

"No one can escape justice. I mean, people try, and some get away with it for a while, but eventually—"

"Justice doesn't always prevail, so don't bother trying to convince me that it does."

"You're right. I'm sorry. I've had cases where we had video evidence of the crime, and yet the perpetrator was found not guilty, or their case was thrown out."

"Exactly."

"But maybe that won't happen in this case. Have you checked to see what he's up to now? Does he still have kids at his house? If he does, we have an obligation to do something to stop him."

"He doesn't have them anymore. We checked."

"Are you sure?"

"Positive. We keep a close eye on his place."

"But ... as far as I know, there's only one person you watch. If you had other cameras set up, I would have found their feeds in your system."

"There aren't any other cameras," I say slowly, watching as realization marches across her face. "The man who hurt me, who hurt us. Me, Scar, Nitro, Talon, and Reaper—"

"Jonathan Blackstone," she whispers.

"Yes. Now do you see why he's untouchable? We've tried and failed more times than I can count. Even that video last year wasn't enough to bring him down. We wanted to kill him, but we've never been able to get close enough."

"Matrix, this is really bad."

"No shit. Sorry." I run my hand through my hair. "Sometimes, I wondered why we even tried to stop him. We made sure he didn't have any more kids, but I knew. In our souls, every one of us knew that a man like Blackstone would never stop. His perversions aren't the kind that just fizzle out with age. If anything, it gets worse."

"And now he's into human trafficking."

"Exactly. We had no idea that was going on until the night I followed you to the campground."

"That feels like a hundred years ago, but it's

been less than a week."

"As far as we're concerned, what he's doing now is far worse than what he did to us in the basement. It was horrific, but he didn't have more than twenty kids at a time."

"That many?" Tears fill her eyes, but she doesn't shed them.

"It's a lot, but it's nothing compared to his current operation. If Lulu's had forty girls during its heyday, how many do you think they're running now? I'm sure it's at least that many, and that's just one location. We don't know how many other houses are operating around the country. Hell, he could have places like that all over the world."

"We've got to stop him." She's on her feet, pacing back and forth in front of the door to the balcony.

"That's why we're here. If we can find your sister and get her to testify against him, then we finally have a real shot at stopping him."

"She might not be here anymore. What if she isn't? Then what?" She stops and looks at me.

"Then we keep searching until we find her. Earlier, you asked me what *we* were." I slide off the bed and cross the room to join her.

"You don't have to answer that. It's okay."

"Honestly, I don't know what to call this. But I do know one thing."

"What's that?" she asks as I take her hands in mine.

"I care about you a lot. You're strong and beautiful, and smart. You hacked my system, which basically makes you old lady material." I manage a quick grin.

"I feel the same way about you."

"Then let's do this together. After we find your sister, we can figure out what we want to be to each other. But I don't want you to think it's going to be easy. We need to consider certain things if we want to stay together."

"Things like my job?"

"That's the big one."

"I've thought about what my life would be like without it."

"And?"

"I'm not sure. I go back and forth. Although I love my work, sometimes I wonder how much of a difference I'm really making."

"You don't have to decide anything tonight. Let's take it one step at a time. For now, let's just enjoy what we have. We can worry about the future later."

"I can do that."

A knock sounds on the door.

Vapor hollers through it. "Talon's back. Church in five."

Daisy runs across the room and pulls open the door. "Please, just tell me, is my sister at Lulu's?"

"Yes."

I grab Daisy as she collapses against the

wall. After pulling her back into our room, I get her situated on the bed. "Babe, lay here while I go to Church. When I get back, I'll tell you everything. I promise. Trust me."

"I do."

Those words warm my heart. Her confidence in me is a balm for my soul. For the longest time, I never thought I'd heal from the pain Blackstone caused. Now I'm starting to wonder if maybe Daisy's the cheat code I've been waiting for my whole life. I don't know how we'll be able to make it work between us, but I'm going to figure it out. Now that I've found her, I'm never letting her go.

CHAPTER 16: MATRIX

I hate leaving Daisy behind after the conversation we just had. Something amazing is happening between us. We're starting to figure out what it is, but we're not there yet. I hope that over time we'll figure out whether we belong together. I think we do, but as I told her, she'll have to reconsider her job. A federal agent and a MC member won't work in the long run. We're not on the same side. Until we can work that out, we won't have a future together.

After I take my seat in the library, I wait for the others to arrive. With all the voodoo stuff in the room, I can't help but wonder if anyone in the club practices Santería. I'd love to make a Blackstone poppet and stab its beady black eyes with a million pins.

"What the hell was up with all the yelling coming from your room?" Scar slides into the chair beside me. Since no one else has arrived, we're alone in the room.

"There was a lot going on. Let's just leave it

at that." I smirk.

"Remember, we're guests here. If you two don't keep it down, they're liable to throw us out. And I wouldn't blame them one bit."

"Sorry, pres. My girl's a screamer."

"She's yours now? You claiming her, Matrix?"

"Who?" Reaper walks in and sits across from us.

"Daisy," Scar says.

"Seriously? The Fed?" Reaper looks at me like I've lost my damn mind, and maybe I have. If someone had told me a few weeks ago that Daisy was an FBI agent and we'd end up together in New Orleans trying to find her trafficked sister, I would have laughed my ass off. A lot has gone down recently. Everything changed.

"You didn't answer my question," Scar says.

"Uh ..."

Claiming a woman is a big deal in a motorcycle club. It makes her off-limits to everyone else, which works for me. But it also makes me even more responsible for her than I already am. If she does anything to fuck over the club, then it's on me. I want to trust her not to screw us, but as long as she's still employed by the US government, is it really worth the risk? Fortunately, members from the NOLA chapter start filing into the room, so I don't have to answer Scar's question.

"Church is in session." Vapor slams the

gavel. "Talon will be here in a second. He said he needed a minute to wash the stink off him."

"Since when is he obsessed with being clean?" Reaper asks.

"No idea," I mutter.

Talon joins us a few seconds later. "Sorry I'm late."

"Tell us what went down," Vapor says.

"Lulu's is fucking crazy. There are girls everywhere."

"How many?"

"I counted forty-five, but I can't be one hundred percent sure I got them all. They kept coming in and out of rooms with customers. It was hard to keep track."

"That sounds about right," Vapor says.

"The last prospect we sent in also said there are at least forty girls. It checks out," Fender adds.

"What about Daisy's sister, Angela?" I ask.

"Found her upstairs in one of the rooms. She was …" Talon's gaze slides to me before it drops to the table. He studies the table's woodgrain as if it's the most fascinating thing in the world.

"Drugged up and beat up, I'd imagine," Bones says.

"She's in bad shape. I didn't get a close look, but I'm pretty sure I saw track marks on her arms. Her eyes were glassy like she's on something."

"They keep most of the girls hooked on heroin to keep them compliant. Even if they could escape, they wouldn't. They're too addicted to getting their next fix. It becomes an obsession," Fang says.

"If we manage to get her out, she's going to need medical treatment. Not just for the drugs, but for everything else." Vapor doesn't have to elaborate. I already know what other issues she might have because she was trafficked.

"We're getting her out." My tone leaves no room for argument.

"Agreed. We just have to figure out how," Scar says.

"They have the whole place locked down," Talon says.

"Digital security?" I ask.

"Surprisingly, no. I looked all over, along doors and windows. Nothing. I was as surprised as you. But that doesn't mean it'll be easy. Armed guards patrol both inside the house as well as around the grounds. I don't know how we're going to sneak her out. And what about the others? We can't just leave them behind." Talon frowns.

"Are you sure the woman you saw was Angela?" I ask.

"The girl was a lot thinner, very pale, and she looked like shit, but it was her. The eyes matched the photo Daisy gave us."

"Okay. Local cops have no interest in busting the place, right?" I ask Vapor.

"They won't lift a finger to help."

"We can't go in guns blazing either. There are a lot of other girls inside," Talon says.

"Trying to rescue them all won't work," Scar says. "We have to focus on Angela for now. Once we get her out, Daisy can alert the Feds. I don't trust them not to fuck it up, but at least this will put the house at the top of their priority list."

"Okay, so if we're only interested in Angela, how are we getting her out?" I ask.

"That's a damn good question," Talon says.

"You were inside. Any ideas?"

"Do they ever take the girls out to entertain men away from Lulu's?" Talon asks.

"It's happened once or twice that we know of," Fang says.

"What were the details?"

"A couple of months back, there was a big crypto convention in town. Crypto billionaires flew in on private jets. They stayed in the penthouse suite at The Canal. It's a very exclusive boutique hotel. You can't book it online. Fortunately, I have access to their registration system." Fang grins.

"Are there any big conventions happening right now?"

"There's a huge medical convention. What are you thinking?" Fang asks.

"What if we pose as high-end buyers looking for girls to entertain us for the weekend?"

"How could we be sure they'd send Angela?"

I ask.

"Give a detailed description of the type of girls you want. Make sure it matches her exactly. There's a chance it won't work, but it should." Fang opens his laptop and starts typing. The hotel's reservation system pops up. "I just need fake names, and we're good to go."

"I don't know anything about medical stuff. None of us look like doctors."

"Those aren't the guys who make the most money in medicine. Pharmaceutical reps bring in the big bucks. Also, it could be an extra lure because they have access to prescription opiates. Cartels will pay good money for that high-quality stuff."

"I like where you're headed with this," Scar says.

"I've been thinking about this all night. I knew we wouldn't be able to just walk in there and get her. We need her to come to us," Talon says.

"Who wants to play the pharma reps?" Fang asks.

"Me." I raise my hand.

"Will you be able to stay objective if shit goes tits up and we can't pull her out?" Scar asks.

"Yes," I say confidently. When it comes down to stuff like this, I can focus.

"Fang looks like a science nerd. Bring him with you," Talon says. "I can't go because they'd recognize me from Lulu's."

"Thanks?" Fang cocks his head. Apparently, he doesn't like being called a nerd, even though that's exactly what he is. I know because I'm one too. Unlike him, I'm proud of it.

"What about Daisy? Can we bring her with us?" I ask.

"It might make them suspicious," Scar says.

"She managed to fly under our radar without raising any red flags."

"Don't remind me."

"I know her. She won't want to sit tight and wait."

"Bringing her along is a good idea. She can identify her sister," Reaper says.

I'm shocked he's on Daisy's side for once. I was starting to think he hated her, not just because she's a Fed, but for some other reason that I couldn't fathom.

"How soon can we set this up?" Scar asks.

"I'll get you, me, and Daisy booked into the hotel." Fang starts clicking away on his keyboard to make it happen.

"They gave me a business card to call whenever I want to go to Lulu's," Talon says.

"We'd essentially be cold calling," I point out.

"No. We'll tell them one of their frequent customers referred you. I've got a list of names we can use, people we've seen coming and going from the house multiple times. You can pick someone from the list. I just sent it to your phone," Fang says.

My phone pings.

"I'm not even going to ask how you got my completely unlisted, unregistered number," I growl.

"Child's play." Fang smirks.

"If you found mine so easily, then why did we have to go to the strip club to get Lulu's?"

"They change it too much. It was the only way we could be sure it was current."

"If you say so." I pull up the list and whistle. "Seriously? All of these people have been to Lulu's? There are politicians, sports stars, actors. Shit, didn't she win some big award last year?"

"Yep. She's a grade-A pervert."

"No shit."

"As they say, the list is long but distinguished."

"More like disgusting," Reaper says.

"Agreed." I stand and walk toward one of the windows. "I'll make the call now and see if we can get the cartel to bring Angela to us."

"Go ahead," Vapor says.

After Talon passes me the card, they sit silently while I call Lulu's. After a lot of explaining and schmoozing, I finally get around to telling them exactly what I want. I describe Angela to the tee. "The girl should be about thirteen. Too much younger, and they cry all the time."

"Go on." The oily voice on the other end of

the line comes through clearly.

"Brown hair. Short. Chin length if you've got it. Petite."

"Eyes?"

"Blue. They always look extra innocent when they're that color." I want to throw up, but I have to be a revolting pig to play the part.

"I think I know just the girl," the man says.

"We're rather picky. The three of us like to share our girls. We have the same tastes, but sometimes we can't agree on just one."

"It becomes considerably more expensive if I have to send extra, especially if they're not chosen."

"You take corporate credit cards, don't you?" I ask, using the magic words that have opened many doors in the past.

"Of course, sir."

"Good. Then charge the company for five. Whatever we don't want, we'll keep regardless. We can make them watch."

"We'll be sending them with security. For their protection, of course."

Yeah, right. They have armed guards to make sure their captives don't try to escape.

"You'll be discrete?" I ask in a perturbed tone. "The hotel assured me we could use service elevators to bring our guests up. Are you familiar with The Canal? The friend who recommended you has stayed there before."

"We're very well acquainted with that

property. We just need your room number."

"The penthouse," I say in a snotty tone as if it should have been obvious.

"Excellent. We'll put a temporary hold on the card today. The girls will be delivered tomorrow night by eight p.m. They will be leaving promptly at sunrise the following morning. You can mark them any way you like; however, if you hurt them in any permanent way, we'll have to charge you the lifetime purchase price."

"How much is that?" I ask.

"One million dollars."

"So, if I wanted to keep my favorite, it would only cost me a million?"

"Yes."

"That's something to consider." I turn around to face the guys at the conference table. They're all looking at each other. I don't know if any of them has that much lying around, but it would be helpful.

"Until tomorrow." The man ends the call.

I check to be sure it's disconnected before I shove it in my cut. "We have just under twenty-four hours. If we do this right, we can rescue all five girls. He did mention a million-dollar buy-out option. None of you happen to have that much extra pocket change lying around, right?"

Everyone shakes their head.

"We'd love it if it were that easy, but it's not. Since you're taking Angela back to Montana, that leaves four more girls if we rescue all of them. We can handle that easily," Vapor says.

"You'll find homes for them?" I ask.

"Another chapter contacted us last week looking for placement for several kids. We wanted to make a swap but didn't have anyone in mind. These girls will be perfect. The farther away we can get them from their abusers, the better. Montana would be ideal, but I don't want there to be any connection between Lulu's and your club. Blackstone can't catch even a whiff of your involvement in this."

"You know our doors are always open if you need a place to hide victims," Scar says.

"Same goes for us," Vapor says. "Now, let's get into how we want this to play out."

"Here's what I'm thinking ..." As I run through several options for rescuing the girls, I keep thinking about Daisy. She's going to be so excited when she finds out what's happening. However, I have to make sure she's not too anxious. This cartel is smart. They were strong enough to get rid of the cartel that owned New Orleans before them. They won't be easy foes.

After discussing the plan and all possible contingencies, Vapor adjourns Church. He and his crew plan to be our eyes and ears outside the hotel. The UV Montana crew will be inside, either hiding in the penthouse or hanging out in the emergency exit stairwell. As long as the cartel doesn't send more than a few guys to protect the girls, we should be able to pull this off without a hitch. It almost seems too easy, which makes me nervous.

I head upstairs to where Daisy is waiting for me. As soon as I open the door, she pounces. "Well?"

"Your sister's at Lulu's. At least, we're pretty sure it's her. Sit down." I guide her to the bed, where she perches on the edge.

"What? Why do you look so worried? What's wrong with her?"

"She's probably addicted to heroin."

"No." She covers her mouth with her hand.

"And she's in bad shape overall. I suspected this could be the case, but I just want to prepare you for what you'll see tomorrow night. You can't lose your shit."

"Tomorrow? I'm going to see her that soon?"

"Yes. Hopefully." I fill her in on the rescue plan. "It should work, but we're dealing with a domestic, and possibly international, trafficking ring. They're not stupid."

"I could call my SAC and get backup."

"No fucking way. Seriously?" I frown.

"You're right. I'm not thinking straight. I just figured we could use the help."

"Not from the fucking Feds. UV NOLA has our backs. Always. I trust these men with our lives. We all swore the same creed—to protect the innocent while taking down the guilty by whatever means necessary."

"That's slightly different from the one I had to swear to," she says wryly.

"Same idea. Different methods."

"Don't remind me." She looks away.

"One of these days, you'll have to pick a side. But not today. We're checking into the hotel at four in the afternoon. That gives us about twelve hours, and I plan on sleeping through most of them. I want to be fully alert and ready for this."

"Me too."

"Then come to bed with me." I slowly strip her down, leaving her panties on so she knows I'm not after more sex. We really do need to rest.

After we settle into bed together, we cuddle. I love the feeling of her in my arms. A man could get used to this. That's the last thought I have before we doze off.

When Scar wakes us in the early afternoon, I'm well rested, and so is Daisy.

"Ready, babe?"

"Let's get my sister."

She laces her fingers through mine, and we walk out the door. Whether she realizes yet or not, we're a team. When we decide we're going to do something, we're unstoppable. Eventually, she'll see it. It's only a matter of time before she recognizes it too. We belong together.

CHAPTER 17: MATRIX

I've never been inside a hotel room like this before. It's ridiculously over the top. In addition to the plush sofas, designer rugs, and fine art in the living room, there's a bedroom almost as big as the entire NOLA clubhouse. A massive bed sits in the center of the room, but that's not the best feature. There's a huge bathtub big enough for four people beside two huge sliding doors leading to a patio. I could have one hell of a party with Daisy in that tub.

I wish we were here for fun, but we're not. Angela and the other four girls we ordered are supposed to arrive in five minutes. According to Fang, they're never late. The one thing this cartel has going for them is punctuality. I can't help but laugh.

"What's so funny?" Daisy gets up from one of the sofas in the living room and walks toward the small kitchen where I'm standing.

"Nothing. I was just thinking about how the lives of rich people are so different from ours. Also, that bathtub in the main bedroom is unbelievable. If we were here for something other than rescuing your sister, I'd make sure we put it to use." I waggle my eyebrows.

"I don't know how you can joke at a time like this. I'm so nervous I feel like I'm going to throw up."

"Don't do that." Fang turns away from the window. He's been watching the street below for any sign of the cartel. So far, he hasn't spotted anyone.

"Of course, I won't. But don't expect me to join you guys for dinner after this is done."

"Babe …" I cross the room and gently grasp her shoulders. "Everything will go according to plan. Vapor has his guys positioned outside the hotel. Scar has ours hidden in various places throughout this place. Nothing bad will happen."

"We have to incapacitate the men who come with the girls before they can radio in or text their men for backup." She steps out of my hold and crosses her arms over her chest.

"They should only have two guards. Fang and I will handle them while you keep the girls calm. We can't afford any distractions. Remember the plan. As soon as we attack, take the girls out of the room and down the emergency stairs. Don't look back for anything, even if you hear gunshots. We're not going to fire our weapons unless absolutely necessary. We have other ways of taking these guys down."

"I've got some martial arts training. They won't know what hit them." Despite looking like a tech nerd, Fang's all business. I respect a man who can code but who can also kick ass. He's just like me. We haven't had many interactions in the past, but he's someone I'd like to get to know better. All the tech guys in UV should meet at some point. It would be useful to cross-train on any skills we have that the others don't possess yet.

"Please be careful." Daisy wraps her arms around my waist. "I don't want anything to happen to you or Angela. You too, Fang."

"I was starting to feel left out," he jokes.

"Never, brother." I release Daisy while nodding at him.

A knock sounds on the door.

"Get into position. Remember, if things go tits up, the girls are our main priority." I slip my hand into my suit pocket. I'm holding a wicked switchblade courtesy of Bones. The man knows his knives. Back in my cutting days, I would have tried it out already. But I'm past that. Too many people are counting on me, and I can't let them down.

Daisy heads to the door and opens it. "You're right on time."

Two huge men wearing matching black, well-fitting suits walk into the room. Five girls, all with their heads down, parade in behind them.

"Gus Cartier." I hold out my hand. "We spoke on the phone."

"You talked to the boss. I'm Horatio, and this is Enrique." He gestures toward his counterpart. "We'll be outside, waiting. We expect the girls to be returned by morning. Earlier is fine. Just call when you're done with them."

As he's talking, Fang slowly circles behind Enrique. That means Horatio's mine. When Fang darts his hand into his pocket, it's on. I whip my knife out and attack. The men react faster than expected, jumping to the side, and avoiding the first slashes of our blades.

"Girls! Come with me!" Daisy opens her arms and uses them to corral the girls into the hall.

I kick Horatio in the stomach, sending him flying into the wall. Gripping the knife, I stalk forward. He pulls a gun out of his waistband. Before he can fire a shot, I shove his arm up with my free hand. The gun fires. A bullet lodges in the ceiling. So much for making this a quiet operation.

Horatio slams his head into mine. Stunned, I stumble back, falling over an end table. It goes crashing to the floor, but I manage to roll to my feet. He leaps over the sofa and lands in front of me. I swing my elbow up, smashing it into his face. His nose cracks, and blood spurts all over the oriental rug. That's going to cost the hotel a pretty penny. Good thing we're registered under false names.

As my opponent grabs at his broken nose, I swoop in to end it. Using a roundhouse kick, I slam my boot into the side of his head. His head snaps back before he drops to the ground. He's out but not dead. I could walk away, but flashes of what happened in Blackstone's dungeon hit me so hard I can't stop my next impulse. His face becomes Blackstone's. I clutch my knife in the center of my fist before driving it through his carotid artery, ending his pathetic, disgusting existence.

"A little help over here!"

I spin to find Fang pinned down, getting the shit kicked out of him. Launching my knife across the room, it sails for a second before piercing Enrique's thigh. He howls in pain as he pulls it out. His fixation on the knife gives Fang a few seconds to crawl out of Enrique's striking range.

Since one shot was already fired, there's no point in prolonging this thing. I whip my gun out of my waistband and shoot him through his forehead. He falls back. I watch him carefully as I advance. When I'm close enough, I fire two more shots into his chest. He's done.

"Let's get the fuck out of here." I whip my gaze to where Fang's struggling to his feet. "You good?"

"Better ... than a ... Swedish massage,"

he gasps, holding his ribs. "Cops coming. Fire escape."

The sound of sirens fills the air.

"Shit. We can't go that way. We'll have to take the stairs. It's the same way Daisy went."

"Go." He grabs his gun from a shoulder holster and heads toward the door. I beat him to it.

Glancing into the hall, I check to make sure it's empty, then jog past the elevators toward the stairwell. As soon as I push open the door, female screams echo up from below.

"Fuck!" I take the stairs so fast I'm half running, half sliding down them. Fang, despite probably having broken ribs, is right on my ass.

I lean over the metal railing and spot Daisy and the girls three floors down. She's standing with her legs spread and her gun drawn. I can't see who she's pointing it at, but it doesn't matter. I've got to get there before the other person shoots her.

As I jump onto that landing, Daisy screams, "Get down."

The girls drop to the floor along with her. I fire at the man standing in the doorway holding a gun on them. I don't know why the hell he hesitated to shoot Daisy. I'm guessing he didn't want to risk killing one of the girls. That probably saved her life.

"Go! Run!" I shout as I help the girls to their feet. They're slow as shit, probably because they're drugged out of their minds. But screaming seems to get through to them because they pick up the pace. We're about to hit the exit door when it bangs open.

I jerk my gun toward the opening. It's Scar.

"We've got about two seconds before the cops circle back and find us," he says.

"Throw the girls in the van," Vapor yells from the driver's seat. He's parked right outside the door in the service alley.

"You're safe. Come with me." Daisy helps lift them into the vehicle before turning to me. "Are you coming with us?"

"No. Scar and I will lure the cops away."

"Be careful!"

"I will." I slam the door and pound my fist on it, letting Vapor know it's time to roll.

Scar and I run to the far end of the alley where our bikes are waiting. There's no time to fuck around with helmets. We hop on our bikes and burn rubber as we burst out of the alley onto the main road.

Out of the corner of my eye, I spot a cop on foot. He starts yelling. He grabs the radio on his shoulder and screams into it. That's going to bring a whole lot of heat. We have to get the fuck out of here.

We mapped out the escape route and ran through various scenarios. The plan included every contingency we could think up. I don't even have to signal to Scar to let him know we're going to plan B. He knows exactly when to turn.

As we screech around the corner, I glance back. Two motorcycle cops and two patrol cars —lights blazing—race to catch up. They know these streets better than we do, but we've got a strategy for that too. We split up exactly as planned. I take north while Scar skids into a sharp turn to the west. We'll meet back up at the clubhouse later.

Driving like the Devil himself is behind me, I use every riding technique I know to gain an edge. My Harley-Davidson CVO Street Glide is black with green flames; not the most discrete bike out there, but I love my baby. I'll be able to lose them as long as I don't lay it down in a turn.

The second I hit the highway, I push the throttle until I'm flying at over 100 MPH. The cops could still catch me, but it's unlikely because I'm about to lose them at the next offramp. I tear down it. When I get to the next road, I hit the brakes. After fishtailing through the turn, I pull into an alleyway behind a body shop owned by the NOLA club. One of their prospects is waiting next to an open bay door. He pulls it shut behind me. Seconds later, sirens fly past the shop.

The prospect is built like a linebacker, all muscle. His grease-stained tank top is stretched to the limit across his massive chest. His long hair gives him that trashy rock star look a lot of twenty-somethings adopt. He's about that age, so it works for him. Anyone older would look like an idiot.

He circles my bike, inspecting it. "Nice fuckin' ride."

"It gets me where I need to go." I smirk and get off the bike. "I'm Matrix."

"Tank." His grip is firm. After all the chaos of the last thirty minutes, I appreciate how it grounds me. "Want a beer while you wait?"

"Sure."

He walks to the other side of the garage and grabs two bottles of Abita from a fridge. When he comes back, he points toward a couple of well-worn stools. After we sit, he hands me one of the drinks.

"Have you heard from Vapor?" I ask before taking a long pull out of the bottle.

"Scar, Daisy, and the girls made it back to the clubhouse."

"How're they doing?"

"Vapor said they're okay, all things considered. Fuck the cartel, and fuck Lulu's. I wish we could shut them down for good."

"Me, too." I clink my bottle against his. "One of these days, you will. Vapor's a smart guy. He'll figure out a way to destroy the cartel."

"God willing." Tank finishes his beer, then tosses the bottle into a huge metal trash can. The resounding racket grates on my nerves. "Another?"

"Sure. I'm going to be here for at least a

couple of hours."

"That's tough. If I were waiting to get back to my woman, I'd be losing my shit."

"She's not my woman."

"Really? I heard you two almost broke the damn bed last night." He hands me an icy bottle while grinning like a fool. *Kids.*

"Yeah, well …" I smirk.

"And she's a Fed?"

"For a prospect, you sure know a lot of shit you shouldn't."

"I'm almost patched in. Vapor says a vote's coming up in a few weeks. If I don't fuck up between now and then, I'm in."

"Congratulations, man."

"Thanks, but I don't want to get ahead of myself. I've been waiting to join the club for years. They kept saying I was too young and wet behind the ears." He shakes his head.

"How old are you anyway?"

"Twenty-two."

"A kid."

"Yeah, but I've seen some shit." His face darkens. I get a glimpse of his demons and can't help but wonder if we're more alike than I'd expect.

"Bad shit makes you stronger."

"That's what Vapor always says."

"Then he knows what he's talking about." I wave my half-empty bottle around the garage. "Is this your place?"

"Nah. The club just lets me work here. They own it now. I was already here before they took over. They liked me, so they kept me on. Then they let me become a prospect."

"Are you a mechanic?"

"Yeah."

"My bike's been rattling a bit. Could you check it out while we're sitting around with our thumbs up our asses?"

"Sure! I'd love to work on your shit for free." His sarcasm isn't lost on me.

"All right, shithead. I'll pay you. *If* you can fix it."

"Just fuckin' with you. If I charged your ass, Vapor would have mine."

I laugh before tossing my empty bottle into the trash. We spend the next hour hunched over my bike. The kid's a fucking genius. He finds the problem and fixes it with time to spare. He may be young, but he's clearly got a head for bikes. I can see why Vapor wanted to bring him on. The kid's gifted at fixing shit.

The old rotary phone on the wall rings.

"I thought that was a decoration," I joke.

"Still works. The old man who owned it before us didn't trust technology. We kept it because, well, why the fuck not? It's kinda cool." He grabs the receiver and lifts it to his ear. "Tank … Yeah … He's still here … Okay … Me too? Fuck yeah!" He hangs up. "We're going to the clubhouse!"

"Why's that so exciting?" I ask.

"Well …" He rubs the back of his meaty neck. "Did you meet Vicki the Hickey yet?"

"Please tell me you don't call her that to her face."

"Fuck no. It wasn't even my idea. But check this out." He sweeps his hair off his neck to reveal a huge red bruise. "Lives up to her name, am I right?" He grins.

"I didn't need to see that shit," I grumble, but mostly because I'm jealous. I want Daisy to give me one of those. I can't wait to have her sexy hands and devilish lips all over my naked body.

"Sorry, man." Tank's neck flushes so red that his hickey blends into it.

"Let's ride."

I grab my helmet off the back of my bike and put it on. The miles between the garage and the NOLA clubhouse are a blur. All I can think about is Daisy. I didn't get a good look at her during the chaos, but she seemed like she hadn't been injured. I'm grateful for that. I'd be a fucking mess if anything happened to her.

When we get to the clubhouse, one of the young, hot blonde girls literally hurls herself off the front steps into Tank's arms. I'm guessing it's Vicki because she's already gnawing on his neck like a rat on cheese. I shake my head as I walk past them.

Taking the steps two at a time, I hurry into the house.

"Daisy's upstairs with her sister and Doc," Vapor says as I walk past him.

"Thanks." I give him a nod.

Daisy's soft voice leads me to one of the bedrooms where Angela is lying in bed. An older woman is sitting by her side. She's probably in her mid-fifties, and she reminds me of Nina. Her spiky, snow-white hair stands out in stark contrast with her vibrantly colored muumuu dress. I haven't met her before. I have no idea who she is, but with the way she's frowning, she's obviously concerned about Angela.

Daisy steps over to where I'm standing. "Hey, babe."

I pull her into a hug before spreading hot kisses all over her face and mouth. By the time I'm done kissing her, I'm ready to drag her down the hall so we can finish breaking the bed. She's not having any of it and pulls away.

"This is Doc Lavine." She gestures toward an older Creole man, probably in his sixties, with toffee-colored skin and short gray hair.

"*Bonjou.*"

"Hello. It's nice to meet you. How's she doing?" I ask.

"Ah, she very bad. But we work with this." Doc Lavine pulls a vial out of his bag. He shakes it, mixing the clear and brown fluids. He opens it, releasing a spicy scent reminiscent of cinnamon, but it's not quite the same.

"What's that?" Daisy asks.

"Petit potion. Fix soul." He dabs the liquid on Angela's forehead before muttering a barely audible chant. "She'll live. But her heart be troubled."

Before I can ask him for details, he leaves the room.

"He'll be back tomorrow." The older woman adjusts her muumuu while eyeing me. "I'm Babet. You must be Matrix. Daisy has told me a lot about you."

"She has?"

"I have?" Daisy glances at Babet before turning to give me a shrug.

"You don't have to say much to reveal everything." Babet smiles. "I'll stay with Angela while you two catch up."

"But—"

"Come on, babe." Daisy grabs my arm and half-drags me down the hall. As soon as we're in our room with the door closed, she lets out a huge sigh. "I swear that woman can look right into your soul. It's like she knows things about me that I haven't told her. It's fucking weird."

"O-kay. How's Angela doing?" I guide her to the bed, where we sit.

"All I know is what you heard Doc tell us. She's going to be okay, but she's bruised up. Everywhere. I hate that they did that to her." Tears fill her eyes.

"Oh, babe." I cradle her to my chest. "She's safe now. Everything's going to be okay."

"Thank you. You saved her life." She presses her cheek against mine. "I don't know what I would have done without you. I would never have found her."

"You're part of our family, Daisy. Fed or not, you're still technically our club girl."

"Is that all?" she asks softly.

"You know it's not." I kiss her trembling lips until she relaxes in my arms. The conversation we need to have is too important to rush. I don't want to have it right now. "We'll talk more when we get back to Montana. Okay?"

"We can't leave for a few more days. Doc said we're stuck here until Angela and the other girls make it through withdrawal."

"So, they were all drugged?" My brow furrows. Even though I knew this would probably be the case, it still pisses me off. Considering what they did to the girls, those cartel guys deserved long, painful deaths. If only I'd had more time with them. I would have made them suffer.

"Doc gave the girls something to help them through the withdrawal process. Angie and the others should be okay. It will just take time. I need to go sit with her."

"Do you want me to come with you?" I ask.

"No. Stay here and rest until I'm back. Then, I want you to hold me all night. I won't be able to sleep unless you're beside me."

"I'm not going anywhere, babe." I kiss her

forehead. "Let me know if you need me. I need to talk to the guys. I'll be right downstairs."

"I love you."

Her huge emerald-green eyes meet mine. There's so much hope and love in them that it takes my breath away. My mind goes blank, and all I can do is respond with what's in my heart. "I love you, too."

She smiles and kisses me before walking out the door, leaving me stunned. For a few seconds, I'm elated, but then reality kicks in. Even though I told her about some of what happened with Blackstone, she still doesn't really know me. She doesn't understand what I went through. Not the worst details. Part of me wants to tell her everything, but it's so dark and fucked up that I don't think I can. She's only caught a glimpse of the demons that torment me. She doesn't realize the full extent of it. She knows about the dissociation and cutting, but she hasn't discovered my darkest secret. If she found out about it, what would she think?

But if we're going to stay together, then she needs to know the truth. I've got to tell her everything. Otherwise, there'll always be an insurmountable wall between us. Sometimes love isn't enough. I wish it were, but that's not always the case. Ultimately, I think she can handle it, but I won't know until I tell her everything. For us to work, I can't hold anything back, and I've got to do it soon. Because if I don't,

I won't be the only one walking away with a shattered heart.

CHAPTER 18: DAISY

Sitting in a chair by my sister's bed, all I can think about are the men who did this to her. Not just the cartel but the customers. What kind of sick people would do something like this? Men like that make me wonder if my faith in the general goodness of humanity is misplaced. But then I remember guys like Matrix, Scar, Vapor, and Fang. They're fighting battles I can't even get close to and in ways I could never comprehend until now. I understand why they do the things they do, not in an intellectual way, but in a visceral way. Their rage against Blackstone makes sense now. I can see why they'll do whatever it takes to destroy him—because he's evil. He's enabling monsters, and he must be stopped.

We must find a way to connect Lulu's to Blackstone. If my sister saw Blackstone talking to the cartel about human trafficking or if she was ever taken to his ranch after being kidnapped, we have him. I just need her to get better so she can talk to me. She hasn't regained consciousness since Doc Lavine gave her medication to help her through withdrawal. He said this would happen, so I'm not worried. Instead, I'm furious at the whole situation.

The only light in the darkness right now is Matrix. I can't believe I told him I love him, but it's true. Honestly, I think I was half in love with him even before he found out I'm an FBI agent. As a club girl, I spent a lot of time cooking and cleaning for him and the other MC guys. Matrix always stood out, not just because he's a talented hacker, but because he's the sweetest man in the club. I fell hard and fast, but I don't regret it. I've been waiting my whole life to meet someone like him.

It's crazy that I'm in love with someone who has committed multiple felonies. I've witnessed several already, but I won't turn him in for any of them. Every man he's killed deserved it. My only regret is that they didn't suffer the way my sister's suffering now. I've never been a vengeful person, but they hurt my sister, either directly or indirectly, and they got what they had coming to them.

I get out of my chair to pace back and forth in front of the window. It overlooks the street below, which is quiet. A stray dog sniffs around a trash can before knocking it over. It hits the sidewalk with a clang, but no one from the house across the way comes out to investigate the noise. It's just another sultry night in the Big Easy.

A soft knock on the door cuts through the silence, and Babet walks into the room, closing the door behind her. "How is she?"

"The same."

"Doc said she'd probably sleep the rest of the night and most of tomorrow. Have you eaten since you got back?"

"No. But I'm not hungry. I'm too pissed off to eat."

"I know all about that." Babet drags a chair next to mine. I sit beside her, but we're both facing the bed, watching over Angela.

"Thank you for being here for us."

"It's what I do. These men are my family. I take care of them, and they watch over me. It works out for everyone."

"How did you meet them?" I ask.

"That's a long, convoluted story. It's best not to get into it unless you want me to talk your ear off." She laughs softly. "How's Matrix doing?"

"He's concerned about Angela and me. I told him that I'm fine." I pause before adding, "Actually, I told him I love him."

"Was that the first time you said it to him?"

"Yes, but I've known it for a while. I just didn't want to admit it." I blush.

"Why not? Is it because of the Fed thing?"

"That's a huge problem. His club and my job don't mix. Hell, I was undercover as a club girl. *Was*, being the keyword. I'm not anymore. I haven't called the SAC since I hung up on him the other day. For all I know, I don't work for the FBI because they fired me."

"How does that make you feel?" She turns her head, looking my way.

"Honestly? Scared. Relieved. I have mixed emotions, but they're all at war with each other. I'm afraid because working for the government is the only real job I've ever had. On the other hand, I'm relieved because, even though I haven't been doing it directly, it feels like I'm playing both sides. I'm failing at my job, but I'm also failing the club."

"You feel an allegiance to them, don't you?" She nods as if she understands, and I suppose she does.

"Yes. Matrix told me a little bit about one of the men behind this trafficking ring. He's a terrible, evil monster. The FBI has been watching him for years, but they don't have anything on him. He's like Teflon. Nothing sticks. There are rumors, and sometimes, even a video surfaces, but Blackstone's smart enough not to leave any real evidence behind."

"Until now."

"What do you mean?" I ask.

"Your sister and the other girls could testify against him."

"They could. But only if they want to. I won't force them to do it, not when they're so young and scared. Also, we're not sure if they can even connect Blackstone to the cartel's operation. We won't know until they wake up. By the way, how are the other girls?"

"About as good as Angela. They're also coming off heroin, which is one hell of a drug. I know from personal experience."

"Really? You were an addict?"

"When Vapor found me, I had one foot in the grave and the other on the proverbial banana peel. He saved my life." She glances at me. "You're probably wondering why he rescued me when so many people need his help."

"I am, but I don't want to pry."

"That's okay. We have time. The long and short of it is that I was working as a madam in a local brothel. It took a long time for me to fall that far, but drugs had a lot to do with it." She stops and gets that faraway look people have when they remember something traumatic. "Anyway, he and his club raided the house and shut it down. They gave me an ultimatum. Get clear or die. They kept me locked up for months."

"Oh, my God." I sit back, shocked.

"It was the right thing to do. Really. If you'd been there, you'd understand it was the only option. I think they took pity on me because of the drugs. Also, I wasn't running the brothel. Not all of it. I was just doing the scheduling, and I kept the girls in line. I hate what I did, and I'll spend the rest of my life trying to make amends."

A single tear streaks down her cheek before she wipes it away.

"I'm sorry that happened. I know enough about drug cases to realize something terrible must have happened for you to be that hooked."

"Yes, but that's a story I'll never tell." She sighs deeply. "But back to Matrix. You love him. Does he feel the same way about you?"

"Yes. He just told me for the first time." I can't help but smile. Other than my family, no one's ever loved me before. It's exciting and amazing and terrifying at the same time.

"Then you have a choice to make."

"Which is?"

"Leave the FBI and commit yourself to him and the club. Or walk away from him and lose the love you two clearly share. I could see it the minute you walked into our clubhouse. You're electric when you're together, like a hot summer storm."

"We have chemistry. That's for sure. I love him, but leaving my job could be a disaster. If things don't work out between Matrix and me, then what? Not only will I have torched my career, but I'll lose my security clearance too. I'll never get another job in the government."

"There are other types of employment," she says wryly.

"I know, but ever since I was a little girl, all I wanted to do was put bad guys behind bars."

"You can do that with the club."

"Not really. The things they do aren't legal. They'd never hold up in court." I lower my voice to a whisper. "They don't wait around for the justice system to deal with men like Blackstone. They kill them instead. I watched Matrix do it." I conveniently leave out the fact that I killed a man too. That guy absolutely deserved it, so maybe my morality is more flexible than I think.

"Yet you didn't report him. If you did, we wouldn't be having this conversation."

"No. But only because the guy he killed deserved to die."

"Sometimes, that's the only real way to get vengeance."

"I know, but if I joined the club, I'd be going against everything I stand for. I believe that justice ultimately prevails. In most cases."

"But not all."

"No. Some criminals are too intelligent, or they're exceptionally resourceful. They have scumbag lawyers who know every loophole."

"Fuck those guys."

"Absolutely." I chuckle.

"I think you and Matrix will be good together. Walk away from that job. You'll make a great old lady for him. He needs a woman like you, someone who can keep him in line."

"Oh, I don't know about that. He keeps me on my toes. That's for sure."

"And based on what I heard the other night, he's damn good in bed."

"Babet!"

"Oh, let an old woman have some fun."

"You're not old."

"I'm fifty-five, and some days, I feel every one of those years."

"Well, I don't see it. Your energy is that of a woman half your age." I give her a one-armed side hug.

"Thank you. I wish I'd made different choices when I was your age, but I didn't. That's what got me into drugs and everything related to it. I thank God every day that Vapor gave me a second chance. He could have killed me, but he didn't. These men, they may look like outlaw bikers, but they have hearts of gold."

"I know. I see how good they are with the people they rescue. They're nothing like what I expected when I first went undercover. None of them even tried to make me sleep with them. I thought I'd have to get close to one of the guys to get more intel, but that never happened. If anything, they were *too* respectful." I smile. "Matrix never touched me until after he found out I was an agent."

"The irony."

"Right? And now he can't keep his hands off me."

"What a *terrible* problem to have." She rolls her eyes but laughs.

"I'm not complaining. Trust me on that."

"Oh, I do. Which is why you need to

hold onto him. I had a guy like him once. A good, kind, honorable man. But I was wild and wanted excitement. He seemed too tame. Too domesticated. I didn't realize it until years later, but if I'd stayed with him, my life would have been so different."

"Have you tried to contact him since you got clean?" I ask.

"No. I never looked him up."

"Why not?"

"Too much has happened. I'm not the same person he knew."

"But you recovered. You're not using anymore, right?"

"Eight years clean."

"Congratulations."

"I still talk to my sponsor every week. She's my best friend now."

"What you did is amazing. So many people are enslaved by drugs and alcohol. You're free of it. I think you should call that man. At least look him up to see if he's married. If he is, then there's no point in calling. But if he's not …"

"I'll think about it," she says noncommittally.

"When I get home to Montana, I'm going to call you. I'll want an update." I raise my brow.

"Hardass," she teases.

"You know it." I beam.

"I'm going to grab some jambalaya. Want me to bring you a bowl?"

"Actually, yes. I'm finally starting to get hungry."

"If you need a break, we could eat in the kitchen."

"No. I'd rather stay with Angie right now if that's okay."

"Absolutely. You're a good sister, and you'll make a great wife. Stay with Matrix. Make the man happy. He deserves it, and so do you."

"I'll keep that in mind."

After she leaves, I turn my attention to my sister. Her chest rises and falls rhythmically. Watching her breathe makes me realize how precious life really is. It could be snatched away in seconds. Today, Matrix could have died. I could have been killed too.

Maybe Babet's right. Would walking away from my job actually be the end of the world? Not really. As she pointed out, there are other employment options. If things don't work out between Matrix and me, I could go into the private sector and possibly become a freelance investigator. It's an option.

Still, I'm not quite ready to make that choice; besides, none of this matters. I don't have to decide today. Angela will need a few days of rest before we can transport her back to Montana. We'll be at the NOLA clubhouse for a little longer, so I'll enjoy my time with Matrix while I have it.

Babet returns a few minutes later with two

steaming bowls of jambalaya. I dig in, enjoying bits of crawfish, shrimp, smoked sausage, and a variety of vegetables in a savory sauce. It's magical, and I can't get enough.

After scarfing down the entire bowl, I'm so stuffed I feel like a sausage. I pat my belly and look over at Babet. "I'm going to need you to send me a vat of jambalaya at least once a month."

"I have a better idea. How about I come up and cook for you? Vapor says we're due for a visit."

"Do you know Acid at the Denver chapter? He's their president."

"I met him once a couple of years ago."

"He also wants to bring his club up to Montana. We should do a huge club meetup."

"Hum, we'd have to consider security for something like that. We don't want criminals connecting all of us together."

"Oh, right. I didn't think of that."

"But I'm sure the boys will figure something out. Either way, I want to visit you this summer. I've always wanted to see Old Faithful in Yellowstone."

"Ugh. Then you definitely want to wait until fall. After Labor Day is the best time. No crowds."

"Sounds like a plan." She yawns, then stretches her arms overhead. "I need some sleep. I used to think fifty-year-olds were full of shit when they said they got tired much faster than when they were younger. Turns out, they were telling the God's honest truth."

"Noted." I smile.

"Angela won't wake up for at least a few more hours. I'll get a prospect to stand guard so you can sleep. You'll want to be alert when she wakes up."

"You're right. I should go see how Matrix is doing."

"He's probably waiting in bed for you. Try to keep it down so the rest of us aren't up all night." A wicked grin spreads across her lips.

"So embarrassing," I mutter while she laughs.

She turns to open the door when a huge banging sound comes from below.

"What the heck was—"

Gunshots pierce the air. They sound as if they're coming from the living room.

"Help me barricade the room!" Babet grabs one side of a huge oak dresser. "Hurry!"

I push my hands against the other side, and we shove it in front of the door.

"What's going on?" I whisper.

"Don't know." She eyes the windows across the room.

"Stay away from those. If anyone's on the street, they could see you."

"We've never had anything like this happen before." Babet's pale and trembling. She crosses her arms over her chest and slides down to sit beside the dresser.

"Don't worry. The guys will stop whoever's trying to break in." I kneel before her and take her hands in mine. "They'll keep us safe."

"Or they'll die trying," she whispers.

Even though I don't believe in superstition, it feels like a portend. I shiver and glance at my sister. After all the shit we've been through, we're not dying tonight. Vapor, Scar, and all the other men of Underground Vengeance will keep us safe. I know they will. But if something happens and they can't, then we're all dying tonight.

Together.

CHAPTER 19: MATRIX

I'm sitting in the kitchen with Reaper and Tank when all hell breaks loose. The back door bursts open, and two men from the cartel run into the room. Within seconds, I'm on my feet with my gun drawn, but I don't get a shot off fast enough. Tank takes a bullet to the shoulder. He drops to the floor, writhing in agony.

Returning fire, I clip one guy, who spins and falls to the ground. The other guy ducks behind the island. As he pops back up, I flip the dining room table and take cover. Bullets bite into the solid oak, sending wood chips flying. I wait for an opening to shoot back. Before I can act, Reaper springs out from the pantry. He fires his Glock at the man behind the island, and the bullet grazes the guy's arm, forcing him to drop his weapon.

I rush forward, ready to take him down, until he pulls a machete from his shoulder strap sheath. The eighteen-inch blade flashes as it arches down. I leap back, narrowly missing its sharp edge. I'm about to fire my gun when a huge body slams into me from behind. My weapon clatters across the tile out of reach.

Reaper pulls the thug off me before tossing him against the cabinets, dropping his gun in the process. That doesn't stop him from finishing off the guy with a boot to the face. We turn toward the man with the machete. He swipes it back and forth in an arc, advancing toward us.

As I step back, my boot connects with a solid mass. I glance down to find Tank lying on the floor with his face contorted in pain. He's pressing his hand into his wounded shoulder, but it's not helping. Blood spurts through his fingers, soaking his tank top. If we're going to save him, we need to act fast.

Suddenly, Reaper surges past me. He grabs the machete guy's arm and holds it above the guy's head. They're locked in a battle of wills. Neither man is winning, so I have to act fast.

"Grab a gun!" Reaper yells.

I scramble across the floor to get my gun. As soon as it's securely in my hand, I aim. I can't get a good shot. Reaper's in the way.

"Drop!" I yell.

Reaper immediately releases the guy and ducks. I fire, hitting the man in the heart. We don't have time to celebrate his death. Screams and gunshots echo through the house, reminding us of the chaos still surrounding us.

As we leave the kitchen and stalk toward the living room, a cartel member attempts to flee. He's holding a knife with a twelve-inch blade covered in blood. I knock it out of his hand before it can do any more damage, and it clatters to the floor. I land a solid punch to his jaw, and he falls face-first onto the ground. He won't be going anywhere for a while.

I kick the knife under the couch in my attempt to retrieve it. "Fuck!"

Trying to make sense of the pandemonium, I spot several pairs of men locked in combat. I search for any cartel members who aren't being handled by NOLA club members. One guy near the front of the house pulls something round and shiny out of his pocket and sends it sailing through the air.

"Fuck! Grenade!" I scream as I dive behind a nearby couch.

The grenade lands in the middle of the room. The explosion is deafening, and the force of it sends me hurtling into a wall. The air is thick with smoke and debris. I struggle to regain my bearings as I cough and gasp for breath.

When the smoke clears, the room has been decimated. Bodies lay strewn across the floor, some of them barely recognizable. I scan the area for any sign of the enemy, but all I see is destruction.

As the ringing in my ears subsides, I become aware of a low groan nearby. I crawl toward the sound and find Ice lying on the floor. His leg is twisted at a grotesque angle. Aside from that, he doesn't seem to have any life-threatening injuries.

"Help the others," he gasps, his voice barely audible over the ringing in my ears.

"Hang on! I'll come back for you."

With all my strength, I crawl toward the couch, searching for the knife I'd kicked under it earlier. My hand finally grasps the handle of the weapon. I stand up, only to find a blur of motion heading directly at me. I have no time to react to the cartel thug. I stagger backward, barely dodging his blade as it slices my shirt. Pain sears across my belly. Blood drips down my abs. I gasp as pain threatens to consume me.

The attacker switches tactics, spinning to deliver a kick to my chest. I tumble backward and hit the ground, rolling. I come to a stop, facing my assailant. His eyes are wild with hate as he lunges for me again.

"You killed my brother!" he screams.

I try to move, but my body's too slow to avoid the knife. It slices my arm, drawing blood. I ignore the pain, allowing myself to disassociate from it until I feel nothing but rage.

Furious, I tackle him to the ground. I punch him in the face, but it doesn't faze him. The guy shoves me away, then jumps on top of me, pinning me to the ground. He slams his fists into my face over and over until darkness threatens to drag me under.

Just as I'm about to pass out, his chest

explodes. He falls forward, covering me with his bulk. I roll him off me and try to sit, but the pain comes flooding back. I can't keep it at bay.

"Stay down." Daisy's gorgeous green eyes come into view, and she glances down at my stomach. Her cry of horror shocks me. How bad is it? "Put your hands here. Oh, my God. Don't move. Babet!"

The older woman from Angela's room appears in my hazy vision.

"More ... cartel," I manage to gasp.

"No. They're dead. It's clear." Vapor's voice carries from across the room. "We've got men down. Work as fast as you can. Babet, call Doc. Get him and his entire team down here. Now!"

I roll my head to find Babet standing over me. She's frantically talking into her phone, but none of the words make any sense. My body feels so light. So empty. So ... floaty.

My spirit rises above my corporal body until I'm hovering near the ceiling. From up here, the carnage doesn't seem so bad. In fact, I feel nothing. The urge to stay doesn't hold any appeal. This is much better than being down there. Returning to my body isn't an option because I know all it would do is bring more pain. More suffering. More of everything I've tried to avoid in the years since I escaped Blackstone's. It's better to be here, away from the others, where nothing and no one can hurt me.

"Matrix!" Daisy slaps my face. "Are you still

there?"

I want to tell her I'm fine. This pain-free place is as close to Heaven as I'll ever get. I just want to enjoy it for a little longer. I could stay here. I've tried it before. Sometimes I can hang out in this realm between the worlds for days on end. Maybe forever.

Yes. That's what I want to do. Stay.

"Matrix, you bastard! Don't do this! Don't leave me!" Daisy's frantic, screaming at me while trying to stop the bleeding. I wish I could tell her that everything's all right. She wouldn't understand, but it's true. I'm perfectly good right where I am.

Time passes. I have no idea how much because time isn't real here. It's something we feel in the earthly realm but not in the floaty place. There's no beginning and no end. Only the existence of this moment. I'm only in the now. Not tomorrow or yesterday. I always have been, and I always will be. I'm forever.

The room changes. It's the bedroom I share with Daisy. I'm in bed, shirtless, with huge bandages wrapped around my belly. I look like a mummy.

Laughter bubbles up from my soul. The freedom of just *being* makes everything better. I could be down there in agony or up here in paradise. I prefer this, so I'm not going back.

Rays of sunlight arch from one side of the room to the other. Darkness falls and rises.

People move fast. So fast. Like frantic ants. Poking. Prodding. The bandages change. Get smaller. Until there's only one strip left.

I know the moment the pain subsides because I become more aware of what's happening in the room. Watching Daisy cry helps me break through the haze. I pay more attention. I don't like seeing her tears. Realizing I need to go back, an unrelenting tugging sensation pulls me down … down … down.

Without warning, I slam back into my body. A jagged cry escapes my lips. My stomach cramps and burns. My parched, dry lips scrape against each other as I try to form words.

"Water," I mumble.

"Oh, thank God!" Daisy jumps to her feet and runs out of the room. "Babet! Hurry! Bring Doc!"

The older woman rushes into the room. When our eyes meet, she gives me a knowing nod, as if she knows where I've been and how hard it was to return from that place.

"I'll get you some water. It's good to have you back." She gently pats my shoulder before leaving the room.

Doc walks in with Daisy and gives me a stern look before pulling his stethoscope out and placing it on my chest. "Heartbeat stronger, now. Less wild." He holds my eyelids open while shining a blinding light into them. I squint and try to roll my head away from the sharp pain caused by the brightness. "Pupils dilating. Episode over."

"Episode?" I ask in a hoarse whisper.

"I call your doc. Dissociation, he say. You go on trip. Escape pain. Welcome back." He smiles. "I come back later."

After he leaves, Daisy rushes to sit on the bed beside me, leaning over and giving me a gentle hug. Although she's careful not to press on my wounds, the discomfort of being back in my body makes me groan.

"Oh, babe. I'm sorry. I just wanted to hold you for a second. Do you hurt still? The bastard who cut you sliced through your abdominal muscles. Doc repaired them, but it's going to suck for a while. He gave you pain meds, but if you need more—"

"I love you," I murmur.

"You scared the shit out of me." She shakes her head, then wipes a tear from her eye. "Why did you do that? I was terrified I'd never get you back."

"I can't control it." While I don't admit it, I *can* shorten the amount of time I spend in the other world. I just have to make an effort to return. She's too angry to hear it, though, so I keep my mouth shut.

"How did you get back? Can you hear and see things when you're gone? Where do you go?"

Her barrage of questions starts a steady pounding in my head. I close my eyes. I want to roll away from her, but even the slightest movement sends flashes of agony through my guts. I can't deal with anything right now, especially not her.

"Go away."

"No. I'm not disappearing on you like you did with me," she says through clenched teeth.

I open my eyes and glower at her, willing her to leave me alone. She doesn't move. Instead, she sits there and glares right back with her arms crossed over her chest. Her eyes are swollen and red from crying, but I can't help her. I'm so messed up I can't even take care of myself. For now, she's on her own.

"I said go away." My stomach's still in knots. The pain is unbearable. I want to curl up into a ball and disappear forever. It's taking every bit of willpower not to let myself drift away again.

"I'm not going anywhere until you tell me what's going on," she says stubbornly.

I let out a frustrated sigh, knowing she won't leave until I give her some kind of answer.

"Fine, but you're not going to like it." I take a deep breath and begin to explain. "When I leave my body, I go to the other world. From that place, I can end up anywhere on Earth. I'm in the room, but I'm not in the room. It's like I'm floating above it. I can hear and see everything going on, but I can't make my presence known. I've been going there since Blackstone's, and I don't know how to stop it. I can't control it. Not really."

"So, you go to a different dimension?" Her brow furrows as she tries to understand.

"Yeah. And I like it there. I can't feel pain or suffering. I'm at peace when I'm in that place. Coming back sucks."

"But you *did* return. You must have done something, so how did you do it?"

"I don't know. It just happens." I pause. "It's almost as if I know it's time to return."

"But you can't make yourself turn back whenever you want to."

"No."

"That sounds terrifying."

"It's not. In fact, it can be very useful."

"How so?"

"Remember what I told you about the dungeon?"

"Yes. And the bad dreams you have."

"They're based on reality. I don't want to talk about what Blackstone did to me or the others, but it was horrific. This one time, I did something that made him so angry that he beat me within an inch of my life. I thought for sure I would die."

"Oh, honey." She slides her hand into mine and gives it a soft squeeze.

"In the middle of the beating, the strangest thing happened. All of a sudden, I was standing next to myself. I watched Blackstone break a wooden paddle over my head and felt nothing. Not one damn ounce of pain."

"That's strange."

"It scared me at first, but then I realized it was a gift. I'd leave my body when things got so bad that I couldn't take it anymore."

"But you couldn't control when that happened, right?"

"Exactly, and that was the drawback. I couldn't do it on command. Still can't. I've tried to get better at it, but it's hit or miss."

"Is that why you cut yourself? Was it practice for disassociating?"

"No. That was functional. When I couldn't take the pain of knowing Blackstone's still out there anymore, I'd cut myself. That feeling would intensify until I thought I'd explode with rage. That's when I'd cut line after line in my skin until I left my body. Sometimes it took two or three cuts. But the last time, after he won the election, I went too far."

"Which is why you ended up in the hospital."

"Exactly. Scar made me promise to stop, and I have. But Daisy, sometimes I want to do it again. I want to cut until I can't feel anything anymore."

"Why?"

"Because it feels like my suffering will never end. Like we'll never get vengeance on Blackstone."

"You will. I believe in you. Scar and the others are all determined to find a way to take him down."

"So far, we've failed."

"But that won't happen this time. We've got witnesses now. At least, I hope we do. The girls still aren't talking."

"How's your sister?"

"Much better. She's almost through withdrawal, but she hasn't spoken a single word."

"How many days was I unconscious?"

"Three."

"Not as many as I thought."

"Did it feel like it was longer?"

"Not really. Time is meaningless in that other place."

"I was so scared. I thought I'd lost you forever." She wipes a tear off her cheek.

"Daisy, there's something else I need to tell you. I've held something back, and I just can't do it anymore."

"What is it?" she asks cautiously.

"You know how I told you I leave my body?"

"Disassociate. Yes."

"Sometimes, I don't stay in the other world."

"Where do you go?" Her tone is guarded.

"I possess another person."

"What?" She stands and moves away from the bed.

"I drop into their body, and then I can control them."

"That's ... that's not possible."

"But it *has* happened."

"When? How?"

"It's been years since the last time. The only time, really. When we were trying to find a way to escape Blackstone's, I tried to leave myself and take over a guard's body instead. It worked."

"Holy shit."

"I've been too worried about the implications to try it again."

"What do you mean?"

"I could get trapped in someone else's body. What if I couldn't leave it?"

"That's a damn good question."

"I was able to escape the guard's body, but I never tried to possess someone again. However, I think I can do it."

"Why are you telling me this? If it's something you don't want to do again, then what difference does it make?" She's slowly backing toward the door, almost as if she's afraid of me.

"I thought you needed to know. If we're going to be together, then you should learn everything about me. Even the weird parts." I stop talking because it's exhausting. I need sleep. Although I've been in bed for three days, I've been conscious the whole time. I haven't rested at all.

"Doc put you on some crazy medications to make sure you don't get an infection. And he gave you strong pain meds. I don't think you're remembering things right. Get some rest, and we'll talk about this in the morning. Okay?"

"Daisy, don't go."

"I have to check on Angela."

"Wait! What happened with the men who attacked us? Who were they?" I try to sit but immediately regret my decision.

"Vapor says the cartel sent them. He told me he made sure we were safe, but he wouldn't give me any details. He claimed it was club business."

"Can you get him for me?"

"Sure. Bye." She's out the door, slamming it behind her before I can get another word out.

Maybe it's for the best. She's overwhelmed right now. This probably wasn't the right time to tell her about the things I've been holding back. However, regardless of when we had it, this conversation wouldn't ever be easy. If she thinks I'm crazy, so be it. This is who I am. If the reality of who I am isn't something she can't handle, then it's better we know now.

As I close my eyes, flashbacks return to haunt me. Sleep is elusive, and for the first time in months, I really, really want my knife. If I had it, I could send myself back to the place where nothing hurts and no one can cause me any pain. Just one little cut, and I'd be free again.

CHAPTER 20: DAISY

After two days of driving, I'm grateful to be back in Montana. I roll down the SUV's window and lift my face into the wind. It roars past, pulling my hair and drying out my eyes. My sister's sleeping in the backseat while Matrix drives. I know he'd rather be on his bike, but he insisted on staying with us instead of letting us straggle behind the others. My thoughts have been a whirl of gratitude and relief but also anxiety.

Before New Orleans, I never thought much about how dangerous Matrix's life can be. Witnessing my sister's rescue, as well as the shootout at the NOLA clubhouse, has brought me to a new level of understanding. If I stay with him, I could be putting not only my life in danger but my sister's life too. I don't know if loving him is worth the risk. My rational side tells me to run away as fast as I can. But the part of me completely in love with him is begging to stay. I don't know what to do.

When we pull up to the clubhouse, I take a deep breath. The tension in my body eases a bit because I'm home. Regardless of whether I stay with him, this has been my family for months. Walking away won't be easy. I don't think I can do it, not after everything they've done for me.

"Are you okay?" Matrix asks softly. "You haven't said a word since Wyoming."

"Just tired," I lie.

If I could explain my feelings, I'd talk to him. But I'm too sleep deprived and too confused to tell him how I'm feeling.

After parking by the porch, Matrix jumps out and opens the back door. Angela's asleep, and when he gently shakes her, her eyes fly open, and she screams.

"It's okay. It's just me. We're home," he says.

"Sorry," she mutters.

"Let's get her set up in my old room," I say.

"Already done. I called Nitro and Holly. They got a bed ready for her. Holly and Nina went and picked up some clothes she can wear while she's with us. If she wants to take a shower and change before bed, she's welcome to do so."

"Thank you," I murmur.

My heart goes soft. When he does things like this, the thought of leaving seems impossible. But then I remember what he said about being about to possess other people, and I can't help but wonder if he's insane. Which version of him is real? The one I fell in love with while living at his clubhouse, or the one I got a glimpse of in New Orleans?

As we approach the door, it swings open, and Nitro steps out, dressed in jeans and his leather cut. His face is hidden beneath a tangle of dark hair. "Glad to see you ladies made it. I wouldn't want to be trapped in a cage with Matrix for thousands of miles. He gets grumpy."

"I'm stiff as fuck, and not in a good way." Matrix makes a show of stretching his legs.

I snort at his comment while Nitro steps aside to let us inside. When the familiar scent of pine and lemon furniture cleaner fills my nostrils, comfort washes over me. Despite everything, being here with Matrix and Nitro feels like coming home.

As we make our way through the living room, I notice a group of guys sitting around the kitchen table. They're laughing and joking, passing around bottles of beer and shots of tequila. I recognize several of the club's prospects. They've been helping Nitro watch over the place while we were in New Orleans.

"Hey, everyone," Matrix calls out. "This is Angela, Daisy's sister. She'll be staying with us for a while."

A chorus of responses fills the air.
"Hey there."
"Nice to meet you."
"Welcome back."
"Sounds good."

"Thank you," Angie mumbles.

"You can stay as long as you want," Scar says. "I know your parents want to see you, but for now, you're safer here."

"That's what my sister said." Her gaze slides to me, so I give her a reassuring nod.

Earlier this morning, I called my parents to update them on her condition. I've been talking to my mom and dad several times a day since we rescued her. They can't wait for her to be able to go home, but they understand the physical issues she's dealing with. Now that she's off the drugs, Doc will have to work on her other injuries. She's been taking a cocktail of medication to resolve any STIs, but we have to retest her every few days to make sure nothing new pops up.

Every time I think about what those men did to her, I want to break something. I wish I could hunt them down and make each one suffer as much as she did. Nothing will bring back her innocence, but getting revenge will help me come to terms with it. I couldn't protect her then, but I can make sure this doesn't happen to another girl from the area. Blackstone must be stopped.

As Nina and Holly walk down the hall toward us, their eyes light up when they see me standing beside my sister.

"You must be Angela." Nina gives her a gentle hug. "I'm Nina, and this is Holly. We're going to help take care of you while you're here."

"They're good people," I tell Angie.

"Okay." She doesn't look at me, preferring to stare at the floor instead. She's been like this ever since she came off the drugs. I know it's a manifestation of shame, but until we can get her to a counselor, I can't do much more to help her. I've already talked to her about how what happened wasn't her fault, but she doesn't believe me. Healing her body won't take long, but healing her soul could take an eternity.

"If you need me, I'm going to be in this room with Matrix. You can lock your door once you're inside. No one is allowed in unless you say it's okay." I give her a reassuring smile.

"All right."

"Matrix and I will leave our door unlocked. If you need us, come in anytime."

"Uh …" Matrix slides his gaze to me. I give him a look that immediately silences him. "Yeah. Whenever you want."

"Go with Nina. She'll help you get a bath," I say.

As Angie walks into my old bedroom, Nina nods at me. I know Angie's in good hands. I've already tried everything I can think of to reassure my sister she's safe. Nina's the wisest person I know. If anyone can get through to Angie, it'll be her.

Exhaustion seeps into every muscle in my body. Being home saps what's left of my energy, and suddenly, I'm so tired that all I want to do is cry.

After we close our bedroom door, Matrix holds out his arms. I go to him. All the concerns I have about our relationship don't matter right now. A rush of emotions threatens to overwhelm me, so I hug him like my life depends on it. My body trembles with the force of my feelings. I wanted to scream, to yell, to cry. I'm so relieved he's been by my side through this ordeal. I'm grateful he was part of the rescue mission. We couldn't have done it without him or the members of either club. They truly are a family.

His phone beeps. He pulls it out and reads the text, then smiles. "Tank's going to make it. The other NOLA guys will pull through too."

"Thank God. How's Tank doing since the surgery?"

"It was touch and go, but the operation on his leg was successful. He's well on his way to recovery. Look, he sent a photo."

He turns the phone so I can see it. Tank's lying in bed with a young blonde woman draped across his chest. She looks familiar. I think she's one of the NOLA club girls. He looks good overall, except …

"What's that on his neck?" I ask, squinting.

"A hickey. And that's Vicki the Hickey."

"Well, that explains the mark. But seriously, do they actually call her that?" I frown.

"Yep. Apparently, she loves it."

"Oh, boy."

"I'll tell him you said hi." Matrix types out a quick message before setting his phone on the nightstand. "I don't know about you, but I'm about to faceplant; I'm so tired."

"Me too." I glance at the door. "Should I check on Angie?"

"Let Nina take care of her. She's got a way of making everyone feel safe. She'll do that for your sister."

He sits on the end of the bed before pulling off his boots. His pants come off next, and then his shirt. By the time he's down to his boxers, my mouth is watering. He's so damn sexy it should be illegal. I'm still worried about what he said about spirit possession, but he had to be out of his mind. It was the drugs talking, not him. Pain meds will make people say crazy shit. That's all it was, nothing more.

"Come here, babe." He slides under the sheets and lifts the corner for me.

I quickly strip down to my panties and get in beside him. Instead of reaching for me for sex, he simply cuddles me against his chest. I bury my face there and listen to the slow, steady beat of his heart. He brushes the hair out of my eyes before trailing soft kisses across my cheeks.

"Welcome home," he says softly.

I nod, unable to speak. I want to tell him how grateful I am for what he did for my sister, but I can't get the words past the lump in my throat. After he was cut, I was so afraid I'd never see him again. All I could do was stand there, watching over his unconscious body and praying he'd come back to me.

"Talk to me, babe."

I shake my head as tears spill down my cheeks.

"Everything's gonna be alright," he says quietly. "We're home now. Vapor's going to hunt and kill every last member of the cartel. He's already got most of them."

"He lost several men that day."

"Yes. Fortunately, none of the patched members. But they lost some friends and some of the club girls too. That grenade …" His whole body shudders.

"Thank God you saw it before it went off."

"After all the shit I've been through, some cartel fuck wasn't going to end my life. I've got a mission to fulfill. Nothing will stop me until it's done."

"Destroy Blackstone."

"Exactly."

"Have you talked to Babet today?" I ask.

"I called her at the last rest stop when you and your sister went inside. She says the other girls are still refusing to talk. They're too scared. Most of them were either your sister's age or younger."

"We can't push them. They're too fragile," I warn him.

"I know. Babe, I've been waiting over ten

years to get vengeance. I can wait a few more days."

"What if it's weeks? Or months?" I ask.

"As long as it takes."

"What if she never wants to talk about it? Or what if she truly doesn't know anything about his connection to the cartel?"

"We'll worry about that after we hear what she has to say. For now, try not to stress about it. I promise you I'm not going to rush her. Everyone in the club is concerned about her well-being. You're family now. So is she. We'll take care of you both."

I nod as a wave of gratitude washes over me. After spending the last year afraid—afraid of not finding her in time, afraid of what the future held for us—I don't have to be scared anymore. I'm safe in Matrix's arms, and Angie will be protected while we're at the clubhouse. These men have done more to help us than the FBI ever did. I'll be forever grateful to them, but I still don't know if I can live an outlaw's life.

"What else is bothering you?" he asks.

"Nothing." I hide my face so he can't see the lie written all over it.

A soft knock sounds on the door.

"Come in," Matrix calls.

Nina walks in. After closing the door behind her, she stands next to the bed. "Angie's sleeping now. I gave her some chamomile tea to help her nod off."

"Thank you." I smile softly.

"Can I get you two anything? Dinner? Condoms?"

"Nina!" Matrix flushes.

"Oh please, like I haven't seen the way you two eye-fuck each other constantly. I'm glad you're finally screwing so the rest of us don't have to witness the endless puppy dog eyes." She smirks and puts her hands on her hips.

"Get out. Please." Matrix grins while pointing at the door.

She laughs as she leaves the room.

"I swear, she still treats us like the kids she saved," he mutters.

"Nina rescued you? From Blackstone's?"

"No. Not directly. After we escaped, we needed a warm place to stay during the winter. We found a huge barn and hid there. Nina figured out what was going on, and she started leaving us food. Slowly, we began to trust her. Eventually, she and her old man, Winchester, welcomed us into their home. They took care of us, and we stayed with them for years."

"I didn't realize you went that far back."

"She saved our lives. Not just physically but also mentally. She knew something had happened to us but never directly asked us about it. She told us if we needed to go to the police, she'd help us. We refused. We'd seen cops at Blackstone's place and knew they couldn't be trusted."

"You never reported him."

"Who'd believe us, a bunch of runaways who fled the generosity of our billionaire benefactor?" Sarcasm twists his mouth into a grimace.

"I'm so sorry. I wish I could arrest him for you right now."

"It would never hold up in court. People still see him as a benevolent billionaire who loves to help children. They won't believe he's really a monster without solid proof. Even back then, he was too cunning to be outsmarted by a few kids. After we escaped, he stopped adopting *helpless orphans*." He air quotes. "As far as we know, he's never adopted anyone since we left. Back then, we were such a mess we couldn't have stood up to him even if we'd wanted to. We were weak, and we didn't have any proof of what he did to us. Right after we escaped, if we'd tried to tell people what he did, they would have chalked it up to us being ungrateful brats.

"Now, we've got a shot at bringing him down because Angie and the other girls don't have any connection to him. There's no reason for them to lie. We're hoping Angie can testify against him because no one can argue with a victim willing to stand up to the monster who hurt them."

"I agree that we need to do this sooner than later. If we wait too long, her credibility will start to wane. I'll talk to her tomorrow and see how she's feeling."

"Only if you think she's ready."

"If she's not, I'll know it." I kiss him softly. "Matrix, I love you, and no matter what happens, we're going to get Blackstone."

"I hope so," he whispers before kissing me back.

***

The next morning, I carefully leave Matrix's bed. I don't want to wake him, so I get dressed in the dark. Talking to my sister will be delicate, and having a man in the room won't help matters. I was up half the night thinking about it, and I'm sure she won't want to talk about her ordeal if Matrix is with me.

I tiptoe across the hall to my old room. I test the door, but it's locked.

"Angie," I whisper. "It's Daisy."

A few seconds later, the door cracks open, and her face fills the space.

"Can I come in?" I ask.

"Sure." She steps back and waits until I walk into the room before relocking the door.

"Did you sleep last night?" I ask.

"Not really."

"Doc could give you something to help with that." I sit on one side of the bed while she takes on the other.

"No more drugs." She shivers and wraps her arms across her chest. She's wearing matching sweatshirt and sweatpants covered in the local college's logo. Nina must have left it for her.

"I need to ask you something. I know you don't want to talk about what happened, and you don't have to. Not yet. Not until you're ready. But there's something very important we need to discuss."

"What?"

"When you were kidnapped, did anyone ever mention the name Blackstone?"

She pales and sways like she's about to pass out.

"Lay down." I gently grab her shoulders and help her to lie flat.

"He's evil," she whispers before dragging a pillow over her face. She screams into it, startling me. The cloth and padding muffle the sound, so it doesn't carry, but I can hear her agony, and it's like a knife through my soul.

"Do you know who he is?" I ask.

"Yes."

"How do you know him?" I don't want to ask any leading questions. She could simply recognize the name because he's the state's governor.

"They took me to his house on a ranch. It had a terrible place in the basement. A dungeon." Her muffled voice comes from underneath the pillow.

"Oh, shit." I cover my mouth with my hand.

"You know about it?" She tosses the pillow

aside and sits with her back to the wall.

"Yes."

"How? Have you been there?"

"No. But …" I'm not sure how much to reveal, so I go with the simplest explanation. "Someone I knew was held captive there once."

"Me too."

"Oh, Angie." I pull her in a warm hug. "I'm sorry I didn't find you soon enough."

"I already told you. It wasn't your fault. I snuck away and went to the mall without telling anyone. If I'd stayed home like I was supposed to —"

"You can't keep beating yourself up like that. Nothing you did was wrong. The only people at fault were the men who took you. I want to punish them. Lock them up forever. But to do that, I'll need your help."

"What would I have to do?" Suspicion fills her eyes.

"Testify that Blackstone is part of the human trafficking ring."

"No," she whispers.

"Angie, you're the only one who can connect him to the New Orleans cartel. You're the only eyewitness we have."

"You have to find someone else. I can't. I'll never tell anyone what they did to me." She starts sobbing.

"It's okay. I'm sorry I pressured you to talk about it." I hug her to my chest and rock her until her crying becomes a whimper. "You don't have to say or do anything unless you want to. I promise."

"Pinky promise?" she asks, hiccuping.

I hold out my little finger until she offers her own. When we wrap them around each other, she smiles, despite her swollen eyes.

"Get some sleep. Don't worry about anything, okay? I love you, and I swear I won't make you testify," I say.

"You promised you wouldn't."

"I won't."

As I wait for her to crawl under the blankets, I silently kick myself for pushing her too hard. This is exactly why I should have waited a few more days. If I'd talked to her with the help of a victim's advocate or a psychologist, they could have helped me keep her calm. Instead, I stressed her out. Now, she might never open up to me again. I really fucked up.

Hanging my head, I leave and return to my room. Matrix is still sleeping. I don't dare wake him. Instead, I sit in a chair beside the bed and run an endless loop through my mind of all the ways I've messed up in the last few months. What just happened with my sister is only the tip of the iceberg of my incompetence. My relationship with Matrix is just one more fuck up in a long line of mistakes. If I don't get my shit together soon, everything will fall apart. I'll be lucky if my sister still talks to me after today. I wouldn't blame her if she wanted to shut me out. She shouldn't have to discuss the details of her kidnapping. If she never wants to tell anyone, then that's her choice. I'm letting my love for Matrix cloud my judgment. That's why we can't work as a couple. He's taking away my objectivity, and it's affecting both my work and my other relationships.

I love him, but I don't see how we can stay together. My sister's healing must be my top priority. As if that's not enough, my job is also too important to walk away from. People like Blackstone will never be brought to justice unless I'm in the fight, battling evil men like him to help victims like my sister. I can't give that up for love. It's just not worth it. Somehow, I have to find a way to break things off with Matrix. It will break my heart and his, but it's the right thing to do.

CHAPTER 21: MATRIX

Talon and I are sitting on the porch, sipping beer while watching the river rush past the clubhouse. For the last few days, Daisy has been trying to get her sister to agree to testify against Blackstone. So far, Angela isn't budging. She doesn't want to tell anyone what happened. I get it. After Talon and I escaped Blackstone's dungeon, we never talked about it again. Maybe it's time we did. We can't go to law enforcement about what Blackstone did to us all those years ago, but it's not too late for Angela.

"Maybe if we talk to her about how we were Blackstone's prisoners too, she'll be more open to talking to the Feds," Talon says.

"I was thinking the same thing, but she's got to be terrified," I say.

"Yeah, I get it. Remember how we were after we finally escaped? Fucked up, big time. We hardly spoke to anyone. There was no way in hell we would talk about Blackstone or what he did." He pauses momentarily before asking, "Have you ever told anyone about those years we spent in his dungeon?"

"Not really. Daisy knows a little bit, but not much. I hate discussing it."

"I've never told a soul. Sometimes I wonder if we should have pushed each other to go to the cops. Nina was so supportive. She would have backed us up."

"Probably, but we can't change the past. All we can do now is try to find a way forward."

I lean back in the Adirondack chair. Staring up at the bright spring sky, I savor the openness and freedom of being outside. After being locked up in a dungeon for years, I never take beautiful days for granted. Every one of them is a gift.

"Do you think Angela would listen if you tried to talk to her?" Talon asks.

"She's thirteen and traumatized. Even if I gave it my best shot, it might not work, and I'm afraid of making things worse. Maybe in time, she'll come around."

"What if she doesn't?"

"Then Blackstone will be free to destroy more people, just like he did to us. I'll never forget being imprisoned. At night, it was so dark I couldn't even see my hand in front of my face. I had to listen to the rats scurrying around and hope they didn't find my toes. I still have terrifying dreams about it."

"Same." Talon's face falls. He chugs the rest of his beer. "Nothing will make the nightmares stop. And believe me; I've tried everything."

"I gave up years ago. Some things just stay with you, no matter what you do."

"Hopefully, Angela's parents will take her to see a good trauma specialist. Even if she never testifies against Blackstone, I don't want her life to end up like mine," Talon says.

"What do you mean?"

"Filled with bitterness."

"You don't come across that way." I turn to study his profile. His jaw's tight, and he's gripping the empty bottle like it's a lifeline.

"I hate myself for not speaking up, for not doing something to stop Blackstone. Even though we were just kids, if we'd told someone the truth, maybe the cops would have done something."

"Don't think like that. We were young and scared. Back then, we did the best we could. Life hasn't been easy, but look at everything we've built. There are clubs all over the country trying to bring men like Blackstone to justice. We haven't stopped him, but we will. Have faith. One day we'll get a break, and it will be exactly what we need to end his reign of terror."

I hear rustling coming from around the corner. In an instant, Talon and I are on our feet with our guns drawn. I motion for him to get behind me. Stalking across the patio, I ready myself for a confrontation.

"Don't shoot!" Angela steps out from behind

the wall with her hands held high.

"Crap!" I stuff my piece in my cut. "Don't sneak up on us like that."

"Sorry." Her gaze drops to the floor.

"Do you need something? Is Daisy okay?" I glance toward the kitchen window.

"She's in there with Nina making lunch. Um … I kind of listened in on you guys. Is it true?" Her voice trembles. "Are you two really talking about Blackstone?"

"Yes," I say softly.

"He kept you prisoner too?"

"Yeah, when we were kids." My throat tightens as memories assault me. I force myself to stay focused. This is the first time she's even said his name in my presence. Maybe she's ready to talk.

"What did he do?" she asks.

"Well …" I glance at Talon. He gives a slight inclination of his chin, so I know it's okay to share our story with her. "When we were much younger, we were adopted by Blackstone."

"Gross." She leans against the railing and folds her arms across her chest.

"He did some really bad stuff to us," Talon says. I give him a look of warning. Although we want to discuss this with her, details aren't necessary. He realizes it and continues, "We were locked up in his dungeon for years. The same place he kept you."

"I was only there a few days. It felt like

forever. You were there for that long?" she asks.

"Yep."

"How did you get away?"

"We made an escape plan. All of us were there. Me, Scar, Nitro, Talon, and Reaper."

"Reaper's scary."

"He's nice unless you're a bad guy," Talon says.

"Glad I'm not one." She flashes a quick smile.

"He makes sure men like Blackstone can't keep hurting people," I say.

"I heard you guys talking about how you wish you'd reported him."

"It's true, but by the time we escaped, we were really messed up," Talon says.

"Daisy wants me to tell the FBI about him." She shifts her weight from one foot to the other.

"What do you think about that?" I ask.

"I want to help. No one else should have to go to his dungeon. It's dark and cold and smelly. I hated it."

"We did too," Talon says softly.

The compassion on his face breaks my heart. I know how hard this is for him. He's never discussed any of it before, but he's willing to do it now because he knows how important this conversation might be. This could be the key to finally getting vengeance.

"I'll testify against him. Anything to make sure he can't hurt anyone else," she says.

Talon and I exchange a look. I can't believe she's willing to go through with this. It's a damn miracle. I'm afraid to say anything to mess this up, so I keep my mouth shut.

"We need to tell Daisy," Talon says.

"I'll talk to her after lunch." Angela's eyes flicker with determination. She may be young, but she's just as strong as her sister. They're both made of steel. Unbreakable. I hope one day I get to meet their parents. I want to know what kind of people they are because they were able to raise two amazing girls, and that's not easy in this world.

"You're so much braver than we ever were. I'm so proud of you," I say.

"I haven't done anything yet." She drags the toe of her shoe across the slats in the deck.

"You won't be doing this alone. We're all here for you. Everyone in this clubhouse knows who and what Blackstone is. He's a monster. The fact that you're willing to stand up to him is amazing." Talon beams at her until a mountain bluebird lands on his shoulder, drawing his attention. He gently pets it. "Oh, hey there."

"Wow! Cool." Angela brightens up. "I've never had a bird land on me."

"Would you like one to?" Talon asks.

"Yeah, but it's not going to happen. Birds don't—Oh, my gosh!" A bluebird hops off the railing before landing on her head.

"Okay, that wasn't your shoulder. I'll just let

him know." Talon gives the bird a pointed look. It flies down to perch on her shoulder.

"Are you, like, talking to it?" Angela asks in amazement.

"When I was a boy, I didn't have any friends, so animals became my buddies. We communicate with each other."

"How?" She turns her head, attempting to look at the bird.

"It's hard to explain. Basically, we exchange thoughts."

"Are you like a witch or something?" She studies him intently.

"No. Not really. I just help the animals out, and they do the same when I need a hand. Or a wingman." Talon grins.

"A wingman!" She laughs.

It's the first time I've heard her do that, but it's exactly what she needs right now. Testifying against Blackstone won't be easy. He'll use every devious trick he can to avoid paying for what he did. Angela has no idea that things won't be as simple as walking in and telling the FBI everything. Blackstone's too smart. We all need to stand behind her because she's going to need us.

"Lunch is ready!" Nina calls.

"Wait until after we eat to tell Daisy, okay?" Angela watches the bluebird fly away.

"Whatever you want, we'll do it," I say, meaning every word.

As we head inside, the aroma of cheesy, black bean nachos gets stronger. Reaper's sitting at the end of the kitchen table in his usual spot. Nitro's sitting beside Holly while she breastfeeds their baby, Robert. Trent, their first child, sits quietly, shoveling macaroni and cheese into his mouth with a fork.

Scar and Julia are across the table, with their son Eli situated between them in a highchair. He's already munching on a grilled cheese sandwich, but he stops to grin at me as we take our seats. He's almost two years old and still as sweet as can be. I hope the terrible twos don't kick in any time soon.

Daisy and Nina carry huge platters of nachos to the table. After setting them down, they also sit. I grab Daisy's hand under the table and gently squeeze it. She gives me a tight smile. I know she's got the weight of the world on her shoulders, but hopefully, it'll get better after she hears what Angela has to say. Part of me wants to just blurt it out, but I have to respect Angela's wishes and wait.

"Be careful because the trays are hot," Nina says. "We just took them out of the oven. Use the tongs, so we don't have to call Doc. You know he'll eat all the leftovers if you let him."

"What leftovers?" Julia asks, laughing.

"I plan on scarfing down this entire pile myself. But if my woman wants a few bites, I'll let her have some," Scar says, teasing his wife.

"If you want me to *let you* have anything later, then you'd better hand that plate over, buddy." Julia playfully slaps his arm.

While this is happening, Angela's watching everyone. She visibly relaxes for the first time since arriving. I think she's finally starting to realize we're a family. Not the big, scary bikers we appear to be. Not when we're with our friends. She's safe here. I hope she understands that because it'll make things easier for her going forward.

After a noble attempt at polishing off all the food, Nina and Holly pack up what's left. Scar and Julia take Eli, Trent, and Robert outside to play. The smiles on their faces warm my heart. Ever since they got together, Scar's hard edges have softened. Not completely. He's still a tough motherfucker, especially when it comes to club business. But when it comes to his family, he's completely whipped, in a good way.

As they walk away, I can't help but feel a sense of relief wash over me. We've been carrying the burden of what happened at Blackstone's for years. I know I shouldn't get too excited because there aren't any guarantees yet, but I already feel like a weight has been lifted off my shoulders. Justice might finally be served. I cling to that hope because it's all that I have. That and Daisy. I don't know how she'll react to her sister's change of heart, but I'm about to find out.

"Um, I want to testify," Angela blurts.

"What?" Daisy nearly drops the glass she's carrying to the sink.

"I know what Blackstone did to Matrix and Talon," Angela whispers.

"You do?" Daisy's gaze snaps to meet mine, and fury fills her eyes. I want to explain what happened, but Angela cuts in before I can get a word out.

"Blackstone is a bad man who hurts kids. I want you to arrest him and take him to jail."

"I want that too," Daisy says cautiously. "But it's not as easy as just walking up to him and slapping handcuffs on him. It might be more complicated than that."

"What do I have to do so he goes to prison?" Angela asks.

"I'll have to call my boss and let him know you're ready to talk. He doesn't even know we rescued you yet."

"Okay. Call him."

"I will. In just a second. Matrix, can I speak with you for a minute?" Daisy grabs my arm and drags me toward the hall. "Angie, stay with Nina."

"I've got her," Nina says. "You're a brave girl. You're going to kick Blackstone's ass."

"Good," Angie says.

Daisy pulls me into our bedroom and closes the door. When she turns to face me, her bottom lip is trembling.

"Babe, what's wrong?" I ask, grasping her

forearms.

"What did you say to her?"

"Nothing. She overheard me talking to Talon outside. That's how she found out about my connection to Blackstone. I didn't try to talk to her about it at all. We never mentioned any specifics about what he did to us. She doesn't know any details."

"Really?" Daisy skewers me with a look. "You'd better not be lying."

"Have I ever lied to you?" I release her and take a step back. I'm wounded. The only person who wasn't telling the truth in our relationship was her. She was the one undercover, lying to my face every day for months. However, I'm not going to point that out and start a fight. In fact, it's almost as if she's trying to pick one with me. What's going on with her?

"No." She sniffs but won't meet my gaze.

"I've never kept anything important from you, and I never will. I love you, Daisy. I don't know why you're pissed off, but I haven't done anything wrong."

"Why did she change her mind so fast? What exactly did you and Talon say?"

After relaying our conversation with Angela as close to verbatim as I can manage, I wait for Daisy's response. She's silent for several minutes.

"Look, I don't have any reason to lie about this. I'm not going to force a kid to testify, especially when I couldn't do it myself. She came to us, not the other way around." I run my fingers through my hair, exasperated.

"I'll call Agent Vale. I don't even know if I work for the FBI anymore, but it doesn't matter. They have to listen to her story. It's the least they can do after totally failing her. I can't fuck this up, Matrix. Everything that happened in the last week … it's just too much. Being around you is too dangerous."

"Around me? What are you talking about? I kept you safe."

"Yes, but at what cost? We almost died in New Orleans. I can't do this anymore."

"What are you saying?"

"I think Angie and I should leave the clubhouse."

"What? Why? The FBI has already proven they can't protect her. They couldn't even find her. We did that." I fist my hands, struggling to control my frustration.

"I know. But your life, club life, it's too risky."

"For Angela? Or for you?"

"Both of us," she whispers.

If she'd punched me in the throat, I would have been less shocked. I thought everything was going well between us. I can't believe she's doing this to me. To us. Is she actually dumping me? We were supposed to be happy together. How did we go from that to this so quickly?

"Daisy, you're not thinking straight. We can get through anything together."

"Not this, Matrix. I can't go to the FBI with the motorcycle club by my side. They need to take her accusations seriously."

"And you don't think they'll do that if we're with you?" Her logic makes absolutely no sense, but I don't want to keep arguing with her. "Fine. Don't bring us. But don't freak out and break things off with me because you're afraid of what the Feds will think. We're in this together. You're my ride-or-die woman."

"I wanted to be." Her voice cracks. "But my sister has to come first."

"She will." Desperation fills my tone because she's slipping away, and I don't know how to stop it. "Babe, you don't have to do this alone. I'll stay in the background. The other club guys don't have to be a part of this."

"What you want is impossible. As long as we're connected, it's a potential liability. I can't risk it. Blackstone has to pay for what he did. No one is going to stand in my way, not even you. I want justice for my sister, and I'll do whatever it takes to get it."

"You're wrong. You need me by your side. Not because you can't do this alone but because you know I can support you in a way no one else can. If you want to deny that, so be it. But I'm not buying this crap for a second." I pull open the door and step into the hall. "When you come to your senses and realize we're better together than apart, you know where to find me."

I slam the door and stomp past everyone's stunned faces. Outside, I grab my helmet and straddle my bike. I've got to get the fuck out of here before I say something I'll regret. Daisy's obviously freaking out because Angela's going to testify. I don't blame her for being scared, but I didn't expect this. Maybe our relationship wasn't as solid as I thought. Could I really have been so wrong about it? I don't think so. I meant what I said. She's my ride-or-die woman, and we belong together. I just hope she realizes it before it's too late.

CHAPTER 22: DAISY

I stare at the door Matrix just slammed. He doesn't understand the trouble I'm in. Although I haven't called my boss yet, I already know how it's going to go. Agent Vale will be furious that I hung up on him in New Orleans. I just need to explain to him why I did it. My motives and instincts were spot on; after all, we found Angie when the FBI couldn't. But Vale's going to be pissed off, and really, I can't blame him. I basically went AWOL.

Reaching under the dresser, I pull a duct-taped burner phone off the bottom. It's my last untraceable phone, but it doesn't matter. I can't stay at the clubhouse anymore. The information Angie has is too important. Even though it's killing me to leave the club behind, it's what I have to do right now. The fact that my heart's breaking into a million pieces isn't something I can focus on. Later, I'll have time to grieve. Until then, I've got to take action and help Angie bring Blackstone to justice.

My stomach churns as I punch in Agent Vale's number. He answers on the second ring. "Vale."

"It's Agent Banner."

"What the fuck, Banner? I've got men looking for you all over the city."

"New Orleans?"

"Where the hell else would you be?" he asks.

"I'm back in Montana."

"What? I just wasted tons of time and manpower scouring those damn swamps searching for you."

"Why were you checking the swamps?"

"When you didn't call me back, I figured you were captured by the cartel."

"Well, I'm fine. Better than that, even. I found my sister, and Matrix helped me rescue her. She's with us—me—at the clubhouse."

"I'm sending a car immediately. Are they holding you prisoner? Should my agents expect a fight?" His gruff voice sends a shiver of fear down my spine. I'm sure he'd love to get a shot at killing these men. He's never liked them, and I've made the target on their backs even bigger with my disappearing act.

"No. I'll come to you, and I'm bringing Angie with me. She has information about the man who held her after she was kidnapped from the mall."

"What man? Who?"

"I'll tell you when we get to the office."

"No. Stay put. I'll drive down to get you myself."

"I'm leaving the clubhouse. For good," I add, barely able to get the words out.

"You're goddamn right you are. Your undercover assignment ended when you went AWOL. The guys upstairs want to fire your ass, but I told them to wait until we heard from you. No one knew what the fuck was going on. My faith in you had better not be misplaced."

"It's not, sir. When you hear what Angie has to say, you'll be giving me a promotion."

"I highly doubt that."

"Can we come in today?"

"No. Why don't we wait until next week?" he asks sarcastically. "Yes, get your ass in here. Now!"

"We'll be there in an hour."

"Fine." He ends the call.

My heart's beating so fast I feel a bit faint. Sitting on the edge of the bed, I look around the room I've been sharing with the man I love. I wish things were simpler between us. Everything's always so complicated. Our relationship has been messy from day one because it was built on a lie. He knows the truth now, and he says he still loves me, but will he still feel that way a year from now? Will he actually be able to trust me long-term? I don't think so. Eventually, he'll start to have doubts, and then he'll have no choice but to leave me.

However, I could be totally wrong about all of this. My mind's such a mess that it's hard to figure out what to do. I could be making a terrible mistake by abandoning him, but I think it's the right choice. I just hope I don't regret it. I could be throwing away the best thing that's ever happened to me.

The bedroom door cracks open. Angie pokes her head in. "Did you call him?"

"Yes. He was furious, but I expected that."

"Did you tell him about Blackstone?"

"Not yet. I want to wait until we're in the office. Everything must be official. I don't want any mistakes. Go pack your things. We're leaving in fifteen minutes."

"Are Mom and Dad meeting us there?" she asks.

"No."

"Then why do I have to pack my stuff? Where are we going after I tell the FBI about Blackstone?"

"I'll drive you to our parent's house."

"But ... I won't be safe there." She eyes me warily.

"I'll be with you. I can protect you."

"There's only one of you, but if we stay with Matrix and Talon and the other guys—"

"Stop!" I hold up my hand. "Look, we can't hide out here forever. No one's going to come looking for you. Blackstone won't know who's testifying against him until we're in court. They won't identify you by name on any of the documents. You'll be known as 'Jane Doe' even when we go to trial."

"No! He'll find out. He knows everything."

"Why do you say that?" I ask.

"He knew who you were. Not right away, but I overheard him yelling at someone for grabbing an FBI agent's sister. We have to stay here. These guys have guns. They can keep Blackstone away from us."

"Let's just go to the office. We can talk about this after you make your statement." There's no point in arguing with her. I just need to get her out of the clubhouse and over to the FBI. We'll figure out what's next after that.

"Okay, but I'm leaving my things here. Nina said I could keep all the clothes she bought me."

"That's true. She's rich and very generous. I hope you thanked her."

"I did."

"All right. If you're not going to pack, then we'll leave right now. We can get the clothes later."

"Do you have a car?"

"Yes. Since moving into the clubhouse, I rarely use it anymore, but it's parked over at the bar and grill."

"Is Matrix coming too?"

"No. He's not, honey. Matrix and the other guys are good men. We know that, but my boss and everyone else on the planet thinks they're criminals. We can't take Matrix with us because they might not listen to you if he's there. They'll be too focused on him and what he's doing with us."

"I guess that makes sense." She frowns but nods.

"Trust me. We'll get through this, but we need to leave."

As we walk out of the room, I can't resist looking back at the bed I shared with Matrix. I can still feel his hands on my body, his lips on my skin, and that tongue. God, I'm going to miss him. With a sigh, I close the door behind us.

"Are you taking off?" Nina asks as we pass the kitchen. She's in the middle of chopping vegetables and tossing them into a pot on the stove, but she stops to talk to us.

"Yes," I say firmly.

"Will we be seeing you again?"

"Maybe."

"You said we would come back." Angie puts her hand on her hips. "Promise we're coming back after I tell your boss about Blackstone."

"I can't make that promise," I admit. "I'm not sure how long this will take or when we'll be done."

"Fine. Then let's go so we can hurry up and be back in time for dinner."

"I think she likes us," Nina says, smiling.

"You're awesome." Angie runs and wraps her arms around Nina's waist.

"Your sister's trying to do the right thing. Be nice to her. She's doing the best she can." Nina gives me a pointed look.

"Where's Matrix?" I ask softly.

"Gone. He took off on his bike a few minutes ago, shortly after he slammed the door." Nina arches a brow. "Boy, would I have loved to be a fly on the wall for that conversation."

"I'll ... I'll call you and let you know how it went."

"Tell me in person when you come home." Nina picks up her knife and resumes chopping the vegetables.

I don't respond to her because I don't know when—or if—I'll step back inside this clubhouse again. I already miss her, but I can't dwell on it.

The drive to the FBI office is tense. Angie won't stop staring out the window. She hasn't glanced my way even once since leaving the clubhouse. I'm worried about her. This situation would be overwhelming for an adult, and she's just a kid. If Vale tries to grill her, he's going to have one hell of a fight on his hands. I won't let him intimidate her.

As soon as we walk into the offices where I work, the whole room goes silent. Everyone stares as we walk past the occupied desks. Vale's corner office has a solid wood door, but it also has glass windows. We're still on display as we step inside. I glance out to see everyone whispering and looking our way. I remind myself that I'm a professional and that I didn't really do anything that wrong. Sure, I didn't check in after I hung up on him, but sometimes undercover agents can't make contact. It's not like undercover work has a set schedule.

Agent Vale looks up from his computer. I'm still standing, which makes it easy to see the subtle dusting of gray along his temples. I haven't seen him in person in several weeks, but he looks like he's aged ten years since I saw him last. He's in his late forties, but the lines around his eyes are deeper and more pronounced than I remember.

"Sit down." He gestures toward the two chairs opposite his desk.

I take the chair directly across from him while Angie sits in the one beside it. She crosses one leg over the other, then swings it back and forth. I reach for her hand and gently grasp it in mine, trying to reassure her that she's safe.

"Before we get into any specifics surrounding your sister's abduction, I need your badge and gun."

I pull my weapon from its holster and set it on the desk. "My badge is at my apartment. I left it there when I moved into the clubhouse."

"You can drop it off later."

"Am I being fired?"

"You're on leave, pending an investigation into your role in the Los Serpientes de Cristal massacre in New Orleans."

I should be upset, but I'm not. If anything, I feel a sense of relief. After spending months being torn between two worlds, I'm finally free from my conflicting loyalties. I don't have to be weighed down by guilt anymore. Also, he didn't say a thing about that guy I killed. He'll probably never find out about him. Apparently, escaping justice is easy when you're careful enough.

Although the FBI hasn't formally fired me, once they find out what happened in NOLA, it will end my career for sure. I'm done. I think I already knew that would be the case, but this solidifies my suspicions. Later, I'll have time to worry about why I don't care that my career is over. Right now, I have bigger issues to deal with.

"What do you know about the cartel in New Orleans?" he asks.

"They were holding Angie in a house called Lulu's."

"We're aware of that place."

"Then why aren't you doing anything about it?" I demand. "Did you know my sister was being held captive there?"

"No. If we'd known, we would have found a way to get her out. We've been tracking them for years, but there isn't enough evidence to bring them down yet. We're trying to get agents to go undercover in their organization, but it's nearly impossible to infiltrate that group. They only bring in people they've known for years."

"My sister spent almost twelve months

imprisoned there."

"And for that, I'm sorry." He gives her a sympathetic look. "But my hands are tied. The NOLA team is doing what they can."

"Maybe you can't help them in New Orleans, but you can do something about the trafficking going on right under our noses here in Montana."

"That, I can do. So," he says, turning to Angie, "Daisy tells me you have information about the man who kidnapped you."

"He held her at his home in a dungeon in his basement," I interject.

"Jesus." His gaze flicks to Angie. "Who is he? Do you know his name?"

"Jonathan Blackstone. The governor of Montana."

Agent Vale's eyes go wide. "Say that again."

"Blackstone kept me prisoner in a cold, disgusting dungeon under his ranch house."

"Here? In Montana?"

"Yes."

"Are you sure it was his house?"

"Yes. He lived there with a bunch of guards. I overheard him talking to other people about moving us to Denver, then to New Orleans."

"Us? There were others?"

"Yes. We rescued four girls plus Angie from Lulu's," I interrupt.

"Where are they at now? Why aren't they here with you?" Vale asks.

"They're refusing to talk about their ordeal."

"Well, they don't get to make that choice. I want them in this office by the end of the day."

"That's not going to happen." I shake my head. "They aren't in Montana."

"Are they still in New Orleans?"

"I don't know."

"Cut the shit. Tell me now, or I'll fire you."

"Honestly, I have no idea where they are. We split up in New Orleans. I haven't seen or heard from them since."

I leave out the details about how they were taken into Underground Vengeance's network of safe houses. The best thing about the club's process is that nobody knows where the girls will end up. Each link in the chain only knows about the next one. They don't know where they came from or, ultimately, where they're going. All they know is that they're still in the network and that they'll be safe.

"You've made one hell of a mess of this," Vale grumbles.

"I did more than this office ever could for my sister, and that's all that matters." I lift my chin and give him a defiant look. All I've ever cared about is finding my sister. I did it with Matrix's help. Vale didn't do shit, so fuck him.

"You said you were being held at Blackstone's house," he says to Angie.

"His ranch." She shifts uncomfortably in her chair.

"Could you lead us back to his house?"

"I don't know where it's at because they blindfolded me before they threw me in the back of their van. But if you took me there, I could show you the dungeon."

"This isn't a lot to go on. It's her word against a very powerful man's." Vale steeples his fingers and rests his elbows on his desk. He stares me down.

"If you get a warrant to search the basement, you'll have all the evidence you need to support her claim," I say confidently.

"Are you sure you were being held at Blackstone's place?" he asks Angie.

"Stop badgering her. She knows it was him. Not only did she see him, but she overheard him on several occasions talking about human trafficking. This is it. It's the break we've been waiting for. We always knew he was up to something, but he was always too smart to get caught. Now, we've got a witness. Get a warrant, raid his place, and find that dungeon. He'll have one hell of a time trying to explain that away."

"I'm really sticking my neck out based on the word of a thirteen-year-old. If she's wrong and we don't find anything, your career is over."

"My sister would never lie about something like this. I believe her."

"Okay. I'll call around and see if any judge is crazy enough to grant a warrant. Sit tight."

Vale picks up his phone and starts making calls. Based on what I overhear, the first two judges laugh him off. But when he calls the third, we hit paydirt. She's a new addition to the bench and not nearly as jaded as the others. More importantly, she's willing to believe my sister. The judge agrees to give him a very limited warrant to search the basement of Blackstone's Montana ranch. After thanking her for her time, he hangs up.

"I'll put a team together. As soon as we get that warrant, we'll move in. I don't want this to get out. Keep your mouth shut, and don't tell anyone what's happening. In fact, stay in my office. I'll send someone over to get you food while you wait. Don't let Angela out of your sight. She must be able to make a positive ID when we get there."

"She will. Also, I'm coming with you." When he starts to protest, I interrupt. "Look, I'm not letting my sister go in there alone. I don't care if every FBI agent in the state is part of the raid. They can't protect her the way I can. Go ahead and keep my gun. I don't care. Even if I'm on leave, I'm not abandoning her. I'll go as a civilian."

"God, you're such a pain in the ass."

"There's nothing you can do to stop me from going. I don't give a damn if you fire me for this."

"Fine. But no gun. And mark my words, if she's wrong about this, it'll be your ass." He slams his fist on the desk.

Angie whimpers, pulls her legs up into her chair, and wraps her arms around her knees, holding herself in a tight ball. I hate seeing her so afraid, but there's nothing I can do other than stay by her side. It's my only option. I don't doubt her for a second. Based on her description of the dungeon and how closely it matches Matrix's, she was there. Now all we need to do is prove it.

Vale leaves the room. A while later, a young agent comes in to take our food order. I'm not hungry, and neither is Angie. I don't blame her. Eating is the last thing on my mind. My stomach hasn't stopped churning since we walked into the office. The sooner we can get this raid over with, the better. My whole life feels like it's in utter turmoil. It's as if I'm trying to outrun a bullet determined to blow a hole right through my heart. I'm sure some of this is because I left Matrix the way I did, but that couldn't be helped. Once we take Blackstone into custody, I'll have time to figure out the rest of my life. Until then, everything's on hold.

Thirty minutes later, Vale pokes his head into the office. "It's a go. We'll leave in one hour. I want you and Angela in body armor, just in case. I'll send someone in to get you suited up."

After he leaves, I turn to Angie. "I know you're scared, but this will be over soon. I promise. All you need to do is point out the dungeon and identify Blackstone."

"Okay. Then can we go back to the

clubhouse?"

"Maybe. I don't know yet."

That's the only answer I can give her because I truly don't know what we're going to do afterward. I'll be able to think more clearly about the future once the raid is over. Right now, I'm taking things one step at a time because it's the only option I've got if I want to maintain my sanity. I just hope we get the evidence we need to lock Blackstone up for good. That will make this entire nightmare worth it. Men like him don't deserve freedom. I can't wait to see him in handcuffs.

CHAPTER 23: DAISY

Angie and I stand beside two agents tasked with watching us while the raid goes down. We're tucked behind the agents' black SUV, waiting for Vale to serve the warrant. Vale didn't want Blackstone to see us right away, so we're waiting for his signal several hundred yards down the road around a bend. I can't see the house from here, but we'll be going in soon enough.

I squeeze Angie's hand. She's frozen, probably petrified, and I don't blame her one bit. Walking back into the house where she was held captive is incredibly brave. I can't wait for this to be over. It's only the beginning, though. Unless he confesses, we'll have to go through a trial, complete with the ensuing media circus that comes with any high-profile case. I'm not looking forward to that part of this process.

Vale's planning on knocking on the door at exactly six a.m. He wants the early morning element of surprise on our side. I agree. This is the best time to perform a search. It catches people off-guard when we show up at daybreak. They're usually not awake enough to think through their response to the warrant, which we can use to our advantage.

Although the sky is getting lighter, the sun hasn't peeked over the mountains. It's nearly freezing, but I'm sweating through my shirt. I haven't worn a Kevlar vest in months. It's heavy as hell, already chafing. Regardless, I'm glad I've got it. Agent Vale isn't letting me anywhere near the action, but I've seen raids go horribly wrong in the past. Blackstone shouldn't know we're coming, but a man like him has eyes and ears everywhere. We've got to be prepared for anything.

Everyone's in place, waiting for Vale's signal. The heavy weight of anticipation fills the air. My heart's pounding. I take a deep breath to steady myself. This is it. The moment we've been waiting for. Blackstone's about to find out what happens to anyone who hurts my sister. He's about to pay for what he did.

The radio squawks. Suddenly, they're going in.

I wait for the sound of gunshots, but nothing comes. It's eerily silent. I was expecting an explosive situation. A shootout. Something. But none of that happens.

"All clear." Vale's voice carries through the radio. "Bring the witness in."

"Let's go." One of the agents tasked with babysitting us leads the way. When we're just outside the front door, he hands us off to Vale.

"Remember, the warrant is very specific. We can't search the whole house, only the basement," Vale says.

"I know. You already told me that." Angie's voice wavers, but she holds her head high. She's trying not to show any fear, but clearly, she's terrified.

"Where's Blackstone?" I ask.

"In the living room. We're going to walk past him when we go in. Are you going to be okay?" he asks Angie.

She nods.

"Did you remember how to get to the door to the basement?" I ask.

"It's through the kitchen," Angie says.

"Okay." Vale walks ahead of us.

As we enter the sprawling ranch house, I can't help but gawk at the splendor. In addition to custom woodwork throughout the grand entryway, Blackstone has priceless art on display. Massive oil paintings line the walls. A huge, fresh flower arrangement, bigger than any I've ever seen, sits on a decorative table in one corner of the living room. It's eclipsed by a massive stone fireplace that covers most of one wall.

Several agents stand over a man sitting on the sofa. When the guy turns to glare at us, I immediately recognize him from his campaign commercials. Wild black hair sticks up from Blackstone's head in every direction. He's over six feet tall with a wraith-like, pale complexion. He's smiling, but pure evil radiates from his eyes. He's giving us the cold, calculating gaze of a man planning a murder. His eyes are almost black, simmering with rage. His innate malevolence shocks me to the core. I knew he was a monster, but this is something else. It's like I'm staring into the eyes of the Devil himself.

"Hello, Agent Banner. It's so nice to finally meet you." He attempts to stand, but an agent tells him to stay seated. Blackstone glowers at the other man before plastering a fake smile across his face. "Good luck with your search."

"You're done, Blackstone." I give him a smug smirk. "I hope you enjoy your time in prison."

"I highly doubt I'll be seeing the inside of a cell anytime soon." His confident tone sends chills down my spine.

"Come on," Vale says, motioning me and Angie forward.

We don't speak until we're in the kitchen, out of Blackstone's view.

"It's through there." Angie points at a perfectly normal-looking wooden door.

"I'll go in first." Vale pulls his sidearm and holds it at the ready.

As he twists the knob, I hold my breath. The door opens, revealing a black void. Vale feels along the wall inside the darkness until he finds a light switch. Pale illumination washes over the staircase, but I can't see anything beyond it.

"Do I have to go down there?" Angie whispers.

"Unfortunately, yes. But let me clear the room first," Vale says.

We wait until he gives us the all-clear signal, then we descend the steps. They creak underfoot as if they've been used many times. Based on what Matrix told me, Blackstone held groups of up to twenty kids at a time. To control them, he employed several guards. That made for a lot of trips up and down these stairs.

By the time we reach the bottom, I expect to see the chains and cages Angie and Matrix described. What we find instead is absolutely shocking.

The floor is covered in a plush, cream carpet that looks as if it's never been stepped on before. The walls are painted a soft, almost institutional green, but somehow the muted color works within the space. Even though it's a basement, it feels open and welcoming. It's nothing like what Angie described. There isn't a single nefarious thing in sight. Even the soft lighting gives the room a soothing feeling. *What the hell is going on?*

"I don't understand," Angie mutters as she wanders through the space. "This wasn't here before. There were chains attached to the walls. The floor was concrete. And cold. It's warm in here."

"It's heated," Vale says, studying her.

"No. That's impossible. It was freezing, even during the daytime, and there were cages with metal bars. Where are they?"

"That's a fucking good question." Vale holsters his gun before placing his hands on his hips. "There's not one goddamn thing here to indicate it was ever a dungeon. You lied."

"No! I swear he kept me down here. The other girls can tell you. They were locked up with me."

"There's nothing here."

"Maybe he cleared it out and remodeled," I say.

"In less than twelve hours? We didn't even know about your sister's accusations until yesterday. Even if he somehow found out about the warrant, he wouldn't have had time to transform a dungeon into this." Vale runs his hand through his hair. "We're so fucked. He's going to have our asses because I believed your lies. My boss will lose his fucking mind when he finds out."

"This isn't right!" Angie looks around the room frantically. "I was trapped down here. I swear. I'm not making it up."

When she bursts into tears, I pull her into my arms. I hold her close while she sobs uncontrollably. "You need to pull up the carpet and check for blood. He couldn't have removed all trace evidence."

"We're not destroying his property to appease your lies," Vale snaps at Angie before turning to me. "You're fired. You're done. What the hell possessed you to trick your sister into making an accusation like this? Have you lost your fucking mind? Did that bastard in that motorcycle club fuck the sense right out of your head? Because that's what it looks like. I knew putting you undercover with them would be risky, but I never expected you to try to blow up my career in addition to your own."

"She's telling you the truth," I say, digging in. I'm not about to let him intimidate me into submission. "Get the techs down here with luminol. If they find blood, you can tear up the floor and look for more evidence."

"We're not ripping up anything other than your badge. I want that on my desk by noon." Vale stomps across the carpet, leaving boot prints in his wake.

"It all looks brand new. Doesn't that bother you even a little bit?" I demand.

"He's a fucking billionaire. Everything in this house looks like he bought it yesterday. That's how people who are richer than God live. Jesus, Daisy. Get your shit together. Whatever they did to you at that clubhouse is going to ruin your life if you let it. Did they put you up to this?" He stops at the base of the staircase.

"No. They didn't have anything to do with

it."

"See, the funny thing is, I don't believe you now. You've lost all credibility. It's too bad because you were a damn good agent before you went into the field. That was my mistake. I thought you could handle it. Apparently not." His feet pound up the stairs as he heads toward the kitchen.

"You believe me, don't you?" Angie asks me as tears spill down her cheeks.

"Yes. Of course. Always. Blackstone couldn't have found out about you and fixed all of this so quickly. He must have changed everything months ago, sometime between when you were taken and now. He covered his tracks because he knew we'd come after him. He realized I'd never stop looking for you and that your trail would lead right to his door. That bastard."

"Now, what do we do?"

"I don't know."

"Can we go? I hate it down here."

"Of course."

I guide her out of the basement into the empty kitchen. Laughter echoes from the living room. When I turn the corner, I'm stunned by what I see. Vale and Blackstone are joking around and laughing like they're old pals.

"You know how kids can be," Blackstone says to him. "Little liars. They do it for the attention."

"I didn't lie!" Angie hurls herself across the

room at him, but Vale catches her around the waist and drags her away from Blackstone. She's kicking and screaming, completely losing it, but I don't blame her one bit. I'd be doing exactly the same thing if I were her.

"She was telling the truth." I narrow my gaze at Blackstone.

"You should take her to a good counselor. She's clearly mentally disturbed." His smirk churns my stomach. As soon as Vale leaves the house with Angie, Blackstone takes a step closer. "Did you actually think you'd find a dungeon in my basement?"

"It was there."

The two remaining agents in the room roll their eyes before heading for the door.

"You'd better watch your step, Agent Banner. Little girls like you shouldn't make accusations against men like me."

"Are you threatening me?" I demand. The urge to get in his face is nearly overwhelming, but my body refuses to move. It's almost as if it knows I'm facing off with pure evil.

"I'd never do something so crass."

"No. You'd just traffic and torture kids."

"Torture?" He laughs. "What on earth are you talking about?"

"I know what you did to Matrix. He told me everything, including what happened to all the other kids you tried to destroy."

Blackstone glances toward the agents, but

they're not paying any attention to him. They're halfway out the front door and aren't even looking our way. We may as well be alone.

"Tell Matrix I said hi. I do miss the little brat. Does he still like to fight back? Do you play games with whips and nipple clamps when you're together? Assuming you're fucking him, of course. He might not be into women."

"Fuck you!" I swing my fist, but he's surprisingly fast, grabbing my hand mid-air and crushing it between his fingers.

"You'd better start looking over your shoulder, little girl. If you think you can ruin my life, then you've got another thing coming. If they haven't fired you already, consider it done. I know people who can make your life a living hell. You won't even be able to get a job at a fast-food restaurant by the time I'm done ruining your reputation. And your sister? That little bitch is going to end up exactly where I want her, on her knees, begging me to stop."

"You'll never touch her ever again." I yank my fist from his grasp and step back.

"Oh, I will. And my hands will be the only ones ever to touch her young, not-so-innocent anymore, body. Her buyer wanted her intact. Otherwise, I would have had her already. But I'll get what I want, eventually. I always do."

"Banner!" Vale calls from the door. "Get your ass out here."

"Goodbye, Daisy. I hope we see each other

again. Soon." A shadow of sinister delight spreads across his face.

Icy fingers of dread slither down my spine, and my blood runs cold. This isn't the first time I've been confronted by a malicious criminal, but I've never witnessed anyone so gleefully depraved. His sadistic enjoyment of my anger and frustration is unlike anything I've ever seen. It's inhuman. Predatory to the point of being demonic. I never used to believe in Hell, but I'm starting to rethink that stance because I'm sure I just met the Devil.

I turn my back on him and try not to run toward the door. Every fiber of my being vibrates with fear, not because he threatened me. I expected that. But because he's truly evil incarnate. I can't believe Matrix and the other men from Underground Vengeance survived years with this man. I couldn't even stand to be in his presence for a few minutes. I hope I never have to see him again. If I do, it's because we're in the morgue, identifying his lifeless body.

Outside, sunlight blankets the landscape in a warm glow. Birds chirp in the trees, oblivious to the human drama playing out below. The day would be gorgeous if Blackstone hadn't ruined it with his treachery. He outsmarted us, and now, we've got no recourse but to leave empty-handed. It's a complete and total disaster.

"I'll take you back to the office." Vale yanks open the rear door of his SUV. My sister's sitting in the back seat, so I get in beside her. He slams it behind me before taking the driver's seat. "I don't want to hear one fucking word from either of you. What you did today was an absolute shit show. I'm sure you'll be hearing from Blackstone's lawyer. I wouldn't blame him if he sued you for making slanderous accusations against him."

"He's evil, and you can't even see it," I mutter.

"The man's a brilliant innovator making Montana better with his sweeping new policies. I can't believe you thought he could be a part of a child trafficking ring. He does so much for kids. He even funded the new pediatric cancer ward at the hospital. There's nothing malicious about him."

"You're so blind. That's what he wants you to think. It's his cover."

"It's a pity you're allowing yourself to be so delusional." He shakes his head and glances at me in the rearview mirror. "If you'd just stayed in the office, none of this would have happened. You'd still be digging through computers, and you'd still have a job. You're going to be the laughingstock of the agency. Your failure is the only thing anyone will talk about for months, if not years."

"You're wrong. I don't know how I'm going to prove it, but I'm going to show everyone who he really is."

"Stay away from Blackstone. You've done enough already."

"No. I won't stop until he faces justice. If you won't help me, then I know who will."

"Walk away, Daisy. If you get caught up with those bikers, they'll ruin your life even more than they already have. Find a new career, something far away from law enforcement and outlaws."

"Thanks for your oh-so-helpful advice." I break eye contact because I can't even stand to look at him anymore. He was my mentor for years, but he's completely turned his back on me. It feels like I'm living a nightmare. But it's all too real.

As soon as we get back to the FBI office, I don't even wait for the SUV to stop. I push the door open and get out with Angie right behind me.

"That asshole was your boss?" Angie tosses a look back over her shoulder.

"Yeah, but not anymore."

"I'm sorry you lost your job."

"I'm not." I open the passenger door of my compact car and motion for her to get in. "Come on."

"Where are we going?"

"I don't know yet. Anywhere but here."

Angie nods and slides into the seat. She's quiet as I drive us out of the parking lot and onto the main road. I can't imagine how devastated she must be right now. She needs time to process everything that happened today, and so do I. With that in mind, I head up the mountain toward one of our favorite hiking spots, a beautiful trail that encircles a large pond. When I need to get clear about what's going on in my head, I walk around it until I get clarity. After everything that happened at Blackstone's, I need to take a long walk through the woods.

As I navigate a curve in the road, I notice a black SUV following us. It's getting a little too close for comfort, which is super annoying. Vale probably sent an agent to follow us. He wants to find out if I'm going back to Underground Vengeance. *Asshole.*

The road straightens. I press the gas pedal to increase the distance between us and the SUV on our tail. Trying to lose the other driver on this road is pointless. It's too dangerous. It doesn't even have side rails to prevent cars from sailing over the edge, so I need to focus. I can get rid of them later when the road is less treacherous.

Going into the next twist in the road, the SUV lurches forward, slamming into the back of my car. A shockwave blasts through my body as the realization hits. The person behind us isn't with the FBI, which means Blackstone sent them. I'd bet my life on it. Whoever's back there isn't trying to follow us; they're trying to kill us.

"Hold on!" I glance at Angie to make sure she has her seatbelt on. She does.

I swerve closer to the mountain to avoid the steep drop-off on the other side of the road. My hands are slick with sweat, but I manage to keep hold of the wheel. The car skids around the turn, kicking up gravel in its wake. Taking the curve too tightly, I scrape against protruding rocks. A cacophony of screeching metal fills the air while friction slows us down.

"He's gaining on us!" Angie yells.

"Shit!"

I gun the engine as the road twists like a snake. The relentless hum of my pursuer's vehicle overpowers the sound of blood pounding through my ears. Gravel crunches beneath the tires as I fishtail around each bend. My heart races as I try to outrun the other vehicle. Every time I think I'm getting away, the guy behind us closes in again. It's almost as if he's taunting me.

I refuse to give in to despair, but I don't know how much longer I'll be able to keep this up. Each turn brings a new set of dangers, from sheer drop-offs and hidden ravines to the sharp corners that force me to slow down and take a careful line. The fear of plunging off the side of the mountain into oblivion is far greater than my anxiety about the SUV behind me. If I make it to a spot where I can turn and fight our attacker, we might have a chance. But if we fly off the mountain, then we're dead. I'm not going to let that happen.

The sound of our pursuer's engine gets even

louder. I can feel his presence behind me like a stalker. I press forward, pushing my car faster as I skid into another turn. The SUV clips my rear bumper, sending us into a half-spin. I attempt to recover, but it's impossible. I'm hurdling toward the edge of the mountain, and there's not a damn thing I can do to stop it. We're not going to make it.

Angie's scream joins mine as we plunge over the edge into the abyss. The car floats through the air, weightless for several seconds, before slamming into the ground.

Everything goes black.

CHAPTER 24: MATRIX

I've been riding my bike for hours, but the pervasive sense of dread I've had since leaving the clubhouse is still with me. Something feels wrong. It's not just the fact that Daisy left me; there's more to it. A sense of foreboding follows me through each twist and turn on the mountain road I know so well. I don't know what's happening, but I need to figure it out.

Earlier, I stopped long enough to hack into the local FBI office's computers. Normally, I steer clear of the Feds, but I wanted an update on Blackstone. Around ten last night, they got a warrant. They were planning on serving it this morning, but I haven't checked for updates. I should be elated because Blackstone can't run this time. But I'm not. It's almost as if I know it won't be this easy. I chalk it up to my anxiety. However, I can't help but wonder how things are going.

I pull off the asphalt into a dirt turnout. There's still a smattering of snow against the north-facing mountainside where the sun rarely shines. Other than that, the road is clear. It's a perfect day for riding. I wish I could enjoy it without worrying about Daisy and her sister.

After sliding my phone out of my cut, I pull up the tracer program I left behind when I hacked the Feds. It's set to notify me of any correspondence related to Blackstone. Five alerts pop up on the screen. I open the first one and almost can't believe what I'm reading. They served the warrant, but they didn't find shit.

No dungeon. No cages. Nothing.

The sick fuck must have cleared it out before the FBI arrived. Hell, he probably got rid of everything months ago. If he's back to trafficking kids, holding victims at his house would be a stupid move anyway. He'd be a fool to keep them that close. He's probably hiding them somewhere else. Or he's paying the cartel to move the kids for him. That's the most likely option.

"If Blackstone's free, where are Daisy and Angela?" I mutter as I text Talon to see if they're at the clubhouse. He responds immediately. They aren't there.

A few days ago, I put a tracker on Daisy's car. At the time, I thought I was overstepping. Now, I'm glad I went the paranoid route. After tapping through several menus, the GPS app on my phone loads, and a red dot appears on the map. I use two fingers to enhance the image, attempting to zero in on their location. What I see doesn't make any sense. The signal must be too weak or something. Her car isn't moving, and it's not even on the road. According to this, it's hanging off the side of the mountain.

I jolt as I grasp the possibility that there's not a damn thing wrong with the app. In a panic, I call Scar. "Are you at home?"

"Yeah, why?"

"I don't have time to explain everything, but I think Daisy and her sister are in trouble. Daisy's car is hanging off the side of the mountain."

"What?" The background noise on Scar's end of the line transitions from cartoons to the roar of his bike within seconds. "Where?"

"You know that hiking trail around the big pond off Old Logger Road?"

"I'm about ten minutes from there."

"The beacon is coming from a few hundred yards south, but it's off the road. I could be wrong, and they could just be broken down—"

"I'll call when I get there."

"See you in fifteen." I end the call and shove the phone into my cut.

My heart thunders as I hop back on the bike. Driving like a pack of wild dogs is snapping at my heels, I race up the mountain. My phone vibrates against my chest. It's the signal Scar sends to get everyone's attention. I'm sure he's rounding up the crew to look for Daisy and Angela. Thank God he's got my back. I can always count on my brothers to come through for me.

By the time I reach Scar, he's standing on the side of the road, looking over the edge. My stomach plummets through my feet. I get off my bike and run across the road to join him.

"They're down there." Scar points to Daisy's crumpled car. It's half-buried in a ravine and covered with mud and debris. The driver's side door hangs open. Two figures sit inside, but neither moves.

"We need to get down there," I say.

"Wait! Talon's bringing the truck with the winch. ETA is five minutes."

"If they're injured, we don't have time to wait. It could mean the difference between life and death."

"Okay, but I don't have any rope with me. I could run home."

"Talon will be here before you get back. I'll climb down."

"No. It's too dangerous."

"I don't give a fuck. I need to know if they're still alive." My voice cracks.

"Be careful," Scar says, knowing he can't stop me.

I have no idea how long they've been there or how they ended up in such a precarious situation, but it doesn't matter. I've got to help them.

Sitting on the edge of the precipice, I reach down until one of my boots finds a thick tree root projecting out from the mountainside. I use it as my first foothold before finding another. Gripping the wall of dirt and rock, I carefully inch my way lower. The car is about one hundred feet below me, but it feels like a million. By the time I reach them, my arms ache, and sweat coats my brow. I drop the final ten feet and roll as I hit the ground.

"Daisy!"

I jump up and run to the driver's side. She's slumped over the steering wheel, with blood seeping from a wound on her forehead. She's covered in the broken safety glass from the shattered windshield. As I move to check for a pulse, she groans, and relief floods me.

"Daisy, don't move, babe. You were in an accident. I need to make sure it's safe before we try to get you out." I haven't had first aid training, but I know enough not to move someone who might have a spinal injury.

"Talon's here!" Scar yells.

"We're coming down. Watch out for the winch." Talon drops it over the edge and slowly lowers it until it reaches the ravine.

Reaper appears beside him. He goes first, gripping the cable with thick work gloves. He wraps his legs around the cable before sliding down it like a firefighter.

While I'm waiting, Angela regains consciousness. Her face twists with fear as she tries desperately to free herself from the seatbelt, which is tangled in the wreckage. "I can't get out."

"Hang on. I'm coming." I circle the car and try to open her door. That entire side of the car is a twisted mess, so the door's wedged shut. I can't get it to budge.

"Let me try." Reaper gives it a valiant effort before giving up.

"Can you move your hands and legs all right? Does anything hurt? Are you in any pain?" I ask her.

"No. I just want to get out." Angie's wide, terrified eyes meet mine.

"Okay, if you can, try crawling over the dashboard through the window. Watch out for the glass."

"Wait." Reaper pulls his jacket off and lays it over the threshold, covering any remaining jagged pieces.

After successfully crawling out of the wreckage, she falls onto the ground, her body limp with relief. Talon lifts her into his arms and carries her toward the winch. I don't know how he's going to get her back up to Scar, but I'm sure they've got a plan.

I quickly turn to Daisy. Tears fill her eyes as she struggles to get free.

"Can you feel your fingers and toes?" I ask.

"I think so."

"We can't move you if you're not sure. I can call a medevac to get you out of here."

"No. I think I can walk. I'm just ... I can't believe we're alive," she sobs.

"You are. Babe, I love you. We'll get through this. Okay?"

"All right." She nods and lifts one shaky hand to wipe away her tears.

Her door's hanging open, but the dashboard is cracked and smashed inward. As she drags her legs out from underneath it, I help her. Fortunately, she wasn't pinned in place during the accident.

She manages to swing her feet to the ground, but as soon as she tries to stand, she collapses into my arms. I scoop her up and turn toward the others. Reaper's rigging up a basket big enough for a single person. He finishes hooking it to the winch line before lifting Angela into it.

"Hang on tight. Don't lean or move," he warns her.

"Okay."

It takes an eternity before Scar's able to pull her to safety. He sends the basket back for Daisy. As we wait, I hold her tightly against my chest. When the basket arrives, I hate letting her go, but there's only one way out. After getting her settled, I give the signal to Scar. He begins to retract the line. I can't take my eyes off the basket until she's free of it.

"You're next," Reaper says.

"Thanks, man."

"If that were my woman, I would have climbed the wall already."

"I thought about it but didn't want to distract Daisy."

He grunts an acknowledgment.

Once we're all topside, I lean to glance over the edge. It's a miracle they survived. People die on this road every year. Rusting metal remnants of destroyed vehicles aren't an unusual sight around here. Her car isn't going anywhere. It will remain in its final resting place and corrode, just like all the others. But unlike most of the drivers, Daisy's still alive. I still can't believe it.

"Talon, can you ride my bike back? I'll drive the girls."

"You got it."

"We'll head to the clubhouse," I say.

"My place is closer. We could meet up there," Scar suggests.

"Yeah, but you don't have enough extra beds."

"True. The clubhouse works. I'll let Nina know we're headed back."

"Is she there already?"

"Never left. She spent the night because she was worried about you."

"About me?" I frown.

"She wasn't the only one." Scar gives me a pointed look.

"Have her call Doc. The girls need to be examined ASAP."

"Done and done."

Daisy's already sitting in the front seat of the truck, while Angela's in the back. They both look dazed and exhausted. I wonder if they got any sleep last night. Based on what I saw earlier, the raid occurred early this morning. I'm dying to ask them about it, but it isn't the right time. I need to wait until after Doc assesses their injuries. That's our top priority right now. News about Blackstone will have to wait.

When we arrive at the clubhouse, Nina runs down the front porch. "How are they?"

"Lots of bumps and bruises. Daisy's got one hell of a gash on her head, but it stopped bleeding." I get out of the truck to help the girls climb the steps.

"Come lay down," Nina says. "You can both fit on Matrix's bed. Doc's on his way. He should be here soon."

After the girls are settled inside, Nina grabs washcloths and ointment for their cuts. While she tends to Angela, I help clean Daisy's head wound.

Doc strolls in about ten minutes later. His face is grim, and he's carrying his medical bag with him. "Everybody out except for the patients."

"I'm staying," I say firmly.

"Let him work." Nina gently grips my arm and pulls me toward the door.

"Okay, but we'll be right down the hall if you

need anything," I tell Doc.

"Sit down before you fall down," he calls as Nina and I leave.

"He's right," she says.

We walk into the living room, where I collapse on the couch and lean forward with my elbows on my knees and my face in my hands. "This is all my fault. I should have insisted on going with them."

"Stop. Even if you'd wanted to go and Daisy had been foolish enough to let you, those Feds wouldn't have allowed you within a mile of Blackstone. Your presence wouldn't have changed anything. It probably would have made things worse."

"He's still free, Nina." I raise my face to meet her shocked gaze.

"No."

"I don't know what happened, but he wasn't arrested. As far as I know, he's still walking around, free as a bird."

"What the fuck?"

"That's what I want to know."

"Did Daisy say anything?" Nina asks.

"No, and I didn't attempt to ask her either. She was too dazed after being pulled from the wreckage."

"Was it an accident, or did someone run her off the road?"

"I don't know. Shit, I have no fucking idea what happened."

"Take a breath while I make tea. You haven't slept either. I can see it in your face. Chill out while Doc does his thing."

"Forget tea. I need a beer."

"Okay." She smiles before retrieving one from the fridge and handing it to me. "Just one, though. You'll need your wits about you when they're ready to talk."

"Sure."

I down the beer in several huge gulps. Setting it aside, I lean back and close my eyes. They're grainier than sandpaper and just as dry. Nina's right. I'm dead on my feet and need to rest. Unfortunately, there's no time for that.

Doc appears a while later and sits on the couch beside me while Nina pulls over a chair for herself.

"Well?" I ask. "How are they?"

"Good, overall. Daisy's got a slight concussion, but she should be okay in a few days. Keep an eye on her. She needs a lot of rest, preferably in a quiet, dark room. Don't stress her out. Now's not the time. Gently massaging her neck and shoulders would be helpful but not necessary. Absolutely no alcohol. I gave her some medication, but she shouldn't take anything else."

"What about Angela?" Nina asks.

"She's going to be fine. Lots of scrapes and bruises, but she's in better shape than her sister. Angela hit her head, but she doesn't have any concussion symptoms. Watch her, too, in case anything changes, but her condition isn't very concerning."

"Thank you." I shake Doc's hand.

"I'll swing by tomorrow to check on them. I'm assuming you're not moving them to another location right away."

"No." I don't tell him this, but if it were up to me, I'd never let either of them leave. They're safer here with us than they are out in the world. I wish Daisy had understood that before she left me.

"If anything comes up tonight, don't hesitate to call me." Doc lets himself out.

"Let's see how they're doing," Nina says.

When we walk into my room, Daisy cracks one eye open to look at us. "Ouch."

"Your head?" I ask.

"Yeah."

"Doc says you need to get some rest. I'll be in to check on you every few hours."

"Matrix, we failed." Daisy closes her eyes.

"Babe, I don't need to know the details until later. You didn't do a damn thing wrong. Blackstone's a piece of shit, and honestly, I'm not surprised he managed to get away with shit once again. I just need you to answer one question for me."

"What's that?" Daisy asks in a sleepy voice.

"When you went off the road, was that because you lost control, or did someone attack you?"

"A black SUV ran us off the road."

"Son of a bitch."

"Blackstone's behind it. I'm sure he is. I met him. He's evil. Worse than I ever imagined."

"I know, babe." I lean to kiss her brow, carefully avoiding the bandage Doc put over the gash on her forehead.

"I'm so sorry."

"You've never done anything wrong. Behind his fake smiles and expensive suits, Blackstone's a monster. We've tried to get him for years. Now you know why we haven't been successful."

"I had so much hope."

"Don't let him take that away from you. Despite everything, I haven't lost faith in our ability to make things right. We will get him. It's only a matter of time before it happens."

"I shouldn't have left you. I love you."

"Me too, babe." I kiss her softly on the lips. "Sleep. We'll talk tomorrow."

I stay by her side until she dozes off. I glance over and realize Angela's still watching me. She overheard everything I said to her sister.

"She's kinda dumb sometimes," she whispers.

"That's not a very nice thing to say."

"Well, it's true. I told her we'd be safer here, but no. She didn't come back to the clubhouse like we should have."

"I'm sure she had her reasons for making

the choices she made."

"I guess."

"You need to rest too. Did you get any sleep last night?" I ask.

"Not really."

"Go ahead. I'll be outside with the other guys. If you want anything or if Daisy wakes up, come get me. Okay?"

"Thanks."

I reluctantly leave the room and join Nina at the kitchen table. Reaper, Scar, and Talon are there too. Nitro must still be at home with his wife. They've been having a heck of a time with their colicky baby, so I don't fault him for not making it. Family always comes first.

"Did Daisy tell you what happened with Blackstone?" Nina asks.

"Not yet. Just that he's still free."

Reaper's shoulders slump, and he shakes his head.

"Don't worry. We'll get that bastard. I know we will," I say confidently.

"How? He keeps slipping through our fingers," Talon says.

"Who the hell knows? But it's going to happen."

Everyone's silent, lost in their thoughts. Since the girls are using my bed, I head into Daisy's old room. So much has gone down since she became one of our club girls. She might still want to leave me, but that's not going to happen.

I love her stubborn ass. Even if it takes me an eternity to do it, I'm going to show her how much she means to me.

In a way, she brought me back to life. I don't have any desire to cut myself anymore. Disappearing into that other, floaty world doesn't hold the same allure. I want to be right here, in the now, with her. I've got to find a way to make her see that no matter what happens with Blackstone, it won't affect our love for each other. He's irrelevant now. I'm still going to help the guys bring him to justice, but Daisy's more important than revenge. She's everything to me. She's what I've been waiting for my whole life, and I want to make her my old lady ... if she'll have me.

CHAPTER 25: DAISY

It's been three days since the accident. I can finally walk without feeling like I've got an icepick stabbing me through the eye. Doc has been back to check on me daily. He's happy with my recovery and assures me everything I'm experiencing is normal. On the other hand, Matrix has been so worried that he's constantly catering to me. He's being so sweet, but it's starting to drive me crazy. I haven't eaten a meal out of bed since returning to the clubhouse. I've been stuck in this room so long that I'm getting cabin fever.

Risking Matrix's wrath, I slide out of bed and get dressed in a flowy pair of cotton pajamas. Angie hasn't been confined to the room because she never had a concussion. She's in the kitchen, eating lunch with the others. I want to be with everyone else too. If Matrix has a problem with it, then too bad. I'm not staying in bed like an invalid for one more minute.

As I pad out of the hallway into the kitchen,

everyone stops talking and watches me take my usual seat at the table. I reach toward a huge tray of loaded open-faced sandwiches and choose one with cream cheese, cucumber, and dill. My second selection includes egg salad with sliced radishes. I drop them onto my plate. Matrix, Angie, Nina, Reaper, Talon, Nitro, and Scar watch every move I make.

"Babe," Matrix says slowly. "Why are you out of bed?"

"Because it's driving me nuts. I feel much better, and I'm sick of being stuck in there."

"I could join you."

"You'd just fawn all over me."

"I wouldn't complain about that," Nina says, laughing. "Let your man spoil you."

"Yeah, babe."

"Please stop. Guys, I know you mean well, but I'm going nuts. All I do is lay around thinking. There aren't any distractions to keep my brain occupied, so it ends up going down a very dark path. I can't stand the thought of Blackstone being out there. He's free to terrorize anyone who stands in his way, and we can't do a damn thing to stop him."

"Get used to it," Reaper grumbles.

"No. I want him dead. He tried to kill Angie and me." I push one of the slices around my plate, but I'm not actually hungry. I just didn't want to be alone with my thoughts anymore.

"We'll get him," Nitro says.

"You know what I realized?" I ask.

"What?" Talon focuses his attention on me.

"Blackstone won't ever be brought to justice through the legal system. It's too corrupt. Even though he couldn't possibly have remodeled the basement in a few hours, someone could have warned him months ago. A lot of people within the FBI knew I was undercover with you. They probably realized it was only a matter of time before I discovered Blackstone's connection to my sister's kidnapping."

"Exactly." Matrix nods in agreement.

"Then how do we do it? How can we finally get him?" I ask.

"We're still trying to figure that out. Nothing we've tried so far has worked, but we'll keep at it until he's either in prison or dead. Trust me, babe. We haven't given up. That's not even an option."

"I want to watch him die." I glance at Angie. She tilts her head slightly, watching me with a curious gaze, but she doesn't say anything.

"You and me both, sister." Talon reaches over the table to give me a high-five. I slap his hand.

"Same," Reaper says.

"I think we're all in agreement on that," Scar says.

"I'd rather we didn't discuss that monster while we're eating," Nina says before turning to me. "Aren't your parents supposed to be here soon? They're coming today, right?"

"Anytime now."

"Do you still think it's safe for Angie to go back to their house?" Talon asks.

"I called some guys I know in Billings. They're going to keep an eye out for Angie and her parents until we deal with Blackstone for good." Scar gives me a nod.

"Thank you. It means so much to me that you care about her enough to put your neck out like that," I say.

"Not a problem. If those guys called us for help, we'd ride out to assist with anything they needed done. That's what clubs do. We're one big family." Scar smiles.

"Well, I appreciate it."

The doorbell rings. Nina goes to answer it. When she returns, my parents are trailing behind her.

"Mom!" I get up slower than I'd like to but manage to stand without inducing another headache. Wrapping my arms around her, I cling to her. I've missed her so much. Since I've been undercover, I haven't been able to call her every week like I used to.

"Hey, pumpkin." Dad joins the hug. "And where's my littlest girl?"

"Here, Dad!" Angie merges into the family gathering, clinging to us.

"Which one of you is Scar?" Dad asks as he untangles himself from the group.

"Me, sir." Scar stands to shake Dad's hand.

"Thank you for protecting my girls." He turns to Matrix. "You'll take good care of Daisy, won't you?"

"Of course. In fact, there's something I'd like to speak with you about privately." Matrix motions for him to go out onto the patio with him. They leave the rest of us in the kitchen, and I watch them through the window. They're standing at the rail, looking out over the river. Their mouths are moving, but the glass is soundproof, so I can't hear a word.

"What's Matrix up to?" I ask, not speaking to anyone in particular.

"Probably asking your dad if it's okay to propose," Mom teases.

"No way."

"And if he asked you to marry him, would you say yes?" Mom arches a brow.

"Um ... have you had lunch yet?"

"Just like my daughter to avoid answering a question by asking a new one. We stopped and had lunch on the way. Angie, finish your meal, please. We'd like to get back on the road before the rain starts."

"I'm ready." Angie clears her dishes, rinsing them in the sink before loading them into the dishwasher.

"Wow! These boys taught you a thing or two while you were here." Mom grins.

"It was Nina." Angie runs to her and wraps

her arms around Nina's waist. "I'll call you when we get home."

"You'd better." Nina pulls a bedazzled, sparkling pink phone from the back pocket of her tight jeans. "I would have wrapped it, but I didn't have time."

"A new phone!" Angie grabs it. "This is awesome! You're the best."

"Who doesn't like presents?" Nina asks, laughing.

"Thank you for everything." Mom embraces Nina. "I'd love to talk too if you ever have the time."

"You're family now. I'll always have time for you."

Dad and Matrix stroll back in from outside. They're both wearing huge, conspiratorial grins. They're definitely up to something.

"What's going on?" I ask.

"We were just talking about your career," Dad says.

"What career? You realize I was fired, right? I told you on the phone. As soon as I get a chance, I'm burning my old badge in the firepit."

"I don't blame you one bit. They treated you like trash. Assholes," Mom mutters.

"Bureaucracy at its finest," Reaper says.

"We'll figure out a job for you later. Right now, all you need to do is rest," Matrix says.

"Exactly." Nina smiles at him.

Dad slowly looks around the room before

clearing his throat. "Before we go, I want to let you all know how much I appreciate this club. You guys helped get my youngest back, and in a weird, roundabout way, you saved Daisy too. She doesn't know it yet, but leaving the FBI will be one of the best things that ever happened to her."

"Why would you say that?" I ask.

"Because you're smarter than anyone I know. They weren't making good use of your talent and computer skills. I know you tried to bring Blackstone to justice legally, but now, it's time to take another approach."

"Dad, you've never believed in vigilante justice before—why now?"

"Because that piece of shit hurt my daughters." Dad's jaw goes rigid.

"But the club saved them. We'll be indebted to you forever for that," Mom says.

"If you want to join these guys, your mother and I will support your choice. I never thought I'd say it, but this group of men has shown their loyalty to you in a way the FBI never did. You know the world's messed up when the law is corrupt and motorcycle gangs are the ones actually bringing people to justice."

"Uh, we're not a gang," Talon says. "We're a club."

"Whatever." Dad shakes his head because he doesn't care about semantics. "We love you all, and we'll never forget what you did for our girls. If you need anything, we'll do what we can to help you."

"Thank you, sir." Matrix shakes Dad's hand again.

"I told you, you can call me Dad. Only if you want to, of course."

"Okay, Dad." The smile on Matrix's face is so innocent and sincere that my heart melts. I know Matrix has never had a father before, but this is super weird. What exactly did they talk about outside? I'm dying to ask, but I'll have to wait until my family's gone.

"You'll visit us soon, right?" Angie asks me.

"Of course." I give her a big hug. "Call me anytime. I'll always be here for you."

"When I get older, I want a boyfriend just like Matrix," she whispers in my ear.

"Oh, boy." I laugh because I don't know if we can handle having two bikers in our family. That said, when she gets old enough, I'll support whatever choice she makes. If I don't like the guy, I'll just send Matrix to deal with him.

Wait? *Send Matrix?* Angie won't be ready to date for at least four or five more years. Ten, if we leave it up to Dad. Will I still be with Matrix in five years? What about ten? Will I even be with him tomorrow? We haven't talked about our relationship since I returned to the clubhouse. I'm still not feeling very good physically, so we decided I'd stay here until I was back to normal. But my recovery shouldn't take more than a couple of weeks. After that, what comes next?

"We should hit the road," Dad says.

It takes a while for everyone to say their goodbyes. Hugs and handshakes abound until, eventually, my parents and sister leave. The rest of the club members, including Nina, return to their seats at the kitchen table. As they dig back into lunch, I glance at Matrix, who's still standing by the front door.

"Want to go outside for a bit?" he asks.

"O-kay." He's up to something, but I have no idea what. I follow him outside.

After we get situated in the Adirondack chairs on the patio overlooking the river, he reaches for my hand. Together, we sit in silence, watching the water flow past. I've always loved it out here. Watching the water flow has a way of carrying your worries away with it. Whenever I felt troubled in the past, I'd come outside and let the river work its magic. I don't know what he wants to tell me, but as long as we're here, everything will end up fine.

"We've been through a lot of shit," he says, finally breaking the silence.

"Yeah, but we made it."

"We did."

"Okay, out with it. What did you and my dad talk about?" I swing my legs to the side and sit up to face him.

"I told him you're the best thing that's ever happened to me." Matrix repositions himself, so he's sitting across from me. He grasps both of my hands in his. "I love you, Daisy. When I first realized what was happening, I hated it. I tried not to notice you, but you were always around, looking so fucking hot that I'd have a constant hard-on. Blue balls for days."

Tossing my head back, I laugh while he grimaces.

"Not funny, babe."

"I'm sorry. When I moved in, you were so mean to me. I had no idea you wanted me. If anything, I thought you didn't want me around."

"You were right about that. I tried to get Scar to get rid of you, but he refused. You made me feel so many different emotions. Shit I'd never experienced before. Feeling all that stuff is hard for me, and you whipped me into a frenzy. I didn't want to acknowledge my attraction to you to anyone, not even myself. But eventually, I couldn't deny it anymore. You forced me to feel everything."

"Your heart opened up."

"You basically tore a gaping hole through it."

"Sorry?" I grin sheepishly.

"Having you in the house, constantly shaking that tight little ass of yours, almost drove me fucking crazy. I wanted you like I've never wanted anyone else. I still do. If Doc hadn't threatened to cut off my nuts, I would have joined you in bed the first night you were back."

"Even with my sister in there too?"

"I would have moved her to your old room."

"Good thing you didn't. I'd have been mad as hell."

"Between you and Doc, I couldn't do anything about how much I wanted to be with you." His light gray eyes meet my gaze, and everything inside me softens. He glances away before looking back at me. "I want to ask you something."

"Oh, I don't know …" My heart thumps wildly in my chest because I know where he's going with this. Why else would he pull my father aside to talk to him?

"Daisy, I'm sure you never pictured having this kind of life. You were married to the FBI and thought justice would always prevail."

"But then Blackstone kidnapped my sister."

"And he showed you what the world is really like. Law enforcement can only go so far. I'm sure you thought people outside the law were terrible human beings, but then you met us."

"Underground Vengeance," I whisper.

"Right."

"And now I know how things actually work, especially for the rich and powerful."

"Which is why we strive to help those who don't have the means to live as if the law doesn't apply to them. That's our entire mission, and it will never change."

"I realize that now."

"Knowing that and understanding that

we'll never drag someone like Blackstone through the legal system, could you still see yourself with a man like me?"

"I could," I murmur.

"Are you sure?"

"Matrix, I also didn't want to fall for you, but there's something undeniable between us. No matter how much I wanted to ignore it, I couldn't. When you finally took me to bed, I thought I would die from all the pleasure you gave me. But it wasn't just the sex."

"No?" He grins.

"Hardly." I laugh. "It was your heart, how you opened up to me about what Blackstone did to you."

"I've never told anyone else. Even Scar and the others don't know everything."

"Your secrets will always be locked up right here." I place my hand over my heart. "They're the most precious thing you've ever given me. That and your love."

"I do love you, Daisy. And I know this might seem old-fashioned, but I believe in family, especially when they're clearly good people. So, I wanted to do this the right way." He slides off the chair and onto one knee. Pulling a small box out of his back pocket, he pops it open.

A glittering, cushion-cut diamond sparkles in the afternoon sun. It's the most beautiful piece of jewelry I've ever seen, with its intricate white gold setting. I hesitate, almost fearful of touching something so beautiful. I almost can't believe it's real. The ring looks like something out of a fairytale.

As I extend my trembling hand, I felt an unexpected surge of emotion. This isn't just about the ring. He's handing me a precious gift, a symbol of his love. My life is about to change forever.

"It's gorgeous," I whisper.

"Babe, you already know what's coming, but before we get to that, I need to tell you something first. I lied to you once. When I told you I couldn't give you hearts and rainbows, I wasn't telling the truth. I want to give you *everything* your heart desires. You're the sunshine to my rain, the light to my darkness. You're the reason I want to live again. When I tried to end my life with that knife, you know what my last thought was?"

"No." My lips tremble.

"It was you. Somehow, I knew you'd be disappointed in me. Until then, you didn't know about the cutting. I never wanted you to realize how messed up I was inside. When Scar let you visit me in the hospital, I wanted to kill him. You shouldn't have had to see me like that, so broken."

"I love every part of you, even the things you want to hide. In time, I hope you'll tell me more about your past. It will help me understand you in a deeper way. And you know I'll never judge you. None of it was your fault."

"You're right, babe. It wasn't. And you helped me accept that."

"Oh, honey." I lean in for a kiss, but the ring box gets in the way. "Oh!"

"Daisy, will you marry me so I can put this ring on your finger and get this box the fuck out of my way?" His voice is serious, but the lines around his mouth and eyes reveal a playful undertone.

"Yes, and yes! I'll marry you."

"That makes you my old lady now."

"What privileges do I get for letting you call me 'old'?" I ask as he slides the ring onto my finger.

"It's a term of endearment, babe." He tosses the empty box onto the chair.

"I know, but 'old', really?"

"Shut up and kiss me."

Without hesitation, I throw my arms around his neck, kissing him deeply. The familiar warmth of his body pressing against mine makes me want so much more from him. As Matrix's strong arms wrap around me, I get lost in the moment. I can't believe I ever doubted our love. I was such a fool.

As we break for air, I look deep into Matrix's eyes. My heart is so full of love and gratitude I'm afraid it will burst.

"Take me to bed, old man."

"Woman! That's not how that works." He scoops me into his arms and carries me toward the door.

"Wait a minute, so you get to call me 'old', but I don't get to return the favor? Who the hell made these rules?"

"Probably Winchester, but who knows?" He chuckles.

"Men." I cluck my tongue.

"I can't wait to make you wrap that around my cock."

"Matrix!"

"Not today, though. This afternoon will be all about you. When you're better, I'll make you ride it, slide it, suck it, bite it …" He breaks into song.

"You're crazy."

"Only for you, babe."

As he carries me through the living room and past the kitchen, I hold out my hand to show off my new ring. The other club members clap and whoop while Nina grins like a proud momma.

"Congrats on the engagement, but keep it the fuck down," Talon yells.

"They won't," Reaper says with a smirk.

"I'm going home to my wife," Scar says.

"Me too," Nitro adds.

"Byeeee," I call over my shoulder as Matrix carries me to bed.

True to his word, he spends the rest of the day—and half the night—making me the happiest woman in the world. When I first moved into the clubhouse, I didn't know what to expect. I never imagined I'd end up in the arms of an outlaw biker, but this is exactly where I belong. Despite all the upheaval, I've finally found the love of a lifetime.

I have no idea what the future will hold in terms of my career, but as long as I get to spend forever with Matrix, it doesn't matter. I'll figure it out later. Right now, the only thing I care about is making love to the man of my most wickedly sexy dreams.

CHAPTER 26: MATRIX

Waking up on my wedding day is easily the most nerve-wracking thing I've ever done. Sure, I survived Blackstone's dungeon, shootouts with human traffickers, and run-ins with violent cartels, but none of that can compare to the anxiety I feel today. I'm not afraid of marrying Daisy. I love her more than anything in the world. My fear has to do with making sure today is perfect for her. I want her to enjoy the most romantic, perfect wedding day ever.

Scar walks into my bedroom, holding two beers. "Thought you might want a drink before you walk down the aisle."

"Do I really look that freaked out?"

"Ha!" He hands me a beer before clinking his bottle against mine. "I remember the day I married Julia like it was yesterday. Almost crapped myself waiting for her to walk toward me. I'm telling you, there's nothing like watching the woman of your dreams choose you for life. It's a high you'll never forget."

"How's the weather outside? I haven't even looked outside yet."

"It's a perfect summer day. I'm so glad she didn't want to wait to get married. Winter's fun for a lot of things, but not weddings."

"Daisy always wanted a backyard wedding. I'm glad she wanted to do it at the clubhouse. How's the yard looking?"

"Talon cut the grass before he went to bed last night. The catering company showed up with tables and chairs this morning. The tent's up, and everyone's waiting."

"What about Daisy? Is she here yet, or is she still with Nina and the girls?"

"They're all here. Daisy and Nina are in a room in the back. They don't want you to accidentally see her before the wedding. Bad luck or some shit."

"Nothing's going to ruin today. I can wait another few minutes to see her."

"Good. Let's get out there and get this done so we can party. I'll let everyone know you'll be out in a few minutes."

"Does the monkey suit look okay?" I gesture at the slate gray suit I'm wearing. I couldn't decide how formal I wanted to go, but after discussing it with Daisy, she suggested a light suit. That way, I'd look fancy enough for a wedding without it being too stuffy. She promised I could take the jacket off as soon as we finished our vows.

"You look like a million bucks."

"Thanks, pres."

The door opens, and Reaper lumbers in. "Hey."

"Hey, man." I give him a bro-hug and slap him on the back.

"You ready to go? This shit's itchy." Reaper scratches at his starched collar.

The one thing Daisy insisted on was that everyone should look good for the photos. Once the party starts, she said we could strip down as much as we want. She might regret not being more specific about exactly how naked everyone can get.

"Almost," I say.

"Hey, I almost forgot to tell you. That contract out on Daisy was canceled."

"Are you sure?"

"Yeah. I had a little chat with a guy from the Demon Riders last night. She's free and clear."

"Did he say who issued the contract?" I ask.

"Nah, but my money's on Blackstone."

"Why would he cancel it after what she did at his house?"

"Probably to get the heat off him. If the Feds caught wind that he's got a contract out on her, they'd want to know why. It's better for Blackstone if he backs off right now."

"That's good to hear, but I don't trust that fucker one bit."

"Me either. Anyway, talking about that guy

makes me want to break shit, and I don't want to fuck up your wedding."

"I hear you on that."

"I'm going to wait in the living room," Reaper says.

"Same." Scar follows him, passing Talon, who is on his way in.

"Bro!" Talon gives me a bear hug. "You ready to get hitched?"

"Damn right, I am."

"Fuck yeah."

"Hey, I heard you've been talking to Vapor from the NOLA chapter. How are they all doing?"

"Great. The guys that were injured during the cartel attack are all back on their feet. He invited me to visit."

"Are you going?" I ask.

"Thinking about it. Did you ever investigate that last lead you had on the people who might be my biological parents?"

"I did, but it wasn't them. I'm still looking."

"Thanks." He smiles, but his shoulders hunch inward.

"Don't give up. We'll find them."

"If they're still alive."

"It's possible you won't like what we discover. Are you sure you want to keep looking?"

"I have to know if they're out there. Even if I find out that they're dead, at least I'll know."

"I've got feelers out to various people on the

dark web. If anyone gives me anything concrete, you'll be the first to know."

"Thanks, brother." Talon's smile returns. "Let's get you out there. I saw Daisy earlier. Smokin' hot."

"Hey, don't even think about checking out my woman again." I playfully punch his arm.

"Wouldn't dream of it. She's all yours."

"You'll find one of your own too."

"Maybe." He chuckles. "Until then, there's pussy for days out there. I don't know who the hell brought all those hot women, but I know I'm not going to be alone tonight."

"Keep it in your pants until after the wedding's over. Okay?"

"Whatever you want, bro."

"I'm ready. Let's do this."

"Hell yeah!" Talon high-fives me.

When we get to the living room, we find Nitro pacing around while rocking Robert in his arms. As soon as he spots us, Robert starts screaming. The kid's got a pair of lungs on him.

"Guys, I'm so sorry. Robert's got colic again. I don't think I'm going to be able to stand up for you."

Tucker, the guy who has been prospecting for us for a year, stands up from the couch. "Want me to take him? I could watch him until the ceremony's over."

"It's not going to be easy," Nitro says.

"How hard can it be? Besides, I've got

earplugs to drown out the crying. I'll be fine."

"The ceremony won't take longer than maybe thirty minutes, max," I say. "We wrote our own vows."

"Sweet. I've got this," Tucker says confidently.

"Okay, but if you need me, come get me." Nitro hands the baby to Tucker. The minute the kid settles into his arms, he goes quiet. "What the fuck?"

"Oh, shit. He's got baby skills too. Somebody patch his ass in," Scar jokes.

"When are we voting on him?" Reaper asks.

"No business talk today," Scar admonishes. "We're here for Matrix and Daisy. Everything else can wait until next week."

"Sounds good, pres." Tucker sits on the couch with Robert. The baby still hasn't made a peep. That's amazing. The prospect really does have a way with kids.

Nina pokes her head out from the hall. "Guys, Daisy says if you don't move your asses, she's going to make me untie the corset and let it out. She'll regret that. She really doesn't want a baby bump in her pics."

"Then she shouldnt' have let Matrix knock her ass up before the wedding," Talon says teasingly.

"She didn't even know she was pregnant until we'd already booked the wedding planners. The show must go on." I grin. "But yeah, let's go. I don't want my wife to be mad at me *during* the wedding. That wouldn't be the best start to a marriage."

"No, it wouldn't." Nina smirks.

"Two minutes." I hold up two fingers. "Then they should start the wedding march song. I just need to haul ass to the front of the aisle."

"Sounds like a plan," Nina says before vanishing down the hall.

"Let's go," Scar says.

As rehearsed, I lead the way.

Outside, the sun's shining down from an endless expanse of deep blue sky. Fluffy white clouds float by on a gentle breeze. The freshly cut grass in the garden is a vibrant shade of green. It starkly contrasts with the huge white tent filled with guests. Laughter and chatter come to a halt as people realize I'm walking toward them. My heart pounds against my ribs, but I can't stop grinning. I'm about to marry the most stunning woman in the world before our friends and family. It's going to be perfect.

I make it to the front of the aisle without tripping over my feet. The other guys from the club link arms with their assigned bridesmaids. Scar and Julia start the procession, followed by Nitro and Holly. Talon accompanies one of Daisy's best friends, while Reaper escorts another woman Daisy has known for years.

When the music for the wedding march begins, I remind myself not to lock my knees. I read a huge list of shit not to do on your wedding day. Passing out made the top of the list. When I first read it, I wanted to know what kind of pussy passes out at their own wedding. Now, I get it. This shit is stressful—in a good way. I certainly don't want to faint like a little bitch and fuck this up for Daisy.

A smile spreads across my face as I anticipate the arrival of my bride. When she steps into view, she takes my breath away. She's positively ravishing in her strapless white gown. It's very tight on top, showing off her best asset before tapering to her tiny waist. I don't see any baby bump. I don't know why she's so paranoid about it anyway, but whatever. Women are very picky about stuff like this. Although I can't understand it, if Daisy wants to hide the pregnancy, so be it. Everyone's going to do the math anyway after she has the kid. They'll know. But if she wants perfect, baby-bump-less pics of our wedding, then she'll get them. Whatever she wants, I'm going to give it to her.

Her long, brown hair is tied with two white ribbons. Seeing those ribbons gets me so fucking hard. I'm sure the bulge in my pants will end up in the pics. I can't wait to tear that dress off her and take her to bed. *Down, boy!*

"You're drooling," Talon whispers under his breath. The other guys try not to laugh while the girls skewer them with death glares. Fortunately, no one's looking at us. All eyes are on my woman.

Walking down the aisle in front of her, Angie tosses red rose petals along the walkway. She's a vision of innocence and purity in her pink flower girl dress. Her blonde hair is tied up in a neat bun. She gives me a shy smile as she walks in front of her sister. I smile back. She's still dealing with a lot of anxiety because of what happened to her, but her parents found a good therapist. Angie sees her twice a week, and she's already doing a lot better than she was after we rescued her.

As Angie steps out of the way, Daisy reaches the front of the aisle. I hold out my hand to her, and she takes it and steps up onto the platform. Doc got his minister's license so he could marry us. He's officiating the wedding, but I don't even hear a word of it. I can't stop staring at my soon-to-be wife.

My heart feels like it's going to burst. Daisy's eyes twinkle as she gazes into mine. It's as if she has a special secret just for me. I can't wait to find out what she's thinking.

Doc finishes talking about the power of our love and the promises we will make to one another, then he turns to me. "Matrix, please share your vows with Daisy."

"Today, I stand before you, before God, our family, and friends; and with all the love in my heart, I make a solemn vow that I will love you for the rest of our lives. Your presence in my life is a gift, and I'm so grateful for it. Your beauty radiates from within, and it touches my soul. You are my sunshine, my comfort and refuge, and my soft place to land. I feel blessed beyond measure that you have chosen me and that I get to spend the rest of my life with you.

"From this day forward, I vow to be your best friend and confidante. I promise to cherish and honor you, to be faithful and loyal, to never take you for granted, and to never stop taking you out on long rides through the mountains."

I pause as the guests chuckle.

"I pledge to love you through any challenge we face. You were there for me in my darkest times, and you never turned your back on me. I'll never stop loving you, and I'll strive to be the husband you deserve."

I wait for a beat before continuing. Daisy and I debated this next part, but ultimately, she decided it would be good to include it.

"I also vow to be your partner in parenting. I'll be the best father I can be to our children, loving them and protecting them, teaching them and encouraging them, and always being their rock and safe haven. I will be there for them in all of life's adventures, and together with you, we will raise them to be compassionate and kind, courageous and wise. I love you, Daisy. Now and forever."

A wave of emotion washes over me. Having a family and children always seemed like an impossible dream, but now, I'm living a miracle.

I can't believe how lucky I am, and it's all because of her.

"Daisy, please share your vows with Matrix," Doc says.

"My heart's filled with so much love and joy as I stand here today and make these vows to you. I couldn't be more excited to begin this new chapter of our lives together. It's been an incredible journey, and I'm looking forward to all the adventures yet to come. I vow to always be here for you. I'll always have your back, no matter what. If you ever need someone to talk to, count on me to be there, even in the middle of the night. I'll never abandon you on your journey."

Tears fill her eyes, but she blinks them away. I want to give her the biggest kiss, but I restrain myself. I know there's more she wants to say, and I'm not about to interrupt her.

"Most importantly, I vow always to love you. From the very first moment I met you, I knew you were the one for me. You are my best friend and soulmate, and I'll love you with all my heart for the rest of my life and beyond. My love for you will never die."

I sniff back tears, but I can hear Daisy's mom sobbing in the audience. I glance at her and give her a reassuring smile. She wipes her eyes with her husband's handkerchief before handing it back to him. He grins at me while stuffing it back in his suit pocket.

"For a bunch of bikers, you sure are a soft

bunch," Doc teases. Laughter spreads through the aisles. As it fades, Doc asks the most important question of the day. "Matrix, do you take Daisy to be your ride-or-die woman for life?"

"I do."

"Daisy, do you take Matrix to be your ride-or-die man for life?"

"I do."

"Well, then, there's nothing left but to kiss the bride." Doc gives me a sly smile.

Gently grasping Daisy's face between my palms, I brush my thumbs over her cheeks. I love the way she shivers beneath my touch. When our lips meet, I stifle a groan of pure pleasure. I haven't been able to kiss her for days. She insisted we sleep in separate beds the last week, which killed me. But I understand why she did it now. I can't wait to carry her off to bed.

As the ceremony ends, the guests erupt into cheers and clapping. As I look around the gathering, I see all the faces of the people we care about. Their happiness and joy bless us with all the love we've ever wanted. I'm so thankful for today and all the support surrounding us. We truly are one big family.

After the ceremony, everyone gathers outside, and the party begins. Music plays while beer and champagne flow like the river. Laughter fills the air and warms my heart, but none of it compares to my beautiful bride. I can't take my eyes off her.

We dance the night away, celebrating the start of our new life together, surrounded by friends and family. As I look into Daisy's eyes, I know without a doubt that this is the beginning of a beautiful journey. I've finally found my soulmate, and I'm never letting her go.

Later, after making love to my gorgeous bride all night, I dream the sweetest dreams about our future together.

***

Sign up for my newsletter at www.LivBrywood.com and get a bonus scene.

Daisy's new career is more fulfilling than she ever could have imagined. With Matrix by her side, they're ready to take on the world. Find out what they're up to now.

ABOUT THE AUTHOR

Liv Brywood

USA Today bestselling author Liv Brywood writes contemporary and paranormal romance. Her scorching heroes love curvy women and aren't afraid to show it. They're loyal, brave, honorable, and above all — sexy. Liv's stories are filled with passion, hope, and everlasting love.

To be the first to find out about the next book in the series, and to get special offers and discounts, sign up for my email newsletter!

To find out more about me, please check out my website.

Friend me on Facebook.

Follow me on Twitter.

Email me at LivBrywood@gmail.com

Printed in Great Britain
by Amazon